Shot in the Buff

Shot in the Buff

Joan Dash

First edition: January 2008

This printing: April 2014

Cover designed by The Barbarienne's Den

Typeset by Swordsmith Productions

This book is dedicated to the 99.9% of nudists who are sane, normal people, and not at all like those described in this book.

Acknowledgments

I couldn't have written this book without the support and encouragement of my daughter, Becky, and my husband, Glen. Thank you, Glen, for enduring endless technical and legal questions.

I'd also like to thank Leigh Grossman of Swordsmith Productions for his help in producing this edition, along with Elizabeth Glover for her beautiful cover design.

Chapter One

My grandfather's wish was to have his ashes spread over a pond at his beloved nudist camp. So here I am, standing with my naked grandmother, on a small rock outcropping overlooking that pond in a nudist camp. A group of people are across the pond looking up at us. I think I'm the only one in this entire place who has clothes on.

My grandmother, at 83, crosses her arms against her flat breasts while I try to open the cardboard box containing my grandfather's ashes. The wind is strong after a thunderstorm blew through an hour ago and broke the August heat. The temperature in this New Hampshire forest must have dropped twenty degrees. My grandmother looks like she's getting cold.

Actually, I'm worried about the wind for a different reason. It has turned and is now coming straight at us. The logical thing would be to go to the other side of the pond, but the other side is a beach crowded with people who are staring over at us, as if to say, "Don't even think about it."

I look around and find a sharp rock and break through the tape. Inside is a sealed, plastic bag which is made of tougher stuff than the tape and does not respond to repeated blows.

"Oh, For God's sake, give that thing to me," says my grandmother.

She grabs the plastic bag and pulls it out of the box. She searches for a suitable corner and puts it up to her mouth.

"Gramma! Don't!" I say. No denture adhesive can be that

strong. But, she clamps down on one corner, gives a quick jerk and says something that comes out like, "Pthaw" before settling her teeth back in place.

"Now give Grampa a good throw," she says. I fling the ashes out of the bag as hard as I can, but the laws of physics rule the day, and the residues of my grandfather stratify in their airborne moment. The lighter ash moves outward for a moment, hangs suspended, and then comes back at us. It lands in my hair. Heavier particles stick to my clothes. For a moment, I wish I was naked because I know I'll never wear these clothes again.

A few of Grampa's teeth have landed near the edge of the rock we're standing on, and I push them into the pond below with my foot. There. At least part of him ended up in the pond.

We stand there in silence, feeling like it would be disrespectful to dump and run, but not knowing what to say. Maybe if there were more people here, it would feel more like a ceremony and less like a task. But my grandfather's wish was to have only family members present. My mother is an only-child, and right now she's deep in the mountains of Peru on an archaeological expedition. Since I'm also an only-child, that leaves only me and Gramma.

The clouds cast flat, gray reflections on the pond below. Underneath those reflections, the water is deep tea brown, colored by years of tannic acid seeping from dead pine needles. I used to swim in this pond when I came here as a girl. Now the camp has a pool, and only toddlers venture into the edge of the pond as their parents watch from the beach.

I wonder if there are still leeches in the pond. As a kid, I pulled a few leeches off my legs after spending a little too much time in the water. You learn to deal with them if the pond is the only water around on a hot summer day. And besides, leeches infuse your skin with a numbing agent. As long as you are in the water you can be in a state of denial about the whole thing.

Of course, men cringe when they visualize leeches at a nudist camp. In the ten summers I spent here as a child, however, I never saw a leech on any part of a man necessary for reproduction. It's not that leeches have a sense of decorum. It's rather that these sensitive parts represent only a tiny part of the total surface area of a man's body. Try telling that to a man.

I practically carry my grandmother down the hill toward the parking lot where her golf cart awaits. Before my grandfather died, he taught her how to use the cart, at least going forward. Going backwards is inconceivable, even to look to her left or right requires her to twist and lean. As a result, she doesn't like to turn. She only likes to go forward.

For a couple of years now, I've been taking care of my grandparents, dropping by almost daily to take care of the little things like food shopping and rides to the doctor. I live in the same town, so it's not all that difficult. When they're not digging in Peru, my Mom and Dad both teach at Stanford in California, so I'm the only one in my family who lives anywhere near my grandparents.

I don't take my clothes off when I come to the camp. My parents used to be nudists here, so I spent a lot of time naked as a kid. But at sixteen, I decided I'd had enough and stopped coming to the camp. I'm 31 now, so that makes it fifteen years since I've officially been a nudist.

I don't have anything against nudism per se. It just happens that I have a tiny waist, slender hips, and long legs. My body attracts a lot of attention even when I have clothes on, and when I'm naked the attention can get annoying. When I was a teenager I complained about it. My mother said I had two choices: I could stop coming to the camp, or I could get fat. For a while, I tried both. Now I'm thin again, but my nudism is limited to the confines of my own house, and only in front of my husband, Jack.

Gramma walks very slowly, and it's taking her a long time to get across the parking lot. Ashes cover her body, making her look like a grainy black and white photo from a newspaper. I must look pretty bad myself. I only hope we can make it to the golf cart before anyone notices us.

Next to the parking lot is a volleyball court where a small crowd has gathered to watch the game. As usual, most of the spectators are there to watch some of the best bodies in the camp bounce around the court. In this camp, at least, both the male and the female volleyball players have physical assets that bounce well, and most of the spectators are transfixed.

Unfortunately, two men look up from the game, wave, and then start walking toward us. My grandmother gives me a poke and mutters, "Now be nice. They always ask about you."

Approaching us are two men who look like Tweedle Dum and Tweedle Dee. Harry has a round belly with a lot of hair, and a round head with very little hair. The smaller guy is Stan, with no fat to be found and not much muscle either.

In this nudist camp, last names and professions are supposed to remain secret, so everyone is known by their spouse's name. Harry is referred to as Harry-of-Harry-and-Janet. In my day, there were very few single people in the camp. Because of declining membership, however, single people are now a lot more common. These singles, mostly men, are named by something distinctive, like Jack-at-the-top-of-the-hill. Stan, of course, is Stan-the-minister since he gives a little service every Sunday in the summer.

As they approach, their demeanor changes since it's obvious that we have either been visiting a smoking volcano, or disposing of ashes. Harry comes up, starts to hug my grandmother, then thinks better of it. He pats her on the shoulder instead.

"I was so sorry to hear about Andrew," he says. "We are really going to miss him. I know the ladies are sure going to miss him. He really had a way with those girls. Did you ever see him, Stan, with that purple walker with the fold-down seat? That walker had two cup holders, one for his sippy cup full of bourbon and the other for a sippy cup of mixer, like he used to call it. It was usually iced tea or something. Anyway, he would invite the ladies to have a seat on his walker and offer them a drink. Eleanor would be standing right there, but you were so good about it."

My grandmother snorts. "It was great fun. Loved every minute."

Stan-the-minister takes a more professional approach when speaking to my grandmother, but even he won't hug her. Instead he takes her hand and holds it between his palms, and, with unwavering eye contact, launches into a soliloquy of expressions appropriate to the occasion, like "difficult time," "someone to talk to," "gone to a better place," "loss of a loved one," and "with you in spirit."

My grandmother looks at him. "I have to pee."

I make rapid excuses to Harry and Stan and hustle my mother to the restroom just in time. Then I quickly help her over to her golf cart. Grandma sits down in the passenger seat, and I drive her down to the single-wide trailer where she will now live by herself. Even though the trailer is tiny, it's going to feel big and empty now. I used to wonder how two people could live in such a small space. Now I'm wondering how one person can be there alone.

As I'm helping her clean up, I look at her. "You going to be okay?"

"I'm going to shoot the next person who asks me that."

"Really, Gramma."

"For crying out loud, I got more people looking out for me now than I ever had when your grandfather was here. It was all Andrew, all the time. Now, I feel like I got eyes all around me even when I'm taking a dump."

"I just don't want you to feel lonely"

"Hey, you don't know how much I'm looking forward to this! I'm going to eat whatever I want, whenever I want. And then I'm going to turn on the TV and watch what I want, and turn it off when I want. And then I'm going to go to bed when I want and I won't have to wake up three times during the night because he has to pee and he has to complain about it all the way to the bathroom and back each time."

I look doubtful, but she goes on, "I know that sounds like I'm just trying to pretend everything is okay. But I think that's the best thing to do. You know the saying, 'When life gives you lemons, decide you want lemons.'"

As I'm driving out of the camp that night I think about what she said. Back in the first century, Seneca said, "Let us train our minds to desire what the situation demands." Gramma said it better.

Chapter Two

Too much money, too fast, can be a bad thing. It can take your self-image and suck the air right out of it. It can make you stumble on your career path. It can cause you to lose your ambition, will, and endurance. This is because money comes with the temptation to ask at every turn, "Who needs this crap anyway?"

When you work hard to make ends meet, you put up with annoying people, frustrating delays, bad cafeteria food, and coworkers that stab you in the back. You *have* to put up with these things because you need the pay check. Meanwhile, your confidence and skills grow. You think about saving enough to buy a house. You feel strong and self sufficient.

But what if you suddenly get a lot of money? Of course, you continue to work because work is the source of so much of your self esteem. But there comes a day when someone spills coffee all over your desk, and you're passed over for a promotion, and a client yells at you over the phone, and you say, "Who needs this crap anyway?" Not you. You don't need the paycheck anymore.

So maybe you try another job, maybe one that doesn't pay so much but is less stressful. But that turns out to be boring and unfulfilling. Who needs it? Then you volunteer at a soup kitchen and discover that some of the clientele there is even more demanding and difficult than your former co-workers. You gradually find excuses not to go.

I have just described the last 18 months of my life. I used to be a competent soil scientist, with a masters degree from the University of Massachusetts. Soil science is not an exciting field, but I've always liked dirt. I can throw some dirt in a jar of water, shake it up, and then tell you whether it's a silty clay loam or a fine sandy loam. And I can be useful, too. I can dig a hole in a field, pour some water in, and tell you whether you can put a septic field there.

A couple of years ago, I was applying these skills at a farm in Maine that had been used as a toxic waste dump a couple of decades ago. Jack Bingham was also there. It wasn't love at first sight, because we were both dressed in head-to-toe hazmat suits with respirators. Jack was dragging his ground penetrating radar back and forth over the site, looking for large objects that might be 50-gallon drums of toxic liquids.

Over lunch, I found out that he had already, at age 29, discovered the work he wanted to do for the rest of his life. I found out he was passionate about peering into the soil and making its secrets visible on his computer screen. Later I found out he was passionate about other things, too, like the secrets of my body, for instance. My girlfriends made lots of comments about his *penetrating* radar. We were engaged a few months later.

A week before the wedding, Jack told me that he was filthy rich. My quick, silent, calculations told me that the money he earned doing radar work was dwarfed by even minimal interest on so large a sum. I asked him why he worked so hard, and he answered that his parents had told him to find something in life that he loved doing, something he would do even if no one paid him to do it. For him, that was finding hidden things under the ground with his techno-toys.

One of my many self-help books said that the thing that

attracts you to your partner is the very thing that will end up driving you nuts. I love Jack's passion for his work. But that work takes him all over New England, New York, New Jersey and Pennsylvania. Which means I'm home by myself a lot. Knowing that we will start a family soon, I haven't wanted to start another job. I'm just hanging around in a kind of limbo.

So when we found this old New Hampshire farm house surrounded by sixty acres on the fertile eastern bank of the Connecticut River, I jumped at the chance of doing something fulfilling. I wanted to throw myself into a frenzy of putting down roots. I know roots are supposed to grow slowly, but damn it, these would be roots on steroids. Besides, it was close to Gramma and Grampa, and I wanted to be useful to somebody, even if they did live in a nudist camp.

Our farmhouse is a two-story, square white building that used to be a tavern, and still has the hitching posts to prove it. It's close to a colonial dirt road which is now our driveway. A state road bypassed the curve of this old road, like a fast flowing river that left our driveway as quiet and still as an oxbow. As a result, our driveway has two openings to the state road about a quarter mile from our house.

The open fields, huge sky, and distant vistas were expansive and inspiring. That's because we bought the house in the spring. If we had waited until now, in August, we would have driven away as fast as the ruts on the old road would have allowed. Now, tall stalks of corn come right up to the house in the back and on both sides. There is even corn in front of the house occupying the rough triangle between the two driveways that run out to the road. Our broad vistas are now visible only from the second floor.

There are a lot of cows next door and they apparently like corn. Our neighbor with the cows, Terry Curtis, paid the previous owners a hefty rent for the use of the sixty acres. He must have assumed it would have been an offer even city slickers couldn't refuse, because the fields had been derocked, plowed, fertilized and limed before we moved in. We had seen fields of corn before. We thought they were pretty.

Corn up close is a different matter. I'm looking at it right now while I sit on the front porch, sewing up one side of a cover for a couch pillow. There is a breeze, but only the second-floor curtains are moving. I hear rustling in the front field, but there's always a rustling somewhere in the corn. No animal can move through corn without making a lot of noise, and we have lots of deer, coyotes, and sometimes even stray cows.

Now the rustling is growing louder and closer. I'm not really worried. Even the coyotes don't bother me. When they finally see me, they turn around and take off fast. I don't like the rats. Rats love corn and they can sound like very large animals when they move together in groups. But this is not a bunch of rats. I already know what something low to the ground sounds like, because the leaves are dry at the bottom and they rustle like newspaper.

This is something bigger, making a swishing sound near the top of the leaves in addition to some rustling. It is also quietly moving down a row, with none of the occasional crashing sounds an animal makes as it tries to get through a row of tightly packed stalks. I stand and feel for my cell phone in my pocket. Then I see the full length of a rifle. To me, it looks a lot like a cannon, but Terry says it's just a semi-automatic, whatever that is.

"Terry!" I yell at him. "For God's sake, can't you yell ahead or something? Scary things come out of corn fields! Didn't you see ET or anything?" It's my neighbor, and, as usual, he walks through the fields with his rifle in front of him so none of the corn hits him in the face. He wouldn't admit that, of course. He says he carries it in case he sees any coyotes.

Terry Curtis steps out into the front yard. He is tall and broad with blond hair that suggests he was trying for a wind blown look this morning. His badly wrinkled tee shirt and shorts look like they were chosen because they were at the top of the pile in the dryer. "How was I to know that you were outside? I thought I was going to have to knock on the door, so why should I yell?"

"So what can I do for you, Terry?" Terry comes around a little too often, given the fact that I'm here by myself most of the time.

"Just checking on my fields." His fields? "I got to keep an eye out for bugs and stuff, see if I need to spray." He was going to knock on my door to check for bugs?

Terry lowers himself slowly into one of the Adirondack chairs on the porch. "Sorry to hear about your grandfather."

"How did you hear about my grandfather?" I'm surprised that he knows. The nudist camp is an entirely separate community located within the confines of Rensford. What goes on there usually stays there.

"The funeral director, what's his name, was talking about it at Ellie's the other day." The director of the local funeral parlor is a model of discretion until he gets to Ellie's Bread and Breakfast, the local coffee shop.

He looks at me, his eyes dancing and his head thrust forward like a chicken. "Is it true he wanted his ashes spread over the nudist camp?"

"Yes," I say.

Terry slaps the arm of the chair. "And did you do it?"

"Yes."

"And, well, did anyone get, you know, covered?"

"No." What was I going to say? Just the immediate family?

I change the subject. "Christopher all ready for the fair? Does he understand the color coding this time?"

Christopher is his five-year-old son, and each year he enters the local agricultural fair in the junior division, showing off a young calf. Last year he won a blue ribbon, but no one had explained to him that a blue ribbon meant first place. When he saw his friend get a red ribbon for second place, Christopher started to cry. His favorite color is red.

Terry sighs. "Yeah, he knows. Blue is good and red is bad. Blue is good and red is bad." Terry is confident when it comes to his calves.

"And will this calf have a name?" The other part of story I heard is that the judge asked Christopher to tell everybody the name of his calf. Christopher said something like, "She doesn't have a name because she's going to be dead tomorrow and we don't name anything that's going to be dead."

"Daisy Belle," he says.

"So does that mean that the life of Daisy Belle will be spared?"

"I suppose," he says with a sigh.

Terry's purpose in life is to provide the world with veal. He's got a hundred or so cows and he impregnates them with sperm that he buys in volume and stores in his freezer. Every couple of weeks or so a white truck comes early in the morning, painted with pictures of a cattle roundup and a western ranch style logo that says Wanna-B-Meat. For about three days after the truck takes away a calf, its mother calls for her missing off-spring with a sound that is a cross between a bellow and a wail.

I hear that sound now. "Another one bites the dust?"

"Hey, after three days the cows forget the whole thing."

I can't stand hearing that wail and I'm always tempted to go find the calf, buy it back and return it to its mother. But then there would be another calf gone and another wailing cow. I'd like to have a discussion about the morality of veal, but I really don't know Terry all that well.

Jack and I were at a party soon after we moved in, and one of the locals told us that Terry was a member of the Manure Mafia. The noise of the party prevented us from getting much information, but we learned that members of the Manure Mafia are into guns. On the way home, we tried to guess what their initiation rites might be.

Terry tries to get the conversation back to the nudist camp. "So I heard over at Ellie's that the cops had to be called in to the camp because of some domestic thing. What was going on there?"

I tell him that I don't know anything about it, even though I heard every detail several times from Gramma.

"Yeah, yeah," he says. "No one wants to air any dirty laundry."

I tell him that there's no dirty laundry at a nudist camp. It takes him a moment or two to get the joke, and then he laughs and bangs his fist on the chair. He says, "That's one for Sally Ann's!"

My eyes widen at the mention of Sally Ann's since I have always assumed he's a happily married man. Sally Ann's is a dimly lit bar, unofficially men-only. Women go in there to earn money, not to spend it.

I'm sitting here alone and isolated, with a patron of Sally Ann's, who happens to have a gun. This is not good. My phone is in my pocket, and I pretend I've got a call coming in.

"It's on vibrate," I whisper as I put the phone up to my ear and get up to go in the house. I pretend to be talking to my grandmother.

"No problem, Grandma.…Sure.…No, it's no bother."

The phone is still next to my ear when it suddenly rings. It's so loud I raise it way over my head and make a face. Terry stares at me. I answer it, looking at Terry, and say, "It's my other line." Terry gives me a puzzled look.

"What? What's your other line?" It's my grandmother.

"Hi, Gramma," I say. Now Terry's eyebrows are up and he's smirking.

Gramma says, "Who were you talking to?"

"Terry, my neighbor."

"Well, I don't want him to hear this. This is bad."

"What, Gramma?"

You know that Wall Street guy, Donald?"

"Yeah."

"Well, he's dead. Shot in the chest."

"What!?"

"And you'll never guess who did it. Stan-the-minister. At least that's what everybody says anyway."

Chapter Three

It takes me a half hour to get rid of Terry and rush over to the camp. I am afraid that Gramma will be upset and frightened. She's just upset.

"The town hall is going to be all over this one. They hate us already. And now somebody gets shot." Gramma is irritated because she's hot. Drops of sweat move down the flat triangles of her breasts, all that remains of her formerly bodacious body.

Gramma used to be a knockout, with long legs and dark wavy hair. I ended up with the long legs and the hair, but not the boobs. Looking at my grandmother, you can still see what beautiful legs she had. Her hair is still thick for her age, but it's hard to tell because it's short and tightly curled against her scalp like an extra-fancy, pale lavender bathing cap. Most of the time I see the back of Gramma's head, because she is so bent over.

"You're worried about the town hall people?" I ask. "The guy is dead, for heaven's sake."

"I'm just saying, this is going to be used against us. We pay all these taxes to the town and we don't send any kids to the schools. You think they'd love us, but no. It's harassment."

I bring her back to Topic A. "So what do you know about Donald? He hasn't been here all that long, has he?"

"He joined about a year ago, and all I know is that he was really rich, from Wall Street. He bought Jane and Tommy's fancy log cabin at the end of Pine Hollow Road."

"Is that where it happened?"

"Yeah, I heard they found him right inside his front door like he opened the door and BAM!"

"Why on earth does anyone think that Stan-the-minister did this?"

"Because they had some sort of big fight yesterday. Really loud."

"Elllaaanoor!"

It's Flo, from next door. Flo is a piece of work, or more exactly, the product of a lot of work. She has silicone boobs, plastic cheekbones and a plastic chin. She has had fat cells removed from thighs, abdomen, and neck. She had lipo on her butt, too, but unfortunately more from one side than the other. She says it forces her to stay skinny, because if she gains weight, one side balloons out and pulls her to the left.

My grandmother yells out, "Come on in, Flo!"

"Well, how's mah little darlin'?" Flo comes from New Hampshire, but her idol is Dolly Parton. "Y'all talkin' about what happened to Donald?"

"Did you hear about the fight between Donald and Stan yesterday?" I ask.

"Hear about it? Darlin', I was right there! Hooweee! Who knew little Stan could get so upset? Him bein' so scrawny."

"What were they fighting about?" I ask.

"Well, they were on the beach and I didn't hear it start, but Donald yelled somethin' about Stan bein' a hypocrite. Then Stan yelled about Donald's bein' in trouble, and then Donald said he would call Stan's church and Stan yelled out somethin' like, 'We'll see about that!' and he got up and stood over Donald and waved a fist. There was a little bit of snickerin' all round cuz Stan looked a little, you know, pathetic wavin' that fist."

I look at my grandmother. "That's it? That's why you're pinning this on Stan?"

"I'm not pinning anything on anybody. I'm just telling you what everybody says."

Both Gramma and Flo have already been to the crime scene, having hopped into Gramma's golf cart and chased after the police cars as soon as they went by. Gramma tries to talk me out of going.

"They won't let you anywhere near the place. They got that yellow tape so far out you can barely see the cabin. I think those cops just don't like being stared at by a bunch of naked people so they pushed us back. But, boy, their eyes popped when they saw Flo."

I decide to go anyway, and I walk down towards Pine Hollow. There are others moving that way, too, and we exchange some nods and greetings. Most people don't mind the fact that I have clothes on. There is a rule that everyone in camp must be naked even if they are just here on a day pass. That's to prevent people from coming in as voyeurs. But hired help, like local carpenters or electricians can keep their clothes on, and most people view me as hired help because I've been taking care of my grandparents.

Others, though, have more of a chip on their shoulder about me and I can understand why. The fact that I used to be a nudist as a kid, but insist on being clothed now, feels like a rejection of their way of life. By wearing clothes, I'm saying, "Been, there, done that, not for me." Gramma goes around telling everybody that my husband won't let me take my clothes off.

Near the cabin, there are police cars and a ring of naked people up against the yellow tape. I see an open spot and prepare to take my place among the gawkers. As I approach the tape, though, one of the uniformed cops comes over and lifts the tape for me to go under. Why is this happening? I can feel the stares on my back as I obediently follow him toward the police cars. Do they think I had something to do with this?

Am I going to see a dead body?

One of the men without a uniform comes over to me and glances casually at the cabin with his eyebrows up as if he's offering me something. I think he's asking whether I want to view the body.

"No, thank you. Maybe later." I say, politely.

He looks at me. "You from Salem?" I shake my head. "Manchester?"

"No, Rensford."

"What are you doing here?"

"Taking care of my grandmother."

He looks over at the cop that led me in. "Are you the one that let in Little Red Riding Hood here?"

"She had clothes on, George. She looked official."

George looks toward the sky, but I'm sure he can't see it because his grey eyebrows are so huge. George is about 60 and he looks tired, tired of trying to lose his beer belly, tired of trying to stand up straight, tired of trying to put up with the local police.

I start to go, and George says, "Wait. You know anything about this place?"

"I've been coming here on and off for most of my life, yeah."

"Well, I got to ask someone some questions and I feel a lot more comfortable looking at you than any of them," he says, tilting his head at the people outside. I've heard better compliments, but I nod okay.

"Okay," he says. "First, how many people are in this, what do call it, nudist colony, camp?

"Camp. There are about two or three hundred members, but only about half that come regularly. And then there are some people here on day passes, people who are traveling from one camp to the next."

"Can I get a list of members and people on day passes?"

"Yeah, at the camp office, although the office is not supposed to give out last names without permission from the members."

"Can't be helped," he says. "Does that mean a hundred or so on a weekday like this?"

"No, maybe fifty or seventy-five. Weekday people are the ones on vacation, or the ones staying here all summer."

"Except for the day pass people, does everyone know pretty much everyone else? Would they notice a new person around?"

"Oh yeah," I say. "Everyone checks out the new bodies." Gramma looks at the new people and can instantly give a complete medical history from their incisions. She can tell if someone has had a hernia, is missing a gall bladder, or has a new hip.

"What about access to this place? We came down a dirt road and had to yell into a squawk box to get someone to come lift the gate."

"All members have a card they swipe to lift the gate."

"Any other entrances?"

"No, and this place is surrounded by some pretty thick forest all the way around. We get a lot of small planes flying over really low, but there's no place for them to land." I tell him about the hired help that's occasionally around, but the fact that they have clothes on makes them highly noticeable.

"What about guns? Any guns around?"

"I've never seen any, but I've heard there are a couple of gun nuts around who have some big collections in their cabins."

George smiles. "We'll get the names of the gun *enthusiasts* later. First we need to figure out how people might carry a concealed weapon. I see everyone around here has some sort of tote bag."

"Pretty much. Etiquette requires that you have a towel with you at all times to put down before you sit anywhere. And then people carry a book, suntan lotion, money, that kind of stuff."

"And so they put it all in a tote bag. Guys, too?'

"Yeah. Some of the old timers are too homophobic to carry a bag, and they carry a towel over their arm. I remember some guys who would wear high white socks and stuff their wallet down the sock on one leg and a pack of cigarettes down the sock on their other leg. But almost everybody carries some sort of tote bag now."

George sighs. "Okay, we got about fifty people around here who could be carrying a concealed weapon. Anybody have a reason to kill Donald? Any disagreements, gripes?" He sees me hesitate. "Come on, if you don't tell me somebody else will."

"Stan-the-minister had an argument with Donald on the beach yesterday."

"Stan-the-minister?"

I give him a two-minute explanation of the naming system and then tell him what little I know about the argument. We are interrupted by one woman, two men, and a gurney. George turns to me, "By the way, what's your name?"

"Catie Bingham."

"Not Catie-of-Catie-and-somebody?"

"My 'somebody' is Jack, but my husband hardly ever sets foot in this place. After his first visit, he said it may him understand why God invented clothes."

George grunts in agreement. "Well, Catie, you're going to need to drive over to Ashton with us so we can take your statement, and maybe give the team a little background on this place. Think your grandmother can spare you?"

"She will be thrilled by my importance."

The body of Donald goes by me. He's zipped up in a big gray plastic bag and strapped onto a gurney. It is the closest I've been to a dead body if you don't count the ashes I was covered with yesterday.

I step away from the police cars and duck under the yellow tape. I am horrified by my lack of horror. To tell the truth, I'm the one who's thrilled with my importance. I can't wait to run down to my grandmother's trailer, tell her all about this, and then run back to be ready to go to Ashton. I feel like a little girl who's just been chosen to be school crossing guard.

A half hour later I'm in Ashton, at the New Hampshire state police barracks. The cement block building confirms the state's reputation for low taxes. On the floor, beige linoleum squares have grimy seams, broken corners, and depressions which indicate previous furniture arrangements. The current furniture is dominated by two-toned, grey metal desks with rounded corners. Behind the desks are large metal chairs which lean back. In front of the desks are small wooden chairs that don't.

I am taken into a small room which is entirely filled by a metal table, with a tape recorder on top and a chair on either side. The only window is a tiny one, laced with chicken wire, high up on the heavy metal door. A very large man named Bruce is in the room with me to take my statement. Bruce works out a little too much. His massive shoulders make his head look like one of those bizarre shrunken heads from some remote Pacific island, but with a buzz cut.

I do not have claustrophobia, despite the assertions of my friends and family. I merely make a rapid, but reasonable, assessment of the total oxygen in the room, and compare that to the rate of usage by me and any one else in the room. Then I look around for sources of air exchange. If I find none, like in this case, I take the rational step of breathing faster and more deeply than the other person in the room. I wish I were more magnanimous, but my object is to take in as much of the finite supply of oxygen as quickly as possible, so that the other person will run out of air before I do.

My rapid gulps of air convince me that there is, in fact, very limited oxygen in the room. It also convinces Bruce that he needs to open the door. Blessed hallway! Bruce waits for me to calm down and turns on the tape recorder. "Tell me about your day."

I start by telling him about Jack leaving for Pennsylvania, and then about the arrival of my neighbor.

"What time did your neighbor come over?'

"About eleven-thirty or maybe closer to twelve."

"And what time did Jack leave?

"About nine."

"Did you see or talk to anyone between those times?"

"No." I don't have an alibi.

"Anybody see you from the road, maybe?

I explain the corn situation. He waves me on, "Okay. Tell me about the visit from your neighbor."

I tell him about Terry, and then go on to tell him about the call from my grandmother and the conversation I had later with her and Flo. I finish up with my account of being ushered into Donald's house by mistake, which is the only part of the story which perks him up and makes him smirk a bit.

"Come on," he says. "The boys are waiting for us." He leads me out of the small room and into a larger room with five men and George behind a desk. George says, "Okay, Catie, if you wouldn't mind filling them in a little. Just tell them what you told me about tote bags and pass cards and last names and stuff. Then there will be some Q and A."

I repeat much of what I told George and then the random questions start:

"What do most people do during the day?"

"On a hot August day, most people are going to go to the pool or the beach, or they're in the canteen where they can get lunch and sit by an air conditioner."

"Does everyone wear shoes?'

"Most people where sneakers or sandals, but, yes, everyone pretty much wears shoes."

"Do the cards that you swipe at the gate carry information about the card holder?'

"I don't think so, because it's easy to go to the office and get another card if you lose yours."

"Who are the so-called gun nuts you mentioned?"

"Don't quote me on this, but I'd say Roger-of-Roger-and-Patty and maybe Dave-of-Dave-and-Carol. They both talk about their guns a lot."

"Know where they live when they're at the camp?"

"Sure. It's like a very small town. Everybody knows where everybody else lives."

George asks me to tell them what I know about Donald. I tell them that I don't think anyone knew him very well. "He wasn't your typical nudist. The camp doesn't get many rich, cosmopolitan types. He kept to himself and didn't attend any meetings or events. There were rumors that he was at camp because he was hiding from the press. I guess he did something spectacularly wrong and he got pilloried by the *Wall Street Journal*."

"Did his wife or kid ever come to the camp?"

"I didn't know he had a wife or kid."

"Tell us about Stan," he paused, "Stan-the-minister."

"You guys are barking up the wrong tree there, but okay, Stan joined a few years ago, and when he found that no one was doing Sunday service at the chapel, he just started doing it."

"There's a chapel?"

"It's more like a little cleared area with a podium and some wooden benches. It's next to a stream and it's really quite pretty, actually."

"People wear clothes at chapel?"

"No, and neither does the minister."

It takes the group a moment to absorb this image, before the next question is asked.

"What was the relationship between Donald and Stan? Did they know each other well?"

"I think Stan wanted to know Donald more than Donald wanted to know Stan. Stan thought it was his duty to reach out to those who might be lonely or unhappy and enfold them in the warmth of the community. I don't think Donald wanted to be enfolded, but Stan can be persistent. Stan visited Donald at his cabin, and would always seek him out if Donald did appear in public, on the beach or at the pool or something."

"You think that Donald felt harassed?"

"Annoyed, maybe. And uncomfortable. Stan is sort of in and out of the closet from one day to the next. Everybody here assumes he's gay. The only one who seems to object to that is Stan himself."

"Do you think he was coming on to Donald?"

"Not consciously. But maybe Donald felt that way."

"Are there a lot of gays in the camp?"

"Depends on what's a lot. To some of the older people, there's way too many already. Other people welcome them with open arms. Some people want more gays because they are the only young people joining nowadays. CNN did a segment a while ago about how nudists are an aging demographic, and that nudist camps are in danger of becoming assisted living places." I don't tell them Jay Leno's response to this – that the way to get young people to join is to tell the old people to put their clothes on.

"Do they do any kind of background checks on people before they're allowed to join?'

"They used to. They would even come to your house to do an interview. Now they're happy with anyone who wants to pay the fee." I explain that the camp sank a lot of money into improvements, like a pool and tennis courts, to attract new members but that it didn't work.

"So anyone, a pedophile or rapist, could join?"

"I guess."

The meeting concludes with assignments for gathering information. One person will check out Donald's Wall Street troubles, another, his family life, and another, his financial situation and will. George will check out the guns, Stan and other people who knew Donald. A young recruit, Kevin, is given the task of tracking down people who were on the beach yesterday and who might have heard the argument between Stan and Donald.

Kevin is clearly uncomfortable with this assignment and tries to convince George that he is better suited to some other task. Kevin is a tall thin man, young enough to still have acne. His shoulders are hunched forward and he seems almost concave in his shyness. Apparently, Kevin has never been to a nudist camp. I take pity on him and offer to accompany him on his interviews, if it's okay with George, and George agrees. He says it will speed up the investigation if they have somebody who knows their way around the place.

I think it has nothing to do with the speed of the investigation. I think I'm allowed to tag along because I'll serve as a bit of a buffer. Having me around will make the camp members feel more comfortable with the police and vice versa. It's got to be awkward for the police to be interviewing people without clothes. Nothing in the police manual prepares them for, say, studying the body language of someone being interviewed, while at the same time being careful not to study the 'wrong' parts of that body.

As I drive home, I feel quite pleased with myself. I have a new identity: Catie Bingham, police escort.

Chapter Four

Jack calls at six, on the dot, every night that he's away. Tonight he talks about the heat in Pennsylvania, sweating in his hazmat suit, and the slim chance of finding anything of significance on this trip. Do I detect a bit of "Who needs this crap anyway?"

Finally, he asks, "And how was your day?"

"I saw the body of someone who was shot dead and I don't have an alibi."

He is silent for a moment and then says, "Okay."

"No, really."

"What do you mean, 'No, really'?"

"No, as in, this is not a sarcastic comment about my dull life, and really, I really did see a dead body today. Inside a bag."

"Who? Where?"

"A guy named Donald at the camp was shot in his cabin."

"Unbelievable. Do they know who did it?"

"No, but I'll be helping the police find out."

"What?"

"Yeah, after I gave my statement at the state police barracks, they asked me to help with the investigation." I'm beginning to get an idea how silly this sounds. "Really," I say.

"Wait. You don't have an alibi, and you've given a statement to the police? Without a lawyer? You went to the police station and talked to them and now they want you to 'help' them? Catie, this just doesn't sound right."

"Did I forget to mention that I am not the killer?"

"You know that's not the point, Catie. Be serious. Don't do anything more without talking to Demers, okay, please?" Phil Demers is the Bingham family lawyer from way back. "Maybe I should come home."

"No." I don't want to tell him that I'm really looking forward to the next couple of days. I don't want to just sit home and miss all the excitement just because Jack was brought up to be paranoid about police. Jack's mother is an aging hippie who still calls them 'pigs'.

"I don't think I'm a suspect, Jack. I think they just want somebody to show them around the camp when they're doing interviews."

"You know I've always loved the fact that you're such a trusting person. But this is crazy. This really is crazy. The police just don't reach out to civilians to 'help' them. Please promise me you'll talk to Demers. I'll call him and tell him to call you right away, okay?"

"Okay. But I'm going over to Maureen's for dinner tonight." I'm too wired up to just have dinner and go to bed. Besides, this way Demers will just have to leave a message and I'll make sure I'm home too late to call him back. A game of phone tag will begin.

"Good. Maureen's got a good head on her shoulders."

I hang up with a promise to be careful, and not trust anyone. The problem is—I like being a trusting person. I like walking through life assuming everyone is a good person. It's a drag to be constantly evaluating people to figure out whether they're going to betray me for some reason.

Needless to say, I'm often proven wrong in my assumptions. And when it happens, I react with shock, and feel even more disturbed than if I had started with more reasonable expectations of human behavior. As a result, I end up being more distrustful of myself than anyone else. I simply can't trust my view of other people, because I'm too lazy to expend the effort to be paranoid when paranoia is warranted.

So I feel more than a little uncertainty now. An hour ago, I was feeling part of a team, a team of good guys trying to chase down the bad guys. Now I don't know.

An hour later, I'm at Maureen's house, a small ranch near the center of town. Maureen is my best buddy around here. She's a reporter for the daily paper in Ashton, Rensford being too small to have anything but a weekly. Her beat is the local hospitals and she's always full of gossip about everybody around here.

At forty-five, Maureen has decided to accept herself as she is. She is a big woman, tall and wide, with black hair that's about one quarter grey. She gets it cut at chin length at the local salon every three or four months. Right now her hair is approaching shoulder length so I think she's about due for another cut. She wears comfortable pants and shoes and she prefers white ankle socks with athletic shoes.

About a year ago, Maureen married Gordon Helms, an English professor at a local Catholic college. Gordon is in his early sixties and is a few years away from retirement, which scares the hell out of Maureen because it means he'll be around all day, everyday. He has only two modes of being – sullen and bombastic. I have no fear of enduring his company tonight, since he has a deathly fear of becoming trapped in a boring conversation, and he sees me, thankfully, as one of Maureen's boring friends.

A number of people in the town of Rensford were appalled that someone as bright and funny and charming as Maureen would marry someone like Gordon, but, unmarried at forty-five, she apparently decided to take what was available. And that was Gordon, short, heavy and balding. Tonight he is wearing seersucker shorts and a short sleeve dress shirt. On his feet are boat shoes over thin white knee socks. It's the knee socks which put him squarely in the species *Academia eccentris,* subgroup *ridiculous.*

Maureen and I are sitting on her screen porch having one of her usual wonderful barbeques, this one with chicken marinated in lime juice and tequila. Gordon is hovering nearby, eavesdropping on our conversation, probably so that he can make fun of me later. He's hovering closer than usual this time, to hear Maureen and I and talk about the murder at the camp.

Maureen, it turns out, has much more information than I have. She's been on the story all day, and she tells me that Donald's real name was Donald James Thaler. He lived in New Canaan, Connecticut, until he sold his house and divorced his wife a year ago. Donald was a mortgage broker, heavily in subprime mortgages.

"But if that's all he did," Maureen said, "he'd be no different than half the people in Fairfield County. No, this guy was a real crook. The *Wall Street Journal* peeled back his layers of shell corporations and found out that he was into sub, *sub*-prime lending."

"What do you mean?"

"What he did was set up a bunch of bank accounts, each with a hundred thousand or so, and then he would *lend* temporary ownership of this bank account to people with false identities and no credit. Then he provided a phone number and secretary to give false confirmations of employment. People got to live in fancy houses for a while before foreclosure, and Donald walked away with the commission."

"How long did he get away with it?" I ask.

"I guess about three years or so. I've got to dig a little deeper."

"Why you? This isn't exactly your beat."

"Something this big? Everybody's on it. Anybody with a computer or even a phone is scrambling to get something on this."

"Well, I'm not here as a source of information, okay?" My conversation with Jack is rubbing off on me. I'm a little wary.

"Catie, of course not! You're here because you need to download. Who wouldn't after a day like yours?"

I draw a deep breath and I'm grateful. Maureen pours me another glass of wine, even though I'm way ahead of her. I need to talk it all out, and this feels like a safe place to do it.

I tell her about the day's adventures. I talk about being mistakenly led into the crime scene, and about seeing the body. I talk about going to Ashton, giving a statement and agreeing to be an escort. I am grateful that she doesn't react like Jack. She doesn't not fly out of her chair and call me a fool for talking to the police. I'm surprised at how relieved I feel.

"So are you going to start your escort service tomorrow?" Maureen asks.

"I guess. I don't know." I'm starting to feel tired. "I'll just have to wait and see if they call."

"So you don't have any specific assignment or anything."

"No. The only thing they want me to do is help this guy Kevin interview people. We're supposed to interview the people who were on the beach when Donald had an argument with someone." I have been careful not to mention Stan specifically.

"He had an argument with someone the day he died?"

"Actually, it was the day before."

"Do the police consider him, or her, to be a suspect?"

"Him. No, it's just a stupid rumor going around. He was just trying to help, you know, reach out to Donald. Bring him into the flock."

"Is it that minister guy, the one who's gay?"

"Maureen, I swear to God, this better be off the record, because it's a stupid idea passed around by silly people."

She lowers her voice and pretends to be prosecutor on TV. "So, Mrs. Bingham, you're not *denying* these rumors. Is that right?"

"I am certainly not denying, Madam, that I've had a long day and I need to go home and go to bed."

Maureen declines my offer to help with the dishes and speedily gets me out of the house so I don't fall asleep at the wheel. It's late and it has been very long day. It seems like a lot of time has passed since yesterday when I disposed of my grandfather's ashes.

At the end of Maureen's long driveway, I stop to straighten out the wires of my Ipod which have gotten tangled around the parking brake. I've gotten one wire straightened out, and I'm working on the other one, when I see a sudden brightness in my rearview mirror. Headlights of a car are flooding a garage door with light. Evidently, Gordon is going somewhere at half past nine.

Not wanting to get caught at the end of the driveway, I take off quickly toward my house. I wonder if he's following me so I pull onto a narrow side street and cut the engine, waiting to see if he passes by. I wait, but no Gordon. Maybe they needed soap for their dishwasher or something. I start the car and drive home. This paranoia thing really is exhausting.

Chapter Five

The phone rings the next morning and the caller ID says, "NH ST POLICE". This is the moment when I should heed the advice left on my machine when I came home last night. The message was from attorney Phil Demers, urging me in the strongest possible terms not to say anything more to the police.

I pick up the phone, "Hello?"

"This is Chief Detective George Myers. May I please speak to Catie Bingham?"

How can I distrust anyone who's so polite? "This is Catie. Am I a suspect?"

"Excuse me?"

"Am I a suspect? Am I on your list of suspects? Should I have a lawyer? My lawyer says I should. My lawyer says I shouldn't talk to you."

"Like you're doing now?"

"Exactly."

"No, you're not a suspect. We are hoping you could help us navigate around the nudist camp, and make both the police officers and the people they interview feel more comfortable. But if you or your lawyer feels the slightest hesitation about your involvement, I'm sure we can proceed without you." He hears no response, so he goes on. "Alternatively, if you would like to bring your attorney along to protect your interests while you help us out, that would be fine, too."

That image makes me laugh. Phil Demers is a bowtie kind of

guy. The easiness of my laugh convinces me that, however wrong I may be, I trust this Chief Detective George Myers.

"Okay, I'm in."

"Great. Can you meet us at the end of the camp driveway on Lee Road in about a half hour?"

"Sure."

A while later, I pull up to George and the others leaning against their cars. Something is not right here. Their faces are very serious as they stare at me approaching. For a moment, I consider just driving by and not stopping.

As I pull to a stop, I see George with a copy of the *Ashton Bulletin*, the paper that Maureen writes for. I get out of the car and he walks over and hands it to me silently. The headline reads in large bold print, "Nude Minister Suspect in Murder." Underneath that, in smaller type but italics: "Local Woman to Help with Investigation," and, underneath that, "By Maureen Helms."

George looks at me closely. "Well, at least you apparently had no idea this was coming. The look on your face is worse than mine when I picked up the paper on the way over here. Let me guess, Maureen Helms is a friend of yours."

Was a friend of mine. "I can't believe she would do this to me. It was all off the record. I just can't believe this. I never would have said anything to her...."

"Spare me."

As George walks away, I look at the article but I can't concentrate. My mind keeps going back to last night. That was Maureen's car that pulled out of the driveway! She must have raced out of the house to get the information to the paper in time for today's edition. I lean back on my car and try not to let the hurt overwhelm me. She was my one good friend around here. It's a total betrayal.

George calls over to me. "So, are you going to help us or

not?" His voice is harsh but I look up and his eyes are kind. I must look so bad that he's feeling sorry for me.

"You still want my help?"

"Yeah, you can handle the press." Bruce, the one with the huge shoulders, has just said the longest sentence I've heard from him so far.

George, Bruce, and Kevin, the new recruit, gather around the hood of one of their cars. George waves me over and points to a blank piece of paper. "Do you think you could draw us a rough map of this place?"

I do my best, drawing the few paved roads, and then the dirt roads, and show them the location of Donald's cabin and Stan's trailer. I draw in the major landmarks such as the beach, pool, sauna, hot tub, canteen, office, etc. They ask me to draw the periphery, but I am stumped. I only know how far the clearing and roads and cabins have pushed out against the surrounding forest. "I'm sure the boundaries must be available at the Rensford Town Hall."

George lays out the plan for the morning. He and Bruce will interview Stan right away, given the heads-up that the newspaper has provided him. I weakly express an interest in being there for that interview because I want to apologize to Stan for having gotten him into this mess. My request is denied. Kevin and I are to talk to as many people as we can, trying to find anyone who saw Donald or might have overheard the argument he had with Stan.

We leave my car by the road, and I get into Kevin's car, and George and Bruce get into the other car. George leads the way down the small, unmarked gravel driveway that is the entrance to the camp. It looks like the plan is to go to the gate and wait there until someone comes to hand out temporary passes to be used during the investigation.

The wait is a long one and it gives me time to become

furious at Maureen. As soon as I'm released from my duties with these guys, I'm going to drive over to her office. I'm not good at confrontations, in general, but in this case I don't even have to say, "How could you?" She is so obviously in the wrong that all I will have to do is stand there and watch her squirm.

I've really worked myself up into a state of righteous fury when I notice Kevin reach into the back seat, get an empty clipboard, and put it on his lap. Then he reaches for a report and puts that, too, on his lap. I'm irritated by all this activity, because I want to continue my fantasies about Maureen squirming under my withering gaze. When he reaches for something else I say, "For heaven's sake, Kevin, you're not going to get an erection."

It's a good thing that his head rest is padded. The back of his head hits it hard and stays there. I'm a little startled, too. Did I just say the word 'erection?' I am about to apologize when he says in a small voice,

"You sure?" He is staring straight ahead.

"I'm sure," I say. "It's every man's biggest fear when they go to a nudist camp, but it just doesn't happen. I've never even heard of it happening."

He shakes his head. "George said it happened to him and some of the other guys and it was really embarrassing and he wished he had worn a big coat to hide it." Kevin gestures toward the back seat where I see a large, heavy overcoat. It's over 80 degrees out there and it's still morning. George and Bruce must be really yukking it up, thinking of Kevin stepping out of the car in that coat.

"Kevin, they are pulling your chain. It didn't happen to them and it won't happen to you." I get no response, so I go on. "Let me guess what is going through your mind – something like, if there's going to be a first, it'll be me. Right?"

"Yeah. You don't know me."

"Okay, let's do a few visualization exercises." I am determined to thwart this prank and get Kevin to step out of the car without the coat. "First, think of being at Wal-Mart or Target or someplace like that. There's one attractive girl behind a register, and as usual, you picture her naked. But, horrors! When you do that, everyone else becomes naked, too. The elderly lady who greeted you at the door is naked. The heavy set man behind you in line is naked. The woman ahead of you has a hundred moles, some hanging skin tags, and a strange rash on her back. Get the picture?"

He lets out a deep breath. I push the envelope a little. "Let's say that you go see an X-rated film. You are looking forward to seeing some gorgeous naked women. But this turns out to be a clothing-optional theater. Just think of every person you have ever seen at a theater, and imagine them all naked. Imagine some of these naked people saying 'excuse me' as you stand and raise your seat to let them go by."

"Okay. Okay. I get it." He takes another deep breath.

I could go on, but a small group of naked people are coming toward our cars. Apparently, providing the state police with gate cards is a thrill to be shared. I am pleased to see that this group represents a random sample of bodies similar to that found in a Wal-Mart or movie theater. I glance down at Kevin's lap. He's got his hand resting heavily on the notebook and clip board just in case.

Four or five of our welcomers huddle around George's car, sensing its greater importance, but a man and a woman recognize me and come back to say hello. I'm trying to remember their names so I can introduce them to Kevin, but I can't think of who they are. The man comes around to my side of the car and I roll down the window and exchange some pleasantries, while the woman goes over to Kevin's side.

Kevin is staring straight ahead and doesn't roll down his

window. The woman, maybe in her late fifties, knocks on the window. Her long narrow breasts hang down to her waist, looking like tube socks filled with sand, and they swing back and forth a little as she knocks. I glance over encouragingly at Kevin, thinking that this is going to be a long day if he can't even take this little bit of nudity. Kevin manages to look at her, but doesn't open the window.

The woman thwacks the top of the car. "Frank," she yells. "Will you ask Catie what's wrong with this guy? He deaf or something?"

As the husband turns to speak to her, I turn toward Kevin, who is staring at his window. Two long breasts are squished against the glass as the woman leans forward, trying to hear her husband. Each time she moves even the slightest bit, the breasts make a different shape against the glass. We are both transfixed. Suddenly he turns to me and then looks down at his lap.

"You were right!" he says to me with a big smile while he pushes the button to roll down his window. The woman steps back, narrowly avoiding a major nipple pinch at the bottom of the window.

"Can I help you, madam?" He is beaming now. The overcoat will stay in the back seat. Before she has a chance to say anything, we see George's car start to pull ahead. "I'm sorry, madam. Maybe we'll have a chance to talk some other time."

Both cars drive into the camp, passing by the office and between the beach and the pool. We pull in next to George's car, and Kevin opens his door. He gets out, takes a long stretch and yawns. "Boy, I could go for a cup of coffee. That took forever at the gate."

There are naked people all around us. I am so proud of him.

Chapter Six

I feel like I'm getting the cold shoulder as Kevin and I walk around the beach asking people whether they knew Donald, or whether they overheard the argument yesterday. I am supposed to be making people feel more at ease with Kevin, but I definitely get the feeling that they'd rather talk to him than me.

When Kevin stops to oblige some children who have called for his help carrying a pail of wet sand, I plop down next to Ethel, a friend of my grandmother's.

"Why do I get the feeling I'm a leper or something?"

Ethel snorts. "You got to be kidding."

"What? What?"

"The *Ashton Bulletin*? You didn't read it this morning?"

"I just saw the headline. Look, I'm so sorry that the whole Stan thing became so public. But I didn't mention his name to Maureen, and, besides, it seemed like that argument was common knowledge. It would have come out anyway."

She shook her head. "This ain't about Stan, honey. It's about you."

"What do you mean, me? Just because the police asked me to help them navigate around this place?"

"Nope, I'm afraid that's not it at all."

Kevin is walking back toward me, and I get up and wipe the sand off my shorts. Ethel reaches over and pats me on the leg. "Read the article, honey."

I have to read that article now. Right now. I ask Kevin whether he can spare me for a half hour while I check on my grandmother, and he dismisses me with a friendly wave. My grandmother will have a copy of that article, probably three copies by now.

I trounce down the rutted dirt road that leads to my grandmother's trailer, kicking up dust that makes a mess of my good shoes that I stupidly wore for this 'work' that I'm doing. Everything is dry, brown and hot. Why did I ever leave my nice air-conditioned cubicle with a water cooler?

Near the center of camp, I pass by cabins, some of them large and one with a fountain out front. Away from the center, there's a polyglot of trailers, cabins, campers and tents. Most are very close to the road with little or no landscaping in front, but lots of lawn chairs and lounges.

For the last 30 years, my grandparents, Eleanor and Andrew, have owned a sky-blue trailer that sits at the beginning of Pine Hollow Road. It's about 35 feet long and eight feet wide, with two doors facing the street. There are worn wooden steps in front of the kitchen door, and a faded wooden trellis tries to hide the concrete blocks that the trailer sits on.

As I approach the trailer, Gramma yells from the bedroom, "Go away. I don't want to talk to you. Go way before someone sees you came in here."

"Will someone just please tell me what's going on?" There is no answer, but I see a copy of the *Ashton Bulletin* on the couch.

Maureen's article is on the front page below the fold. It trashes the camp. And it makes me sound like I'm the one providing the trash. It's written very carefully, quoting what I really did say to her, but then starting the following paragraphs with words like 'additionally' to suggest that these comments also came from me. I am referred to as "Ms. Bingham, a frequent visitor to the camp, but no longer a member."

Some of it really did come from me. Over the year that I have known Maureen, we have occasionally talked about the camp. I've told her how membership dropped in the camp, leading them to add amenities which in turn increased the dues, which then lowered the membership. Murphy's Law as applied to nudist recruitment.

I did not say that this made the camp so desperate for members that they were "advertising online at a number of obscure websites." Casting about for weird, fringe types? That's what she made it sound like. Nor did I say that "families now make up a small portion of membership." That's absolutely not true. And even if it were, what's wrong with people who are single?

Some of the information she must have gotten from others. For instance, she made a big deal about the domestic dispute that drew the police to the camp. That information she could have obtained from police records. She must have been scrambling yesterday to dig up dirt on the camp, *before* I came over for dinner.

"Gramma, I didn't say most of these things. She made stuff up and made it sound like it came from me. And you were the one who told me about Stan."

She emerges from the bedroom, arms crossed in front of her. "I didn't go running out of here to tell an *outsider*. And a reporter!"

"I figured she was a hospital reporter. She only writes about hospital stuff. At least that's what I thought."

"A reporter is a reporter is a reporter. They're worse than car salesmen. You should know that by now."

"How would I know that? I'm a soil scientist. The press doesn't beat down the door of a soil scientist. Maureen's the first reporter I've ever known." And the last one I'll ever be friends with.

There is a tiny knock on the wooden edge of the screen door. It's Roland, Flo's tall, skinny husband, from across the street. Roland's not the warm and cuddly kind, but right now I feel like going up to him and asking him if he will, please, pretty please, be my friend.

"Come on in, Roland," I say. "Want some coffee? A beer?"

Roland is the opposite of his wife in every possible way. Where she is obsessed with her appearance, he is stoop shouldered, with limp hair and a blank expression behind rimless glasses. Where she is outgoing to a fault, he only feels comfortable with his computer. He spends most of his time inside, so he is pale except when he is sunburned. He wears multicolored athletic shoes with heavy white socks.

"No, I was just looking for Flo. It's time to call my father at the home, and I want her to get on the phone."

Normally this expression of filial duty would get at least a grunt of approval from Gramma. But her arms are still crossed and she doesn't look happy. There is no point in trying to convince her that I didn't trash the camp when I talked to Maureen last night.

The next couple of days are going to be hard on Gramma. My grandparents have always had to defend my right to wear clothes in a nudist camp. Now it will be that much harder to stick up for me, and she has to do it alone. But even if I stand here all day, she won't forgive me and I have to get back to Kevin on the beach.

As I'm walking back up the dirt road, I consider taking off my clothes in a show of support for the camp. The feeling passes. I look up, and coming down the hill straight at me is Stan. First my grandmother, now Stan.

He looks like he has something to say and he gets right to it. "What you did, Catie, was a horrible thing. As a man of the cloth, of course, I totally forgive you. It is my duty to put this behind me, and of course I will. Just don't expect me to ever, *ever*, talk to you again."

Chapter Seven

As i get near the beach, I see a man approaching Kevin with a red face and his hand covering his penis. I hurry to get to Kevin before the man reaches him. Kevin is squatting down between two women while he takes some notes. He stands up as he sees me approaching, but he doesn't get any words out before this man taps him on his shoulder with his free hand.

"Officer, I would like you to arrest that woman over there for assault." The man is probably in his forties, with a narrow frame and thick red hair. I don't recognize him. Before we can answer, he turns and walks back across the beach as if there could be no question that we would follow him.

Kevin looks at me and I shrug in bewilderment as we dutifully follow the man. He stops in front of woman whose face is hidden by a large straw hat. She's about the same age and height as the man, but carrying considerably more weight.

From under the straw hat, the woman says, "Look, I never saw this man before, but I figure I'd do the guy a favor. And this is what I get?"

Kevin stands up straighter, trying not to look like the brand new rookie that he is. "Ma'am, could you sit up and take your hat off?"

Her hat comes off and reveals short hair that's been bleached far too many times. When she sits, her belly comes out in front of her, forming a resting place for her breasts as well as her folded hands. She heaves a dramatic sigh and looks at the red-haired man.

"There was a horsefly on your dick. I was supposed to just leave it there while you slept?"

"You could have shooed it away," says the red haired man, spitting the words out.

"I tried. Didn't I try?" she asks, looking at her friend on the next blanket. "I kept shooing and shooing and the fly just sat there, and I kept getting closer and it still sat there, and then I thought maybe it didn't look so good, you know, in front of those kids over there."

"You could have woken me up."

"I said, 'sir, sir,' over and over again, but you didn't wake up. Meanwhile this thing is about to take a big bite out of you, and believe me, I know how that hurts, although maybe not, you know, right there."

"Why didn't you just give me a shove or something?'

"I'm shooing it away, saying sir, sir. And now you're telling me I should have shoved you?"

"You didn't have to roll up your magazine and whack my dick."

She rolls her eyes and looks at Kevin. "Time was of the essence."

The red-haired man also turns toward Kevin. "But it really hurts!"

I figure I should say something to take the focus off of Kevin. "Why don't you put some ice on it?"

Both Kevin and the red-haired man physically recoil, and I get the idea that I'm not being helpful. Kevin surprises me by taking charge of the situation.

"Sir, you are free to file a complaint and get a restraining order requiring her to stay a certain distance away from you. Keep in mind that she will be able to challenge that order in front of a judge if she chooses to do so. In the meantime, I suggest you two take your lounge chairs and move to opposite ends of the beach."

They both comply as if being scolded by a teacher. When they've gathered up their belongings and left, I smile at Kevin. "Wow, I'm impressed."

"I was great, wasn't I?"

"And they were both naked. Didn't seem to bother you at all."

He shrugs. "I feel like I've been here forever. Thanks for that little talk in the car. By the way, I've been wondering how I'm going to tell my wife what you said and how it helped me so much. It's hard to make it sound right."

I picture his wife coming after me with a heavy object in her hand. "Why don't you just say you figured it out all by yourself? If I ever meet your wife, well then, mum's the word."

When George and Bruce drive up and want to go to lunch, Kevin is still flying high and he insists that I go along, too. "Wait till Catie and I tell you what happened this morning."

George says okay, and he and Bruce drive off with instructions for us to meet them at Ellie's. When we arrive at the restaurant, everyone stares at the three uniformed state cops and me. It makes me feel uncomfortable, but these guys seem to be used to it. We finally get our pizza slices and head outside toward an out-of-the-way table where we can talk.

"I feel sort of responsible for getting Stan named so publicly as a suspect." I say. "Mind if I ask what you found out?"

"Airtight alibi," says George. "He was 'administering to the sick' at one of the cabins near the pool. Somebody with psychological problems or something. Anyway, they sat on the porch all morning, and not only does this sick guy confirm it, a lot of people at the pool could see him, too. Stan was on that porch from about 10AM right through lunch."

"And the time of death was. . . ."

"About eleven."

I catch Bruce giving a look to George, and I realize that George is not supposed to be talking to me since I'm a civilian. But, I press on anyway. "What was the fight about anyway?"

George gives a dismissive wave to Bruce. "Catie is serving as police consultant."

"I don't know, George," say Bruce.

"So Stan is in the clear?" I ask.

"Yup. Stan is officially off our list of suspects."

"You have a list of suspects?"

"Yeah, the fifty or so people who were in the camp that morning."

"I wasn't in camp that morning."

George smiles. "I know."

"You checked?"

"Yeah, it was easy. You stick out like a sore thumb there with your clothes. It irritates some people, especially some of the men. One guy I talked to complained that you have one of the best bodies in the place and you insist on wearing clothes. Doesn't seem fair to them, I guess. Not that *I'm* saying you have one of the best bodies in that place. That would be sexual harassment."

"Tell you what. I won't sue you for sexual harassment if you don't put me in jail for Donald's murder."

"Deal."

It's silly, but I actually feel somewhat relieved by this exchange. "What else do you know?"

"The gun was a pretty common .32 caliber revolver with a silencer. My guess is that there was no argument, Donald just opened the door, stepped back to let the guy in, and got shot."

"How do you know it was a guy?"

"Turns out that Donald was a neat freak and you could eat off his floors. But we found foot prints all over the place made by a size ten plastic sole of some kind, like from beach shoes or flip flops. Donald was a size twelve. By the way, you said you were a dirt scientist, right? You might be interested in the fact that the foot prints contained some fine sand like from a beach, and some coarse sand from the dirt road."

"Wow. 'Fine' and 'coarse'. You could join the Dirt Science Society."

"I aim to impress."

"Can you figure out anything about the guy? Like was he short, or tall?"

"From the angle of entry, we can pretty much rule out your grandmother."

"Me, Stan, now my grandmother. Progress. Anything else?"

"The gun was probably in one of those tote bags we talked about. We found fragments of a plasticized canvas material all over the place, which suggests that he shot the gun through the bag. That way, the gun was concealed the entire time Donald was opening the door and letting him in, and there was no reason for there to be a scuffle that might have attracted attention."

"So he walks away with big hole in his tote bag?"

"Not if he brought along a bigger one to put it in. My guess is that he was walking around with the inner bag inside the larger one until he got near Donald's cabin. Then he took out the smaller bag, put it on one shoulder and put the large bag on the other shoulder."

"What about the fragments?"

"Well, it looks like it was a hunting bag, made out of canvas, with a plastic coating. It was printed in a camouflage pattern, not an army green one, but a mottled brown one, meant to blend in with dead leaves."

"This place has a lot of dead leaves."

"Yeah, but we'll find it, and hopefully it'll still have the gun in it."

We leave Ellie's and drive back into the camp, using the new passes to open the gates and go directly to Donald's cabin. The place feels very different now without any gawkers. Yesterday, I was suddenly drawn into the center of things, and all I could feel was excitement. Now, the place feels like death.

I think about my grandfather and the slow wasting away of his body that helped prepare us for his death. But even then, the finality was jolting. One moment my grandfather existed, and the next moment he didn't. It must be an even bigger jolt when the death is unexpected.

Donald's cabin is very quiet. The people who originally built it were obviously looking for privacy. The cabin sits on a large lot at the corner of Pine Hollow Road and Sandhill Lane. Across from the corner there is a steep drop off next to a heavily forested ravine. The cabin sits diagonally on the lot, with a broad view of the forest below.

George is talking to two men who have come out of the cabin with various kits and cameras. He waves me over, and I hear him say, "Let's ask our resident expert in the nudist experience."

He introduces me to the two forensic guys. "Catie, these guys here say there is no sign of forced entry or defensive wounds. Usually that leads us to the conclusion that the victim knew his visitor. But I'm telling them it may not be true in a nudist camp. Assuming the visitor was naked and looked like he was a member of the camp, do you think that Donald would have opened the door and let him in even if he didn't know the guy? Would your grandfather let him in?"

"My grandfather would open the door and say, 'C'mon in. How 'bout a drink?' Then he would wait for the guy to introduce himself. But he would only do that if the guy was naked. If the guy had clothes on, he might open the door, but he'd say something like, 'Can I help you?' and wait for him to answer before letting him in."

"Think that's typical in this camp?"

"Well, my grandfather was a lot more social than Donald, but, yeah, I'd say that was generally true. If you're naked, you are generally considered part of the club. The only person I can picture Donald turning away would be a reporter from the *Wall Street Journal*, someone clever enough to get a day pass and brave enough to take his clothes off."

"But how would he know if it was a *Wall Street Journal* reporter if the reporter was naked?"

"Good point," I say.

Kevin and I start on the house next to Donald's on Pine Hollow. We are supposed to find out if anyone was around yesterday. If they were, George and Bruce will interview them. I ask Kevin whether he minds such low-level work.

"Are you kidding? Only a few months on the job and I'm on a murder in a nudist camp? I thought maybe I'd get some a meth or crack investigation in my first year, but this? I just hope that I don't look back on this a year from now, and think it was all downhill from here."

The idea that this could be one of the highlights of his young life makes me feel better about the lack of excitement in mine. At least I don't consider this to be one of my peak experiences, especially since we knock on door after door with no response. Very few people are in the camp on a Tuesday afternoon, even in August.

We finally get an answer. A woman in her twenties with spiked hair opens the door and a male of about the same age comes up behind her. Both are heavily covered with multiple tattoos tangled around various parts of their bodies. Barbed wire seems to be the artistic theme, penning in fertility symbols from various ancient cultures and Japanese lettering.

Kevin is rendered speechless as he lets his eyes roam. He must have suddenly realized he was staring at some inappropriate part, because he stands up straight, and quickly asks if either of them were around yesterday. The answer is no. Again, Kevin is at a loss for words. I step into the vacuum and explain the reason for our visit.

The woman with spiked hair says that they didn't know Donald all that well and they were sorry that they had missed all the excitement by arriving this morning instead of yesterday as they had planned. The girl launches into exhaustive detail about why they were delayed by one day. This is definitely not one of my peak experiences.

I hear the quiet whine of a golf cart and turn around to see my grandmother approaching. She drives right up to the door so she can join the conversation without getting out of the cart. For the hundredth time this month, I worry about her ability to differentiate between the gas pedal and the brake. She guesses correctly.

My grandmother looks at the woman with the tatoos without smiling. "Hello, Melissa."

Equally frigid is Melissa's response. "Hello, Eleanor. I'm sorry. I've got to be going." She tries to think of some reason and can't, so she turns to her male companion, and says, "Don't I?" He nods blankly. She seems to think this is sufficient, so she steps back and says a crisp goodbye before shutting the door.

I turn to my grandmother. "What was that all about?"

"Isn't it obvious?"

"What?"

"The tattoos, silly. The 'tats,' the 'ink.'"

"You seem to have the words down. But why?"

"I'm trying to reach out to these people, to save them from making bad decisions."

I don't have any tattoos but I've never felt that people who have them show poor decision-making skills. "Okay. What's wrong with tattoos?"

Gramma's mouth is open in wonderment. "Look at me!" She turns to Kevin and says again, "Look at me!" He does, but then looks at me, not sure of where he should be looking and what he's supposed to be seeing.

I shrug. "I give up. What?"

"Look at this skin. Do you see one square inch of my body that isn't all saggy and droopy? Now, imagine if I had gotten tattoos. All those tattoos would be mushed and stretched out, like that artist guy who painted the oozing watches, whatever his name is. What I'm trying to tell these people is that it ain't going to be pretty. They don't believe me. They think they're going to be young forever." She gives a dismissive wave with her wrist.

"It's a personal decision, Gramma. You've got to live and let live."

"I'm not saying don't get a tattoo. I just want a person to be required to at least ask. At least ask their grandparents to send them a picture of themselves naked. Then you can get an idea of what they're going to look like in fifty years and plan accordingly. Like maybe tattoos on your upper back would be the thing to do. The hump will stretch the skin but at least it won't sag."

Kevin has developed a fascination with his feet. At least that's where his eyes are fixed. I'm not sure if that because he's hiding his face or trying to keep his lunch down.

"And that Melissa you were just talking to," says Gramma.

"Her entire body! Can you imagine what she's going to look like in fifty years?"

The mention of Melissa brings me back to reality. "Gramma, we need to get on with our interviews. I'll come see you later, okay?"

"You better come see me. Nobody wants to be with me because of you, so you're all I got."

That reminds me. It's time to go see Maureen.

Chapter Eight

Righteous indignation is one of my favorite feelings. I've been thinking about Maureen all day, and my resentment has been building up with each hour. It's helped me get through a boring afternoon. The police work that I thought was going to be so exciting has turned out to be pretty tedious. Kevin and I have not been able to find anyone on Pine Hollow Road who was around yesterday morning. After knocking on about twenty doors, I'm relieved when George and Bruce drive down and tell us it's time to leave.

Kevin gives me a ride out to my car, still parked on Lee Road. I'm relieved to see that it hasn't been spray painted with angry messages. I had pictured my car covered with anti-nudism statements from passersby, and pro-nudism statements from people leaving the camp. Fair and balanced graffiti.

I drive back into the camp to see Gramma like I promised. Flo is there—I can see her platinum beehive through the screen door. I once thought that she wore a wig, but she said it was her own hair, just sprayed to withstand a category five hurricane. Gramma and Flo are talking about Melissa's tattoos, and Flo adds her two cents.

"You are so right, honey. I swear those girls don't know a ship from shine-olah. What are they going to do when they're baggin, saggin, and draggin? How they gonna get fixed up? Me, I'm gonna get pulled up and tucked in, first sign of it. But what are those Japanese letters gonna spell out if the skin gets snipped? Parts of those tattoos are going to end up in the hospital trash, you know."

Flo plans on spending every last cent of her money to fight the tides of aging, and maintain optimal measurements of every part of her body. I have no doubt that those balloons in her chest will be periodically hoisted to maintain proper alignment. One of Flo's favorite quotes from Dolly Parton is: "It costs a lot to look this cheap."

I've had enough information on the effects of gravity on skin. I change the subject and tell them that I'm going to stop and see Maureen on my way home.

"I read the article twice," Flo says. "And she really did a number on you, Catie. She made it sound like you were creeped out by this place. Like you thought it was a sleaze-pit. I think *she* thinks it's a sleaze-pit but couldn't just come out and say it."

"But I've known her for over a year and she never said anything like that," I say. "Maybe she'd laugh a little at some oddball stuff, but she never let on that she felt this kind of, you know, contempt."

My grandmother snorts. "People change. The whole town is changing. Rich people are moving in, and when rich people move in, the place goes down the toilet."

Although Maureen has never expressed it that way, those are her sentiments, too. She has a real chip on her shoulder about rich people moving in—myself, I had thought, excluded. And she isn't alone. At the first yuppy sighting, the whole town got together and produced a frenzy of new ordinances, called the Smellies and the Uglies. Be forewarned, these ordinances conveyed to the newcomers—farms can smell bad and people can put whatever they like in their front yard. Don't start complaining.

Flo taps her fake red nails on the table in annoyance. "But we've been here longer than anybody! Compared to us, they're all newbies."

The nudist camp has been in this town for almost seventy years, deeply hidden in the heavily forested northeast corner. People usually live in town for a few months before even hearing about it, and their response is always, "You're kidding, here in Rensford?" Until yesterday, the camp had kept a low profile.

"And you know what happened, don't you, at last year's town meeting?" Gramma doesn't wait for an answer. "They said that some guy got up and complained that the camp wasn't good for property values. Property values, my foot. With the taxes we pay he should get down on his knees and thank us."

I was at that town meeting last year and heard the discussion which followed this man's complaint about property values. A town selectman said that he didn't think the town could get rid of the nudist camp, even if they wanted to, because it had been grandfathered in when zoning was adopted.

While there was no action taken, the discussion itself was disturbing. I had no idea that so many people felt such ill-will toward the camp. The murder is going exacerbate those feelings. Rensford is now famous for murder and a nudist camp.

My grandmother shakes her finger at me. "You go tell that friend of yours that her property values probably took a dive because of her own damn article."

After leaving the camp, I drive to Maureen's office which is in a small plaza called the Birches. The Birches consists of a long narrow building, and two young white birches struggling to grow in one corner of the large parking lot. Maureen's office is above Lupiens drugstore which takes up most of the lower part of the building. I see Maureen's car, so I go on up and knock on her door.

She opens it up and greets me with a wide smile. "Catie! Come on in! What brings you here?"

"I read your article this morning. I'm a little upset."

"Upset? Hey, I made you the hero of this town. Come on! My editor loved it. And wait till you see what I've got for tomorrow! Want coffee?"

"Maureen. I'm serious. You made it sound like I was trashing the camp. Nobody there will speak to me."

"And you care?"

"Of course I care. It's not only my grandmother. There are good people there."

"They're all weirdos and you know it. You've been telling us stories about them for a whole year. I know what you think of them."

I'm beginning to regret my attempts to be entertaining at cocktail parties. "Okay, maybe there are some strange characters there, but you made it sound like they are all a bunch of sick loonies."

"Catie, the only thing I did was condense a lot of what you've told me before and make it sound like you told me yesterday. Big deal."

"It is a big deal. With the murder and all, the camp doesn't need any more bad publicity."

"Wait. Let me get this straight. I'm supposed to pass up the biggest chance I'll ever get to move up in my newsroom, because I should be sensitive to the needs of the nudists in town?"

"No, you should be sensitive to the needs of your friend."

"The same friend who makes fun of these people, but who now wants to be seen as supportive in their time of crisis?"

"Maureen, come on, you know that all those stories I told you, even the ones last night, were meant to be just talk between friends, not fodder for your career."

"Fodder for my career? You make it sound like I was purposely using you."

"Bingo."

She's silent for a moment. "You really think that?"

"Yeah."

She looks down at the floor. "Okay, I guess that's it then."

"Yeah. That's it."

I turn and go down the little hallway, down the stairs, and step out into the bright parking lot. I sounded strong a few minutes ago, but inside I'm a quivering mass of protoplasm. I can never think straight when I'm in the middle of a fight with someone. It'll be hours before I figure out if I did the right thing.

I'm driving home on one of Rensford's narrow roads and ahead of me is another example of how the town is changing. The car in front of me is an open BMW convertible, and in front of it is a very slow manure spreader creeping up the hill. The outside of the manure spreader is coated with a thick layer of manure. Inside the spreader is a slurry of manure, urine, and soured milk – whatever ends up below the metal grate that the cows stand on. This slurry can be sprayed from the back of the tank as the spreader moves up and down the fields.

Following a spreader is unpleasant to the point of causing your eyes to sting, and most locals will find another route or stop for a cup of coffee to avoid it. The woman in this convertible seems to think she has a better idea. She thinks the spreader should pull over to let her by. She is flashing her lights, honking her horn, and veering into the middle of the road to let the guy in the spreader know that she wants to get by.

The spreader moves toward the center of the road to prevent her from going by. This is not going to be pretty, and I start pulling back. Like the periscope on top of a submarine, the release chute slowly turns toward the rear and the brake lights come on. The convertible has to stop fast, and when the convertible closes in, the sprayers are turned on. A brown spray is released from the spreader about ten feet from the ground in a wide arc 30 feet across.

Although I am far back now, I can see that the spray has reached into the back seat. The convertible slams on the brakes and veers into a small culvert. I know it sounds coldhearted, but I dial 911, turn around, and find another way home. I'm usually pretty good about helping my fellow motorist, but not her. She's going to stink for days.

When I finally get home, I fill a large glass full of ice and then pour chardonnay over it. My grandfather always warned me not to drink alone. He prided himself on being a social drinker, but that led to his addiction to society. To me, wine goes nicely with solitude. I'm going to need some quiet solitude before I talk to Jack.

It's ten minutes to six, and I feel like I am about to walk into the principal's office. Why am I so nervous? After all, this is my husband, my equal, not someone I have to answer to. But here's the problem. Since one half of me agrees with him, I feel like I am being outvoted by the whole of Jack and, secretly, by one half of myself.

Here's the side of me that agrees with Jack – it's not a good thing to confuse the state police with a support group of best buddies. I'm sure they would make good friends individually, but collectively their object is to solve this murder. If for some reason, they go down the wrong path and think I did it, they will turn on me and pursue me until I am locked up.

Here's the other side. I'm lonely and feeling betrayed and ostracized, and the police are the only ones being nice to me. Case closed.

Chapter Nine

"I give up," Jack sighs. "Trying to keep you safe is like trying to bolt the door with a boiled carrot, as my mother used to say." I would be surprised if Jack's mother ever boiled a carrot, but I hold my tongue. "All it took was one phone call from the police and you were off and running."

I have given him a synopsis of the ups and downs, mostly downs, of the last 24 hours, and I'm surprised to find him less upset than I would have thought. I'm not getting the loud, high-pitched concern of our last conversation, just deep, low sighs. I'm beginning to worry. Why isn't he upset?

"So here's what's going to happen," he says. I mentally brace for impact. "I've asked Phil Demers to come up and hang out with you for a few days until I get back."

"What! You've got to be kidding? Phil Demers? Here? Where's he going to stay? Do I have to make him dinner?" In any emergency, the first thing is to eliminate the possibility that it will mean cleaning the house or going food shopping.

"No, he's going to be staying in the Rensford Inn, but it would be nice if you had dinner with him there once or twice."

"Phil Demers? Really? I mean, he's a big shot Boston lawyer and he's just going to drop everything and come be a babysitter up here? Why would he do that?"

"Because we pay him a ton of money, that's why."

"But why? That's silly!" I've seen Phil Demers once, at a stuffy Bingham family event, and he could have won the door prize for best costume. It wasn't just the bow tie, the manicure, and the cuff links, it was the way he held his wine glass delicately at the base of the stem. Above all, it was the fact that his dark hair was parted in the *center*.

"It's not silly. I love you, and the only way I can be away from you right now, without going nuts with worry, is to have Phil up there with you."

"But why Phil? Look I promise, I'll hire a local lawyer to follow me around, if you want, but please, not Phil."

"Phil is the one I trust, Catie. And if you have to be roped in a little, he's the only one I know who can do it."

"Why can't he just talk to the police by phone?"

"He's already talked to them. When you didn't call him back, he called me, and I told him to talk to the detective in charge of the case. They finally connected late this afternoon."

"And?"

"You're right, you're not a suspect at this point, but Phil thinks it would be prudent to have someone there to make sure you don't become one."

It occurs to me that I can hide from Phil in the camp all day and then just report back to him at dinner. During the day, Phil can monitor the activity of the police in Ashton or do whatever else he feels like doing.

"And, Catie, he is committed to staying by your side throughout this adventure until I get home."

"Surely, not...."

"Yup. He knows this whole thing takes place in a nudist camp, and, like I said, he will be by your side."

It's unimaginable. Putting Phil Demers together with my grandmother in a normal setting would require some sedation on my part. But Phil Demers and my naked grandmother? Phil Demers and Flo?

Jack speaks gently. “It’s okay. Remember to breathe. It will all be over soon. I’ll be home in a few days.”

“Jack, please....”

“Phil has some things to tie up tomorrow morning, but he should be there by noon. He’ll call you on your cell phone. I have to say goodbye now, honey. The guys are waiting to go to dinner.”

I hang up and sit there staring for a while. Damn it. Jack won. The obvious thing for me to do is stop helping with the interviews, and stop being ‘the resident expert in the nudist experience.’ Jack knows what a horror it would be for me to bring someone like Phil Demers into camp, and he knows I will do anything to avoid it.

I get more ice and more chardonnay. I wasn’t that big of a help to the police anyway. I was supposed to help Kevin feel at ease, but now he’s perfectly comfortable being around naked people. And any questions they have about the ‘nudist experience’ they can ask by phone. I have to admit I’ve been hanging around mostly out of my own interest.

I’m worn out from the confrontations with Maureen and Stan, and all the other events of the day. Maybe I should start looking for a real job tomorrow. It’s going to be hard to go back to sewing couch pillows after this excitement.

But by next morning, the old Catie is back. God damn it, if Phil Demers is going to get paid a lot of money to be my babysitter, let him earn it. Jack probably told Phil there’s no way I would bring him into the camp. They probably figured I would withdraw my help from the police at the very thought of it.

And that’s exactly what I was thinking of doing last night. But I, Catie Bingham, am going to call their bluff. I am going to drag Phil Demers into that camp, introduce him to my naked grandmother, and then take my own sweet time while I go to the bathroom. Then I'll let him exchange genteel pleasantries with my grandmother while I go across the street to get Flo.

George calls. "Your lawyer got you under house arrest?"

"No, I am ready and available to report for duty."

"Okay, meet Kevin at the parking lot of the camp in an hour. And stop and get a copy of the *Ashton Bulletin*."

"Oh, no, not again. It's not about me, is it?"

"Mostly, no," he says and hangs up.

Mostly no? What has Maureen done this time? I get in the car, and the first stop is the Rensford town hall. I don't think anyone has yet obtained a map of the camp's boundaries. I am fired up, damn it. I am going to be useful to this investigation. Step aside, Phil Demers, and try not to get in the way.

The town hall is a tiny brick building, formerly a library built by Andrew Carnegie when he decided to donate a library to every town. It is now one large room crammed with desks and computers. One desk and computer is up against a wall under a sign that says 'Town Map'. I sit down at the desk and realize I don't know what name to look up. Who owns the camp anyway?

A pregnant woman in her mid-twenties asks me if I need any help. I describe my problem and she says, "Type in American Association for Nudist Recreation."

I do, and what comes up is a map of a large piece of property along Lee Road in the northeast corner of the town. I recognize the pond and the dirt road leading into the camp, but none of the roads within the camp are mapped. There are several large, undeveloped parcels around the camp, owned by individuals and entities that I don't recognize.

"That map is out of date, though. The camp is now much bigger." The woman points out a large piece of property which wraps around the back of the camp, marked on the map as belonging to B & R Gellerman, Inc. "They just sold their piece to the camp. Now the camp extends all the way over to this property, owned by Mountville Trust."

"Who's Mountville Trust?"

"I don't know. I could ask around if you want me to. Maybe someone else in the office knows."

"I'd appreciate it," I say. "I'd like to know who the new neighbors are."

I print out copies of the map of the northeast corner of the town where the camp is located. Where did the camp get enough money to buy that land? Did they get a loan from the national association? Why would the national association want to invest in expansion of an enterprise that is struggling financially, especially when land prices are so high?

I make a mental note to check in at the camp office for an explanation, and then drive down the road to get the *Ashton Bulletin* at the town's only gas station. One glance at the paper and I can see that Maureen Helms is definitely moving up in the world. She co-authored the lead story entitled, "Murder Victim Swindled Fellow Nudist," and underneath, in smaller type, "Camp Member Lost $200,000 in Mortgage Fund Scam."

I skim the article for any mention of my name and I'm relieved to find none. Before I read it carefully, I want to find out if my name is mentioned anywhere else in the paper. I flip through the pages and find my name in the 'Corrections" column:

"CORRECTION: In yesterday's edition Ms. Catie Bingham was incorrectly named as the source for a number of facts about the murder of Donald Thaler. Ms. Bingham later denied being the source for those facts. Furthermore, she stated that she wants to support the camp in their time of crisis, and that she feels that the camp doesn't need any more bad publicity. We regret the error."

Great, just great. By going to see Maureen yesterday, I succeeded in lowering myself even further in the eyes of the camp. Maybe I should have walked in and said, "Hello-Maureen-this-is-off-the-record." Would it have done any good?

Thumbing back through the pages to get to the lead story, I look at the "Letters to the Editor" page. About twenty emails relate to the nudist camp, and only one defends the camp. It's from "Anonymous" and contains just one sentence, "These people shouldn't be denied the right to something that's natural." My guess is that Anonymous likes to walk around in the buff.

The rest of the emails are uniformly negative, and divided into two groups. Some people think that the nudist camp lowers Rensford in the eyes of God. The others think that it lowers Rensford in the eyes of Mammon. Mammon, in this case, being your typical real estate buyer.

I turn back to the front page to read the lead story. A camp member named David Dechesne lost $200,000 when Donald Thaler's mortgage fund collapsed. I don't recognize the name but that's because there are a lot of Davids in the camp. Most of the article details Donald's scam, but at the end of the article it gives some information about David Dechesne.

David is 48, lives in Litchfield, Connecticut, and his parents are also members of the camp. Their names are Roger and Patty Dechesne. As far as I know, there is only one couple in the camp name Roger and Patty. David's father is Roger, the gun collector.

When I get to the camp, I park my car and get into the passenger's seat of Kevin's car. He's been reading the paper.

"I didn't know that this place was so unpopular with the locals."

"Me, neither."

"So this is recent?"

"From what I've gathered, Rensford has always been a kind of Yankee libertarian place. You know – you mind your business and I'll mind mine. For a long time, the locals even voted down zoning because they felt that everybody should have the right to do as they please with their own property. Zoning just got voted in a few years ago."

"How did they classify the camp?"

"It got its own special category, I think it's called 'recreational residential' or something like that." This reminds me of my trip to the town hall and I show him the map of the property lines, including the new purchase by the camp. "I want to go to the office and find out about why and how they bought such a big chunk of land when they can hardly afford to pump the septic tanks."

"George wants us to continue knocking on doors near Donald's, but I think we can go to the office first, if you want."

"Where's George now?" I ask.

"Talking to Roger Dechesne."

"That was fast."

"George is a fast reader."

As we are walking to the office, I warn him about the imminent arrival of my tag-along attorney, Phil Demers. "This was my husband's idea, not mine. He thinks I should be protected from the big, bad police."

Without a hint of humor in his voice, he says, "Your husband is a smart man."

This was not the reaction I was expecting, and there are a few moments of silence before he goes on. "Are you going to help him with the entry process like you did with me?"

"No." I would have made some kind of sarcastic remark at this point but I'm still reeling from the idea that Kevin thinks I might actually *need* a lawyer. We walk without saying anything

further until we reach a small, one-room cottage overlooking the pond, probably the original building from before this place became a nudist camp. The building shows some neglect with a roof covered in pine needles and small plants growing out of the gutter.

The camp's bulletin board is on the front of the cottage, under the roof of the wide porch. Labor Day weekend is coming, which accounts for the predominance of campaign literature by candidates for camp president, treasurer and the like. There are also announcements of upcoming events like the barbecue cook-off and the Miss Nude New Hampshire pageant. The door to the office is open, and a man small, thin man in his eighties welcomes us in with a booming voice.

"Well, look who's here! Come on in, Catie! Is this one of your law enforcement friends I've been hearing about? Come on in, sir! Take a load off. How can I help you people on this fine day?"

Ellsworth calls himself the office manager. He has no family in the camp, and for years he has stationed himself here to answer the phone and hand out maps. He welcomes the day pass visitors and patiently goes through the camp's welcoming pamphlet. The new version of the pamphlet contains the same list of rules, like no nude dancing, and no alcohol in public areas, but now also includes a tear-off back page to be signed by visitors as a liability waiver.

"Hi, Ellsworth. This is Kevin, or maybe I should say, Officer Branagan."

Kevin reaches forward to shake hands, but before he has a chance to say anything, Ellsworth says, "I'll just call you Kevin, if you don't mind, sir. It's easier for my old brain to remember and I can always use the excuse that we don't use last names in this place."

"That's fine," Kevin says.

I show Ellsworth the map I got at the town hall, and ask him if he knows anything about the purchase of the abutting property.

"All I know is that it happened fast, way too fast, and Bernie is going to have to do some fast talking to explain it at the meeting. Bernie is our president," he explains to Kevin, "at least till Labor Day." I get the feeling that Bernie is not going to get Ellsworth's vote for reelection.

"When did they buy the land?" I ask.

"A month, maybe six weeks, ago."

"Have you got the records for it? I'd be interested in seeing just how much they had to fork over for it."

"Nope. I keep asking Bernie and his crew to give me the paperwork because a lot of people are getting wind of this, and they're coming in here asking about it. I've got nothing. Your map at least tells me who sold it to us."

"What are people saying? What's on the grapevine?"

"They're saying that it was some sort of fire sale, you know, a really good bargain, but only if the camp was ready to act fast. But, like I used to say over and over to my wife, if you don't need it, it's not a bargain at any price. And we sure as heck don't need any more land. We're not exactly bulging at the seams as it is now."

Kevin looks at the map of the roads within the camp, and then turns to Ellsworth. "This is where Donald's cabin is, right? How close is his cabin to the edge of the camp's property, the original property line, not the new one?"

"Boy, oh, boy, that's not an easy question to answer. I couldn't tell you."

There are quick staccato steps on the porch and a very erect woman comes in wearing sandals with low heels. Her hair is in a neat ponytail and expertly highlighted. She slaps a photograph down on Ellsworth's desk.

"There," she says. "There's proof."

It's hard to see the photograph and I lean forward. Ellsworth sighs and hands it to me, but even close up it's hard to tell what it is. I hand it to Kevin.

"Bernie is not going to get my vote for president until he does something about this woman. Every time I talk to him, he says he'll talk to her next time he actually sees her do it, but it only happens on weekdays when she knows she can get away with it."

The picture appears to be close up of the back end of a very large woman. There are pink lines about three inches wide and an inch apart running across the back of her legs and the lower part of her butt. My guess is that the picture was taken just after she got up from sitting on a bench with parallel slats. The woman with the ponytail turns her head toward Kevin and me without turning the rest of her body.

"Sorry for interrupting," she says to us, in a voice that's shows she's not sorry at all. "It's disgusting! On her own chair, fine, but not on the benches and not on the chairs at the canteen."

Ellsworth shakes his head. "You know that there's no regulation against sitting down without a towel."

"There certainly ought to be, and I'm going to pin Bernie down on where he stands on this."

"Did you get her permission to take this picture?"

"Oh, sure," the woman says, sarcastically. "I asked her if she would turn around so I could take a picture of that derriere. It's not like it's the kind of picture that will end up on the internet."

Silently, I disagree. I look down at the picture which Kevin has handed back to me. This is exactly the kind of picture that would end up in some gallery in New York, blown up to a huge size, and called 'Modern Impressionism: Butt on Bench' or something.

Ellsworth is doing his best to address her concerns but even he is losing his patience. "Why don't you just talk to her yourself?"

"Believe me, I have, repeatedly. She says that if I don't want to sit in her sweat, then I should put my own towel down after she gets up. But it's not just sweat, you know," she says, making a face and turning her head to the side, "it's, you know, whatever, ugh."

We hear another set of foot steps on the porch and Phil Demers walks into thc officc.

Chapter Ten

Phil looks as eager and excited as a kid arriving at Disneyland. He's got a big smile and a bounce in his step. "They told me at the gate to drive straight to the office to get my day pass. Is this where I get it?'

The woman with a ponytail looks at Phil with his bow tie and Kevin in his uniform. Realizing that her particular complaint will not be high on the agenda of this crowd, she turns on her heels and walks out, grabbing her evidence as she goes. Phil nods politely and steps aside to let her out.

"Hi, Phil. Good to see you again," I say and introduce him to the others. I'm floored by the breezy grace of his entry into a nudist camp. I can see that Kevin is impressed, too. "You don't need a day pass. You're my guest."

"But I must insist. How else will the water cooler crowd at my office believe me when tell them about this place? And I want some sort of souvenir for myself. This is an amazing place. I feel like Margaret Mead when she first landed in Samoa."

I'm not sure that camp members would consider this is a compliment, and I hope he's not going to go around laughing at the primitive natives. One thing is for sure, though. The natives are going to be laughing at him. Phil has still got the center part in his hair, along with the black rimmed glasses that make him look like a Harry Potter wannabe. His bow tie is blue with yellow stripes to compliment his pale yellow shirt and the pleats in his navy trousers make them balloon out a little before tapering down to dark brown wing tips.

I watch to see if Phil flinches as the naked lower half of Ellsworth comes out from behind the desk. Not even a flicker of embarrassment crosses Phil's face. Do they teach these social skills at Harvard Law? Do they practice maintaining eye contact even if the judge comes out naked?

"Please don't let me interrupt whatever you were doing," Phil says as he looks down at the maps spread out on the table.

Kevin stands up. "I think we've gone as far as we can with this for now. Ellsworth, can you make a copy of the map that Catie drew? I want one to show to George, and Catie will probably want to keep this for herself."

I look up at Kevin, surprised and pleased with what he just did. In just a few sentences he sent a message to Phil that I really was helping out with the investigation. Actually, I'm not sure whether the map is worth showing to George, or whether Kevin is just a kind soul who wants to make it appear that I'm helping out.

Ellsworth makes a copy, and Kevin, Phil and I say goodbye and step out on the porch. What are we supposed to do now? Is Phil just going to walk around with us all day? Is Kevin comfortable talking with me while my lawyer is monitoring the conversation? Is Kevin going to want my help, as insignificant as it is, if Phil has to tag along?

Kevin answers all my internal questions. "Well, Catie, why don't you show Phil around this place? George has given me another assignment any way, so I won't need your help with the door-to-door interviews today. I'm going to be checking out gun dealers in the general area. So, I'll catch up with you later, okay?"

I know it's immature, but I feel like the cool kid on the playground has just dumped me because of the dorky guy who has attached himself to me. Yesterday, I thought George and Bruce were the cool guys and I was stuck with Kevin. Now Kevin is gone and I'm stuck with Phil. I seem to be moving down the social ladder.

Phil and I walk out into the open area between the beach and the pool, and all eyes turn toward him. Children openly stare as if Phil was naked and everyone else had clothes on. I wonder if he is the first person in the camp to ever come in wearing a bow tie. I am about to hustle him off when he stops me and points to a picnic table.

"Could we sit over there a moment? I just have to stop and take this all in."

Oh, great. Phil gawks at them while they gawk at Phil. We walk over to the table and I sit facing away from the crowd and he sits on the other side, looking at them over my shoulder. Neither of us says anything for a minute or two. Finally, I can't stand staring down at the table anymore, and say, "Well?"

"Absolutely fascinating."

"What?"

"I don't know where to start. For one thing, I am amazed by the variability of the female form."

"Just the females?"

"Yes. Yes. I'm sure I would have come to the same conclusion if I had studied people closely at a supermarket, but it's more obvious here. All the males become heavy set in the same way, while females are very individual in their fat distribution."

I can't help myself. I turn around to look. "You mean all the men have big bellies?"

"Yes. All their weight appears to go onto the front of the abdomen, and then when that area fills up, so to speak, the additional weight goes to other parts of their body. But the women put on weight everywhere. Look at some of those women—some truly lovely and unique curves."

I will never again form any preconceived notions about a man who parts his hair in the center. I had Phil to be uptight and acutely embarrassed. Instead, I'm sitting across from an explorer, who feels he has come upon an entirely new civilization.

But let's see how he does when he's up close and personal. "I'd like you to meet my grandmother. Do you want to drive down?" I ask, looking at his wing tips.

"No. No. And don't mind these office shoes. They aren't my good ones. I had a hard time figuring out what to wear this morning, since I didn't know if we were going to be spending time here or in a police station."

I'm not going to get paranoid. Lawyers are paid to be paranoid for you. If he wants to worry about the police, well, that's fine. There's no way George and his crew are suddenly going to decide I'm a murderer. It's ridiculous that Phil is even here.

We walk down the dirt road, and Phil nods and smiles at everyone he sees. I see Roland across the street from Gramma's trailer, and I yell out, "Flo?" He points toward the trailer. Phil is going to get a double whammy: Gramma and Flo together.

I'm about to knock on the screen door when I hear crying and see Flo with her arm around my grandmother. I'm in the door before I know it, and Phil is left standing uncomfortably outside.

"Gramma, what's the matter?"

Flo answers for her. "Oh, that Alice down the street is just a mean old catfish, all mouth and no brain." She gives Gramma an extra squeeze. "Now you never mind about her, you hear?"

"Holding a balled up tissue, my grandmother says softly, "I miss Andrew."

"Course you do, honey. If Andrew was here he'd punch her eyes out."

Alice has never been one of my favorite people. "What did she say?"

"I swear she went on and on, like she always does."

"What did she say?"

"She said the town is going to shut down this place and it's your Gramma's fault," says Flo.

"Why is it her fault?"

"Because she gave birth to your mother and your mother gave birth to you."

I sigh, and then yell out the door, "Phil! We need you in here!"

Phil opens the door and comes in. "How can I be of assistance, ladies?" His eyes widen at the sight of Flo, but his professional training takes hold and he concentrates on my grandmother. "How can I help you, Mrs. – "

"Eleanor," my grandmother says.

"What seems to be the problem, uh, Mrs. Eleanor?"

Flo's boobs bounce as she laughs. "Lordy! We got a genuine newbie, here! Catie, honey, you want to introduce us to your friend?"

"Gramma, Flo, this is Phil, a friend of Jack's. He's an attorney sent here to make sure I don't get into trouble. Phil, this is Eleanor, and Flo, who lives across the street." I explain to him about the camp policy against last names.

Gramma looks at him. "If you're sent here to keep her out of trouble, you're too late. She's in a heap of trouble with everyone."

"Why is that?"

"People around here don't like her in the first place because she's got clothes on, and then she bitches about the camp to her sophisticated townie friends, and then one of those townies turns out to be a reporter, and now the whole town wants to shut us down."

Flo says, "You're a lawyer. Can they do that?"

"Local regulation of nudist camps was not covered in law school, but I'll be happy to go to the town hall and see what their options are, if they choose to go in that direction. What makes you think they want to shut this place down?"

Roland opens the door and Flo makes room for him on the little couch. Flo pats Gramma on the shoulder. "That rotten Alice said that there was a petition or something. Something to force the town to do something about this place."

After I do the necessary introductions, my grandmother raises her head and looks Phil straight in the eye. "It was that idiot scumbag, Donald Thaler. He gets himself killed here and the rest of us have to pick up the pieces."

Roland has been using his search engines. "Do you know Thaler was originally a German word for a unit of currency? When the colonists were choosing a name for an American currency, they chose the unit popular among Germans settled here. They pronounced it 'tahler' and thus our currency became called the dollar."

Phil's face betrays some confusion, but again his professional training kicks in. "Is that so? I wasn't aware of that."

I try to get the conversation back on track. "But what could the town do? The camp has been here so long. The town can't suddenly start changing its mind about things."

"Well, the town could easily do some small things, like revoke a liquor license."

"That's everyone's first idea, but the camp doesn't have a

liquor license," I say. "There's no drinking allowed in public places within the camp."

Gramma snorts. "That didn't stop Andrew and a hundred people like him."

"What about zoning?" asks Phil. "By any chance, is the camp classified in its own zoning category?"

"Yes," I say. "I think the town didn't know what category to put it in so they made up one for it."

"That could be a bit of a problem, because the town may have regulations that allow it to change the restrictions or tax rate for a zoning category, as long as they apply it to all properties within that category. That's something I can find out at the town hall."

"Well, then. What's keeping you?" My grandmother can be so gracious.

Phil and I leave them and walk back to my car. We head off to a restaurant in Marshfield, a place far enough away to allow a greater chance of privacy. On the way, I learn a little about him and his wife, who's also a lawyer, and their two kids, both in a private elementary school and into sports. This weekend Phil will watch his daughter play hockey and his son play lacrosse.

As we enter Marshfield, I am surprised to feel a wave of relaxation. I hadn't realized how much Rensford was getting on my nerves. At the restaurant I order a glass of wine with my soup and salad. Drinking before five o'clock is usually a no-no for me, but I need this. My shoulders feel like they are up around my ears, and I worry that I'm starting to look like a turtle trying to pull its head in.

"We can talk about the murder over dinner tonight, if that's okay with you," says Phil. "But for now I want you to fill me in on those three strange people I just met in that trailer. Beginning with your grandmother."

I tell him all about my grandmother and grandfather and how they ended up using the trailer as their retirement home after she quit her job as a teacher and he quit his job as an advertising salesman for the Yellow Pages. I tell Phil about my grandfather's recent death and the disposal of his ashes only three days ago.

"So your grandmother is still reeling from his death?"

"Reeling is not a word I would associate with Gramma, but, yeah, she's right in the thick of it."

"Does she want to stay at the camp?'

"I think so. At least she never talks about going anywhere else. But most of her friends are gone now, and many of them were really Andrew's friends anyway. My mother is out on the west coast, and so Gramma's got just Roland and Flo, and me"

"Okay, what about Roland?"

"Roland works as a librarian in a high school on the other side of the state where he and Flo live during the school year. He loves to look things up. Flo says the kids take advantage of him when they need to do a term paper. They ask Roland a question, and then they ask him another question, and pretty soon they have the whole term paper done just by writing down what he says. He really can't help himself."

"And Flo?"

I tell him about her obsession with Dolly Parton, her long list of plastic surgeries and her fierce determination to remain youthful, no matter what the cost. "And, of course, the accent is as fake as everything else, since she was brought up nearby in Marshfield."

"Does she work?"

"Not that I know of."

"Do either of them come from a wealthy family?"

"Heavens, no," I say, picturing the relatives who I've been introduced to.

"Then where does the money for all that surgery come from? We're looking at multiple procedures, each maybe five to twenty thousand dollars, with more to come. A high school librarian doesn't make that kind of money."

"I've never thought about that. I don't know."

Chapter Eleven

"Is it just me, or are we making everyone here nervous?" I am sitting with Phil in a room at the town hall. Between us are piles of folders containing everything which might relate to the interaction between the town and the camp. This is the first time we've been left alone.

"I always make people nervous. All lawyers make people nervous." He is marking the pages he wants copied, and he doesn't look up. I am amazed that he can be so focused on something so boring.

"But I never make people nervous – it's always the other way around. Maybe they think I'm the murderer."

"Believe me, they would prefer it."

"What do you mean? Compared to what?"

He sighs and looks up. "How do you think this looks to them? A rumor about a petition to get rid of the camp goes around. Within a day, one of the wealthiest people in town, whose grandmother is in the camp, comes to the town hall with her fancy-pants, out-of-town lawyer."

"Fancy-pants?"

"They never get past the bow tie. They make assumptions. Anyway, they figure you're going to take legal action against the town if they try and close the camp down."

"They think I'd sue the town to keep the camp open? Everybody hates me in camp!"

"The town people don't know that. They look at you and

they see someone who goes to the camp a lot and whose grandmother is there. And they think you immediately called your lawyer, who dropped everything and came up here to get the process going."

"And you *did* drop everything to come up here and I haven't even thanked you for that. Thank you."

"You're welcome. The point is, they look at you and see some costly legal battles ahead of them. So you make them nervous. Now can I get back to looking at the documents?"

It is three o'clock by the time we're through copying the necessary documents. We have agreed to meet for dinner at the Rensford Inn at seven, and Phil wants to get settled in and make a few calls to his office. I want to use the time to do some emergency food shopping and house cleaning just in case Phil comes to the house.

We drive back to pick up his car and I head off to the local super market, wondering whether I was expected to ask him to the house for a drink or even offer to make dinner. It's hard to know what to do with a lawyer. A lawyer can easily start feeling like a friend, but then you remember that you are paying this person to be your friend. Even worse, if your enemy hired this same lawyer, they would feel like friends, too.

And yet, Phil does seem like a friend already. Maybe it's because he's been the Bingham family lawyer for a long time, and doesn't want to kill the Bingham golden goose, but he feels like someone I can trust. I've been feeling much more relaxed already in the few hours he's been here. Whatever the reason, loyalty or money, this guy is on my side. Jack, I know, is always on my side, but Phil is *here*.

I pass the office of the realtor who sold us our house, and make a quick turn into the parking lot to see if Janine is there. Maybe she'll know something about the camp's land acquisition from the Gellermans. Janine is there and we hug like old friends, and it occurs to me that realtors can become paid best friends just like lawyers. Cynicism is my new middle name.

I ask her about the property transfer, and she shakes her head. “I don’t know too much about it. Phyllis, the one with the office on Main Street, handled that one.”

“Did you hear anything about it?

“Not much. I know it wasn’t on the market long. The camp bought it, right?”

“Yeah. Any idea how much they paid for it?”

“No, but I can look it up.” She sits at her computer and a minute later says, “Whoa! The camp got a deal! The property was sixty-two acres and they got it for $72,000! Normally, that would go for more like five or six hundred thousand, assuming it was developable.”

“Why would it be that cheap?”

“I don’t know. But something must have been really wrong with it.”

“Anything wrong with the other properties around there? Any of them have trouble with getting permits?”

“Not that I know of. But you should call Phyllis about it.”

I get the number from Janine, and promise to have lunch with her soon. When I’m in the car, I call Phyllis and find out that she happens to have an opening in her schedule at nine the next morning. I’m anxious to talk to her because I’m wondering if there is something seriously wrong with the camp’s property.

As I drive into the supermarket parking lot, I see a folding table next to the front door and a group of people around the table. When I get out of the car I see that the person behind the table is Maureen’s husband, Gordon, and he’s into his bombastic mode. A couple of months ago, I talked to someone from the Catholic college where he teaches, and she said everyone was eager to get rid of him. If this is how he lectures to students, I can see why.

As I get closer, I can hear that the topic of his lecture is the nudist camp, and he's urging people to sign a petition against it. His rant accuses the camp of every possible sin including being a source of strange diseases, being a bad example for children, and, most important, lowering property values. I am waiting to hear whether nudists turn into vampires at night, but he catches sight of me first.

His sudden silence is deafening and everyone turns to look at me. I smile and wave my fingers and say, "Toodle ooo!" as I walk into the store. It's not my most eloquent moment, but I'm tired of being public enemy number one.

I'm startled by Gordon's new soap box. He's never given me any idea that he is so adamantly against the camp. Maybe that's why Maureen has been so nasty to the camp in her reporting. She is using her stories about the camp to advance her career, but maybe she's also been getting a little push from home.

I leave the supermarket by another door and drive back to the house. I have enough time to unload the groceries and run around the house and do a quick 'degrossing', picking up anything that's really disgusting, doing a quick swish in the downstairs toilet, and getting rid of the dishes in the sink. I am hoping that Phil will not ask for a tour of the house, because I don't have time to degross the upstairs. I just run up there and change into some nicer clothes for dinner tonight.

At six o'clock, right on time, Jack calls. He doesn't tell me about his day, he doesn't even say hello, he just says, "So?"

"I don't even know where to start."

"Are you okay? You're not in any trouble?"

"Nope. Phil Demers scared away the big, bad policeman

that I had previously been working with, and now I'm shut out of the investigation."

"Good. And how did he react to all those naked bodies? Did he run off screaming, or did he declare that he had found true freedom and take his clothes off?"

"Actually, I was very impressed. He was fascinated by everything. He made observations on the comparative variability of fat distribution in males versus females."

"I'll be sure to ask him about it at my parents' next party. How did he react to Gramma? Did he meet her neighbors?"

I explained the circumstances of their encounter, and our trip to the town hall. "Phil seems to be genuinely interested in helping. He's really quite a nice guy."

"Remember, he's married."

"Got it."

We talk for a little more about his day, and then I tell him I'm meeting Phil at seven, so we sign off. I'm glad to hear the old, relaxed Jack. I don't think I was ever in any real danger, but whatever it cost to bring Phil up here was worth it, just to ease Jack's mind.

I arrive at the Rensford Inn, a rambling white colonial house with views of the Connecticut River. I join Phil in the dining room where he is studying the wine list. He wants my opinion on a particular vintage, but I plead ignorance.

I want to talk about the reason he's here. "I just talked to Jack by the way. He seemed much more relaxed about everything."

"That's because I've already talked to him once today, and told him you were not yet shackled and wearing orange."

"Both of you are totally overreacting. I was just helping the police with their investigation."

"Catie, you really need to study up on your clichés. Haven't you ever heard the phrase, 'helping the police with their inquiries?' That's what journalists write about a person who's being questioned by the police."

"So when I say I'm helping...."

"Jack thinks that you are this innocent, eager, gullible creature who's being led into a trap."

"He thinks I'm a dupe."

"He loves you and is worried about you. Now, can you tell me about the day of the murder?"

I go over my activities on Monday morning. When I get to the part about approaching the crime scene, he asks me to slow down.

"Why did they let you go beyond the yellow tape?"

"I had clothes on, and so they thought I was an official."

"It's a common mistake. Why didn't they just usher you right out after they found out you were not an official?"

"Because they had some basic questions about the camp, and they felt more comfortable asking me than the circle of naked people staring at them."

"This is important. Did they throw in some questions about you, or was it all about the camp?"

"At that time, it was all about the camp. They only asked about me when they took my statement at the police barracks."

"We'll get to that. What kind of questions about the camp?"

"How many people are generally there, its access roads, and lots of general questions. I gave them a sort of Dummies' Guide to Naked Life."

"How did they ask you to go to the police barracks and give a statement? Was there any coercion at all?"

"No, they just asked me if I'd mind coming to Ashton to give a statement and educate the rest of the team about life in a nudist camp. Actually, I was thrilled."

Phil sighed. "And I assume that they did not read you your Miranda rights at any time?"

"They didn't. And see? Doesn't that get me off the hook? That means that anything I said couldn't be used against me."

"That's why I asked you about coercion. They only have to read you your rights if they are forcing you to talk or come with them. If you go willingly, if you are *thrilled* to go with them, then they can use anything you say against you without your Miranda rights."

"Come on! That means that if I'm a good, cooperative citizen, I make myself more vulnerable than if I refuse to cooperate?"

"You got it."

I'm feeling a little deflated. My puffed up image as an important part of the investigation is beginning to sound more like, "Little Catie Goes to the Police Station." I still don't believe that George and the rest of them were trying to entrap me, but I'm beginning to feel a little silly.

I relate the rest of the day, and Phil asks me a lot of questions about my statement. I tell him about how quick Bruce was to open the door when he realized that there was not enough air in the room for the two of us. I tell him how Bruce practically skipped over the fact that I didn't have an alibi.

At the end of my story, I ask, "So, what's the verdict? What are you going to say to Jack?"

"That he doesn't need to come home tomorrow. He can stay the extra day and come home on Friday as planned."

"And you?"

"I will stay until he comes home, as planned."

When I get in the car that night, I've decided that I like Phil Demers and I'm glad he's staying. This has been a strange couple of days, and I don't have Jack around, or even Maureen now, to talk to. He's a very expensive rent-a-friend but I'll take what I can get.

It's nearly ten o'clock when I shut off the car in front of the garage. I can hear some loud music and laughter from Terry's house. There's some partying going on outside, enough to scare away any 'critter' that Terry could ever worry about. As I'm climbing up the steps, the noise stops and I hear a truck starting up. I'm looking for my keys when I hear the crunch of tires on the rough gravel of our driveway. Then I see headlights.

Chapter Twelve

Headlights turn the green of the corn to gray. They flicker so fast against the dense foliage that the corn in front of the house looks like waves of static on a TV screen. The patterns get lighter and lighter until my sight is flooded by the high beams directly on me. With the keys still in my hand, I feel around in my purse for my cell phone.

The engine stops. With the beams on there's enough reflected light to see three men get out, but I can't see their faces. They lean up against the truck, about twenty feet away from me. Nobody speaks.

I can't stand it any more. Getting trapped in the house would not be a smart thing to do. But I feel like a small animal that should be still, but gets too scared and tries to run. I have to move, and I turn toward the house.

"Hey!"

I try to sound confident, but the tension makes my voice a squeak. "Hey, what?"

"Hey, there. Misssusss Bingham."

I am relieved to hear how drunk the voice is. Men who are drunk can be dangerous, but if they're too drunk, they're stupid.

I try for real composure. "To whom am I speaking?"

"To whom? To whom? Does her high falutin' highness always talk like that?"

Gaining more confidence, I take a guess. "Okay, Terry. Who are your friends?"

"That's better!" It's the first voice again. "You gotta talk boonie talk here, cuz we here are boonie men, from the boonies."

"Terry?"

"How ya doing, Catie girl?" It's Terry, alright.

Another man speaks up. "Whoa, whoa, whoa, Terrance, my boy. You said we had to say Misssuss Bingham when we talkin' to this lady, right?"

"Yup." It's another voice I don't recognize.

"Terry?" I try again.

"Just checking on my corn." This gets a round of laughs from Boonie Man.

"Your corn is fine. Now leave."

"Wait. We're cool here, right Terr? We just came over to ask about your grandmother."

"What about my grandmother?"

"Do you go see her because you like *her*, or you just like being *naked*?"

"Terry, it's time to take your friends and go home."

"Because I like bein' naked myself. We could all be naked right here, right now."

"Take it easy, Ralphie," says Terry.

"Ralphie's right. No reason we can't all be naked, is there?" It's the second voice, and this one doesn't sound drunk. He comes forward, enough for me to see him, but I don't recognize him. Slowly, he pulls off his tee shirt and throws it on the ground. He's a big guy, maybe forty, with a beer belly gut. Still looking at me, he unbuckles his belt and drops it.

My hand folds around the reassuring curves of my cell phone. "This is ridiculous. Come on, now. Go home," My voice is so high pitched it sounds like I'm whining. "Please, Terry."

"You think Terry's going to be your knight in shinin' armor, here?" asks Ralph. "Hell, he's the one who's been gettin' us all juiced up. He says you run around naked here all the time, struttin' your bare ass outside even."

"I do not!" I stop myself from protesting further. The last thing I want to do is start participating in this conversation.

Ralph gives a little laugh. "Terry says he comes around here nearly every day. Now why would he do that, if it wasn't to see you?"

"Tell them the truth, Terry. You come to check on the corn." This gets a big laugh from all three.

"Yup," says the one without the shirt. "Terry comes and says – hey, the corn's still here!" More laughter.

"If you don't go now, I'm going to have to call the police."

"Oooh, I'm real scared now," says Ralph. "Real scared. Wish I had a gun to protect myself. Terry, you got that rifle of yours?"

"Terry don't take a piss without that baby," says the other. "I think it's in the back seat." He turns to get it.

Terry's voice is tired, like he's already feeling the hangover. "Let's just forget about it, alright? Amanda's coming home soon from shopping. Let's get out of here."

"Hey, Terr, shut up. You don't like it, walk home. Leave us the truck," says Ralph with a smile at me. "We'll use the back of it."

I pull out my phone. "I'm going to call the police now."

Ralph comes toward me. "Now, now. Give me that thing."

I do the quickest, automatic thing. I speed dial Jack. Terry steps in front of Ralph.

When Jack answers, I say, "I'm in front of the house and there are three guys and I'm scared and I have to call the police."

Jack speaks firmly, like he's talking to a child. "Hang up, dial 911, and say there's a fire. We've talked about this before. You know what to do. Hang up, call 911, and report a fire. I'll call Phil."

"I don't..."

"NOW!"

Terry has managed to hold back Ralph, but the other guy is now coming back with the rifle. He says, "Did ya call your Gramma? Sure doesn't sound like you called the police."

I stare at the guy with the beer belly and say to the operator in a calm, defiant voice, "I'd like to report a fire at 695 Old Forge Road, Rensford."

"Shit! Guys, in the truck, fast. Let's go! Let's go!" Terry knows as well as I do that a volunteer fireman, Paul Basley, lives only a few doors down. The other two are not interested in leaving. They start arguing, but their words are soon drowned out by blasts from the fire station, only a mile away. The sudden deafening noise sobers them up fast and they move quickly back to the truck.

By now, that volunteer fireman, Paul Basley, will be getting up from his chair and checking for a text message of the fire's location. When he realizes it's only a few doors down, he's going to race to here as fast as possible so he can be the first on scene. Terry will be lucky if he can get out of our driveway without being seen by Paul.

Knowing which direction Paul will be coming from, Terry guns the engine and churns up the gravel, heading out the other entrance to the road. Then the truck brakes hard. Terry backs up too fast, veering wildly from side to side, and ends up backing into some corn. Ralph gets out of the front seat and grabs the tee shirt and belt still lying on the ground. With Ralph barely back in his seat, Terry guns it again.

I see Terry's truck pull out of the driveway a few seconds before Paul's truck pulls in the other entrance. Pretty soon, I hear sirens in the distance. It's going to be embarrassing to tell everybody that there is no fire, but all I can feel now is relief. Paul Basley's truck pulls up in front of me and he jumps out, pulling on the last of his gear.

"Any people or pets inside?" His adrenaline is pumping as he quickly looks over the whole scene, and moves past me towards the front door.

"There's no fire," I say.

He stops and looks at me, clearly crushed by the news. "No fire?"

"I'm sorry."

Another pickup has arrived. I can hear the fire truck kill its siren as it approaches, its spinning blue lights dazzling as it moves up the driveway. Paul Basley gives a dismissive wave of disgust, to tell the newcomers not to rush. He's waiting for me to go on. "Why did you report a fire?" he finally asks.

"Because I was scared and there were three guys and a rifle and my husband told me…"

"Wait. Who were these guys and what were they doing here?"

"One of them was Terry," I motion toward his house. "One of them was called Ralph. But I didn't get the name of the other one."

"Terry? Terry Curtis? What were they doing? Why were you scared?"

"Because they were talking about being naked and one of them took his shirt off and his belt and went and got a rifle."

"Terry? That doesn't sound like Terry."

"Well, it was mostly his friends and not Terry. He was trying to get them to go."

By now a small crowd has gathered around, and Paul repeats my story. Every one has basically the same reaction. It doesn't sound like something Terry would do. My cell phone rings and it's Jack. He is upset and almost yelling.

"This stupid flea bag of a hotel! Are you okay? I couldn't get a line out. Over and over. No line! I *just* reached Phil. He'll be there soon. Are you okay?" He pauses for a breath, and I start to sob. Hearing his voice has pushed me over the edge, and I hand the phone to Paul.

Paul asks who he's speaking to, and then he listens to Jack for a while. He says, "She's okay; really, I think she just got scared." He listens for a while longer and says, "No, there was no one here when we got here." After a pause, his tone sympathetic, "I completely understand. It was a smart thing to do."

My sobbing has greatly increased my credibility with this crowd. One of the female firefighters has come over to put her arm around me. Paul hands the phone back to me and, as I move away, I hear him explaining what Jack said. I get back on the phone, and this time I'm able to reassure Jack that I'm really okay. He tells me he wants to come home right now, and I really, really, want him to come home, but I say, no, it's okay, I'll be all right.

The crowd is breaking up when I see Phil drive up in his rental car. I've only really known Phil for one day, but the sight of his familiar face is wonderful. It's not Jack, but it's the next best thing. Phil introduces himself to Paul Basley, describing himself as a family friend, thankfully, and not my attorney.

Paul is the last one to leave, but before he does, he has one piece of advice. "I'd be careful about the things you say about Terry and all this stuff that went on tonight. I'm not saying that he didn't do this. I just want to tell you that Terry's pretty well-liked and respected around here, and his family's been around forever. You being relatively new around here...." Phil thanks him graciously for his candor.

Phil gets a small bag from the car, saying that he has orders from Jack to spend the night in the guest room. Now I wish I had had the time to clean up the second floor. We sit at the table for a while over a glass of wine, one for him and two for me, while I recount every last detail of the night. Only then, a little after midnight, can I finally go to sleep.

Chapter Thirteen

I don't look good in the morning. Picture a sleepy-eyed, blowfish with thick glasses and pillow creases, and you get an idea of what I have to face in the mirror. With a shower, some coffee, and my contacts, I begin to assume a less frightening appearance, but it takes some time.

I can hear some stirring in the guest room so I know Phil is up. Maybe I can hide here in the upstairs bathroom long enough so that he is forced to use the half-bath downstairs. That way he will be spared the sight of me in my subhuman form. He will also miss the sight of the rusty ring-around-the-collar in the toilet bowl.

My plan is a partial success. I hear Phil emerge from his room, go down the stairs, and use the half bath. But then he calls up to me at the bottom of the stairs. When I reluctantly appear at the top of the stairs, we arrange to meet at Gramma's trailer later in the day. He also instructs me to call him if I have the slightest fear of trouble. Now, of course, I feel guilty for being an inhospitable host, but guilt is always easier to bear than embarrassment, especially when it comes to a toilet bowl.

I'm out of the house in time to meet Phyllis at her office at nine. I find a parking space across from Village Realty, and Phyllis waves at me through the large glass window. She bounces up from behind her desk to usher me in and seems thoroughly glad to see me. Rensford's population is growing, but not as fast as the number of new realtors in town. Phyllis's near monopoly is long gone.

Not wanting to dash her hopes too quickly, I tell her that Jack and I are thinking about buying some land in town as an investment. I tell her that we are interested in the northeast corner, because we believe that the property values there are less inflated than in the rest of the town. She immediately begins the standard realtor's soliloquy designed to convince buyers that prices are generally higher than they might think. The other version, of course, is designed to convince sellers that prices are generally lower.

Phyllis goes to her file to get a map of the area. Her black hair is gently curled into a precise page boy, and her long red nails pick gingerly through her folders. When she brings the map over to show me, I point to the property labeled as being owned by B & R Gellerman, Inc. "I heard that one went for a really low price."

"Well, yes. But that was under exceptional circumstances. You certainly won't find that kind of deal on any other properties in that area."

"What kind of circumstances?"

"Oh, very unusual. Some sort of pressure on the Gellerman family to sell by June 30th because of tax considerations. Usually, we get that kind of thing around the end of the year, but this time it was at the end of the second quarter." Phyllis opens a drawer and rummages around for something. "The property had been on the market for a few months, and then the national nudist association stepped in and made a deal with the Gellermans."

"And you still got your commission?"

"Such as it was."

"What do you mean?"

"They got $72,000 for sixty-two acres, so it didn't turn out to be a big deal for me."

"Wow. Why so low? I mean, beyond the need for a quick sale. Was there something wrong with the land?"

Phyllis looks away and crosses her legs. "No. I don't know. I wasn't part of the negotiations."

"What do you mean?"

"All negotiations were private between Mountville Trust and the Gellermans."

I remember hearing the name of Mountville Trust from the woman at the town hall. "They're the ones who own the property on the other side of the Gellermans, right?

"Right. I think they were trying to buy the Gellerman land to make sure they had a buffer between their property and the camp's."

"But the Gellermans sold to the camp."

"That was unexpected."

"Do you think it was the camp that talked down the price?"

Phyllis starts moving some papers around. "I don't know. Like I said, I wasn't part of the negotiations."

"And you were okay with that?"

"The Gellermans promised to pay my commission anyway."

"Would you mind if I talked to the Gellermans and this person from Mountville?"

Phyllis just shrugs. She is clearly not happy with the idea, so I don't press her for phone numbers. I thank her and tell her I'll give her a call so we can go look at some land parcels.

I walk down the street to a small supermarket and pick up today's copy of the *Ashton Bulletin*. The headline reads, "THALER WAS STALKER AT R.H.S.," and, underneath that, "Murder Victim Followed High School Girls." The byline is Maureen Helms.

The article says that the parents of two local highschool girls claim that the murder victim followed their daughters home from school during the past few weeks. These parents say that they recognized the photo of the murder victim as being the same person seen loitering around their homes. The article goes on to say that the names of these families are not being released to protect the privacy of the minors involved.

I don't think that Donald Thaler was the type who would stalk high school girls. He seemed to be intent on keeping a very low profile. But how can a dead man issue a denial? I can't believe they made a lead story out of something so easily concocted. All it takes is two adults against the camp, who happen to have daughters in high school.

Why would the editor allow this kind of flimsy information to pass as a lead story? For a moment, I think that Maureen and her editor might be having an affair. He does seem to be elevating her from a mere hospital reporter to a front page crime reporter. Reading the editorial, however, I can see that romance is not the reason. It's a meeting of minds that accounts for her elevation to page one.

The editor is calling for the town to close down the nudist camp, and he wants a referendum to that effect before the town meeting in September. In the meantime, he proposes that the town's attorney begin investigating legal options for closing the camp. He says that Rensford should be able to shape its own image, and not be known as the town with the nudist camp.

"Even if the nudist camp were a model of clean living and high moral values," the editorial says, "it would generate an understandable uneasiness for most people. The recent murder has transformed that uneasiness into fear and abhorrence, especially when it turns out that the murder victim himself was of disreputable character in business, and now, possibly, in his personal life as well (see story, page one)."

I fold up the newspaper and go back to my car. Gramma has to be told about this quickly, and by me. Otherwise she will hear about it from someone who will tell her that it is all the fault of her granddaughter. I'm probably too late already.

Phil and I have agreed to meet at the trailer at 10AM. I want to thank him for staying with me last night. I know that there was little chance that the Manure Mafia boys would have returned, but fear takes a long time to dissipate when the human body has to break down all those fight-or-flight chemicals. Whenever a caveman saw a saber-toothed tiger, I'm sure he was up all night, too.

The dirt road leading into the camp is dry and throws up dust all around the car. The road is too deeply rutted to enable me to get ahead of the dust and, my black SUV is now gray. When I reach the trailer, I leave my clean, cool cocoon and step out into the thick, hot air. It feels like 90 degrees and 90 percent humidity and it's not even noon.

Flo is at the trailer door, trying to get my grandmother to go up to the beach. "Come on, Eleanor. It'll be good for you. We can sit at the edge and put our feet in the water."

"I'm not going to sit in the sun. I told you, it causes premature aging. And I don't want to listen to a bunch of old biddies playing 'name that scar.'"

Clearly, the heat is getting to Gramma—right now she looks like a limp dishrag. I'd love to put her in some nice air conditioned assisted living place, if I could count on her to keep her clothes on. I'm not hopeful.

I hand her the *Ashton Bulletin*, and say, "Not good."

She gives me yet another disgusted wave with her wrist. At this rate, she's going to get carpal tunnel syndrome. "I saw it. A bunch of twaddle. I can't see that hoity-toity guy getting in his car and chasing the local skirts. Loitering around these girl houses? Please."

"I'm talking about the editorial." I turn the page and show her. "They're calling for the camp to be shut down."

She snorts. "More hot air. They can't close this place down. We got our rights. They can't just say to some Joe Shmoe, hey, we don't want you here, go away. And we're bigger than any Joe Shmoe, let me tell you."

I'm glad we won't have to rely on Gramma to argue the case in court. "There may be ways for the town to make it financially more difficult to exist. And the camp is in pretty bad shape to begin with."

"I told them not to build that hot tub the size of Texas! It cost a fortune. Even Andrew thought they went way overboard, and he loved looking at the ladies in that hot tub. He always said that no matter how time had pulled them down, the bubbles would pop them right back up. He was talking about boobs of course, his favorite topic. He'd walk around that hot tub checking out the long ones, short ones. He said even flat, saggy ones looked good in a hot tub."

I can see that Gramma has made a random turn in her synaptic connections. There's no need to go back to the original topic, so I recount a little of what happened to me last night. I want to tone it down a bit, in case Phil says something that would scare her. I give my account, and she's scared anyway.

"That's it, Catie. I want you to move in with me on the nights that Jack is gone. You're by yourself too much. I like Jack. I think he's a nice guy and not just because he's loaded. But he leaves you alone too much. All by yourself on that huge farm? You could scream your bloody head off and no one would hear you!"

"Thanks, Gramma. That's a comforting thought."

"I'm not kidding about this. You hear me? I mean it. You're much safer here."

"As I recall, there's just been a murder here."

"That was because he was a dirtbag, not because this is a dangerous place. You know as well as I do that if you go around pissing enough people off, you're going to get it in the end. He could have been knocked off in a damn nunnery, and that wouldn't make the nunnery a dangerous place."

"So you think he was killed over some business deal?"

"Stop trying to change the subject. I'm telling you, I don't want you in that house all by yourself night after night."

"Thanks Gramma. I really appreciate it. But I like my house and most of the time I feel great there." Although after last night, I'm not sure I'm going to feel so great there for a while.

"You either move in here or you get a big dog."

"What shall I name it?"

"Funny, ha ha. But go back to last night. Why did you call the fire department anyway? I don't get that."

"Jack and I had heard that the police can be a little slow to show up. They have six people on the force, but between day shifts and night shifts and days off, there are usually only two people on duty, and only one car. So if they are in the middle of something, it can take ten or fifteen minutes to get across town, even in an emergency."

"And it's a guaranteed half hour before they show up in camp."

"Really? Why?"

"Dunno. And when they get here, they're kind of sullen, like, 'What do you people want again?' I know Mabel had to call again and again to get them to come over about that punch-drunk son-in-law of hers, beating up on her daughter. One cop even told her that the camp should have its own police force and not mooch off the town."

"Mooch off the town?!"

"Yeah, we pay all these taxes and we get no snow plowing, no trash pickup, no road maintenance, nothing. But if we call 911, we're mooching."

We hear steps and Flo flies in, slamming the door behind her. She waves a piece of paper and spits out the words:

"I have to pay a friggin' fine for indecency!"

Chapter Fourteen

'A fine for what?" I've never heard of such a thing before.

Gramma sighs. "It's part of the new campaign to show everyone what a 'family friendly' place this is. The fines got approved last September and this is the first time I've heard of one being given out. You must have done something really out of line," she says, looking at Flo.

"But I didn't. How could I be indecent if I was covered up? I cover up the sexy parts and I'm indecent?" Apparently, Flo no longer channels Dolly Parton when she's under stress. She sounds like any pissed-off girl raised in New Hampshire.

"Don't be an idiot, Flo," says Gramma. "You start covering up and the puritans come out of the wood work."

I must be Alice, placing a call from Wonderland. "So the way to avoid a fine for indecency is to remain absolutely buck naked?"

Flo ignores me. "But everyone put something on. It was the costume party given by Sylvia and Ron last Saturday."

"What was your costume?"

"French maid."

Gramma drops her head and shakes it. "Flo."

"I was tryin' to be funny, okay? I found this cute little g-string with the most adorable little lace apron attached to the front. And then for my nipples, I found these cute little pasties with brooms on them. They were supposed to be for a witch's costume, but I thought, hey, this'll work. Get it? Brooms? A maid?"

"Pasties and a g-string, Flo?" asks my grandmother.

"I don't get it. I *just* don't get it. If I show my nipples it's okay, but if I cover them up, it's indecent. If I show my crotch it's okay, but if I cover it up with the cutest little apron you ever saw, it's indecent."

"It makes men think of sex," says my grandmother.

"That's *their* problem!"

"Flo, what was that quote you're always givin' us? What did Dolly Parton say about where a man has his brains?"

Flo recites, "Just about every guy I've ever been around has his brains in the head of his subpoena."

"Exactly."

"So I'm supposed to go around making sure that when guys look at me they don't think of sex?"

"Fat chance," I say.

"Thank you, Catie," says Flo. "Why do you think I go through all this surgery, for heaven's sake?"

"Which means you gotta be a little careful, that's all I'm saying. With that body you've gotta be a little more lady-like than the rest of us. Just stay away from costume parties and keep your clothes off."

"But damn it, I like costume parties."

"Just no more g-strings and pasties, okay?" says Gramma. "Even I would set off alarms if I pranced around in a g-string and pasties. Right, Phil?"

We all turn toward the screen door where Phil is standing, not wanting to reply to that question or even touch the handle of the door. I smile at him and say, "The witness is instructed not to answer that question. Come on in, Phil."

Phil enters, a little tentatively, and Flo makes room for him on the little couch. She pats him on the knee. "Phil, here, is one of these real, upscale lawyers. I betcha if he represented me I wouldn't have to pay this ol' cockamamie fine." The slow Dolly drawl is coming back into her voice.

"What fine?"

I break in. "Can we talk about that later? Phil, did you get the chance to go over any of the documents that we got at the town hall yesterday?"

"Yes. I did. And the results are both good and bad. The good news is that the town cannot simply tell the camp to leave. They have no legal authority to simply shut down the camp. On the other hand, they can make it intolerable for the camp to stay."

"How?" I ask.

"First let me say that they have to treat all properties within a zoning category the same. The camp's problem is that it is the only property within the category of "recreational residential". The town can now make things difficult by changing the requirements for that category."

My grandmother is impatient. "Quit your tap dancing and cut to the chase, will you? We're not paying by the word."

Phil smiles. "Of course, Eleanor. I am saying that the town can make things hard for the camp by requiring special permits, or by raising taxes."

The mention of taxes has its usual effect on Gramma. "You're kidding me! You mean to say that they can raise taxes just on us?"

"Yes. Some towns can only raise taxes across the board. Rensford is the other kind of town, with the ability to raise taxes on a single zoning category."

"How high can they raise them?"

"Pretty high, subject to voter approval, of course."

I close my eyes and shake my head. "But that means, instead of having a referendum on getting rid of the camp, they could simply have a referendum on increasing the taxes on the camp."

"Yes."

Gramma, Flo and I are silent; each of us thinking of the effect this would have on our lives. Alarm bells are going off for me. There is no way my grandmother is going to move into our house. I don't care how many people are worried about me being alone so much. It would only make things worse, because it would guarantee that Jack *never* came home. Jack is sweet and everything, but he didn't marry me as a package deal – me and my naked grandmother.

Gramma is tearing up. "I miss Andrew. He would know what to do."

I know she is worried about where she would go if the camp shut down. I have to change the subject before my heart melts and I blurt out an invitation to live with me. "Hey, Flo. You never did tell us how much you have to pay for that indecency fine."

"Those Neanderthals want a hundred bucks! I can't afford a hundred bucks! We're having a hard time with the cable bill. How am I going to watch Nip'n Tuck? I love that show. A hundred bucks. How am I goin' tell Roland?"

Phil and I glance at each other. Where is she getting the money for plastic surgery if she can't pay her cable bill? Out of the window I see a car that could be Kevin's going past, kicking up dust that soon blows into the trailer. I don't know whether it's the humidity, or the dust, or the depressing thought of a homeless grandmother, but I have to get out of there. "Phil, there goes Kevin. You and I have to go talk to him."

I tell Gramma I'll be back in a while, and Phil and I step out of the trailer. We walk in silence, and then Phil asks, "What are we going to talk to Kevin about?"

"Nothing. I just needed to get out of there. But we might as well go see him because my grandmother will be asking for a report. I promise I won't make any incriminating remarks. I'll just ask how things are going."

"How are things going with the investigation?"

"I have no idea. I haven't talked to anyone since yesterday when you arrived at the office and Kevin turned tail and ran. It's weird, but the whole murder thing doesn't seem important anymore, except that it brought down the wrath of the town on us. It's like the town was waiting for a triggering event. I find myself feeling almost angry at Donald Thaler."

"Understandable," says Phil.

"And it didn't help that the murder victim was not the camp's finest citizen."

"The camp's finest citizen probably wouldn't have been murdered," says Phil.

A large family passes us, their sandals and flip flops tapping out sounds like fast hands at a keyboard. Phil turns slightly as they go by. "I've noticed that footwear correlates with age," he says. "Starting with teenagers, sandals are open with a separation between the toes, and young adults wear sandals with something stretchy over the top. Then baby boomers wear sandals that wrap around the heel, and seniors wear athletic shoes with socks."

"I'm truly impressed by your ability to be fascinated by whatever is before you."

"As a great Roman said, 'To marvel at nothing is just about the one and only thing that can make a man happy and keep him that way.'"

"My friend Horace!"

It's Phil's turn to be surprised. "Ah, and I thought you were just some sort of environmental scientist."

"Soil scientist. I slipped into graduate school before they realized I was interested in the classics. Dead white males are a no-no."

"I won't tell. Attorney–client communications," says Phil.

"Speaking of dead white males, Donald was probably murdered by someone younger rather than older, if we apply the Demers' Law of Nudist Footwear."

"Why is that?"

"They found size-ten footprints that had patterns on the bottom that would suggest some sort of plastic or rubber footwear. I think it had tiny surfing waves or something like that."

"And who is the latest suspect, and how old is he?"

"Last I heard it was David Dechesne, son of Roger Dechesne, the gun collector. David's in his late thirties, so that means he's probably still a plastic sandal guy. His father is in the socks-and-athletic-shoes age group, so that eliminates him."

"Ah," Phil continues with a smile. "But perhaps the murderer bought plastic shoes for the very purpose of confusing the authorities!"

"All I know is that no senior citizen will walk around with something between their toes."

"But I don't like anything between my toes, and I'm not a senior."

"It's not a one-to-one correspondence."

We are approaching the yellow tape and Kevin's car parked outside of the cabin. I stride up to the area confidently, since I want to show Phil that I'm one of the team. I may have been benched when he came along, but at least I'm not on the opposing team like he and Jack have feared.

On the other hand, I'm not about to go beyond the yellow

tape without permission, so I yell out, "Hey. Kevin! You in there? It's Catie." There's no answer so I try again. We hear a door shut, and Kevin comes around the back wearing plastic gloves. He is not delighted to see me, and he looks warily at Phil. Phil, in turn, puts on a friendly but guarded smile. This isn't going to be a love fest.

"Okay, guys," I say. "Let's all just relax. I just wanted to say hello and ask how things are going, that's all. Kevin, how are things going?"

"Fine."

"You said you were checking around at local gun shops. Anyone buy anything like the murder weapon in any of them?"

Kevin nods, but doesn't answer. I turn to Phil, "Is there any way I could be allowed to talk to Kevin privately? I mean, I don't want to violate your professional code of duties or whatever. . . ."

Phil nods, "Just as long as you ask the questions and he answers them, and not the other way around." He steps away.

"Well?"

"Catie, you know I'm new to this. Once you have an attorney I think the rules change."

"Kevin, do you remember how I helped you a couple of days ago? Without me you would have been walking around in a heavy overcoat with not only your buddies, but the whole camp laughing at you."

"Okay. Okay. I owe you. And the fact is, we did find that a .32 caliber Smith and Wesson revolver had been purchased about a month ago at East Bank Outfitters, not too far from here. It's a pretty common gun, though."

"And, and? Who bought it?"

"Roger Deschesne."

"Wow. And what does Roger have to say about that?"

"I don't know. George and Bruce have been doing the interviews, and they haven't been sharing a lot."

I would let him continue, but I know Phil is getting nervous. "What about your interviews up and down these streets. Was anyone here that morning? Did they see anything?"

"Yeah, there were a couple of people. And one of them is this widow named Margaret, who's apparently desperate for company and watches for people to go by so she can waylay them with lemonade. And she didn't see anyone go by the whole morning."

"She must have looked away at some point. What about when she went to go to the bathroom?"

"She wears a diaper. Do you know how strange it is to interview an elderly woman wearing a diaper? I had just gotten used to talking to naked women, but that diaper threw me."

I pat him on the arm. "Still, it's only been about 48 hours since you set foot in this place. I think you're doing better than either George or Bruce would have done. You're very kind and respectful, and I haven't heard one complaint about you."

"Thanks, Catie. I appreciate that. And I wish I could just sit down and talk to you about all this, but you're kind of on the opposing team now."

Phil comes over at this point, and smiles. "Time's up, you two, or her husband will sue me for malpractice."

Kevin excuses himself, and Phil and I start back up the road toward my grandmother's trailer. I look at him and say, "I hope I didn't make you too nervous back there."

"No, in fact, it was great. I like to I see my client listening to a policeman sympathetically and then patting him on the arm to say, 'there, there' or whatever you were saying. Very reassuring."

When we get back to the trailer, we find Gramma across the

street with Flo, watching someone sell jewelry on television, while Roland sits at his computer. Gramma asks who would bid on 'such a piece a junk', while Flo declares the piece to be 'too tacky for a hooker'. As they revel in their fashion superiority, I go over to Roland.

"I need some information," I say. If Roland were a dog, he would be wagging his tail right now. "I need the phone numbers or email addresses of B & R Gellerman, Inc. and something called Mountville Trust. Think you can poke around for me, and see what comes up?" He nods enthusiastically.

"What was that about?" asks Phil.

"Tell you at lunch. I'm hungry, so let's just make a quick run over to Ellie's."

Gramma looks up. "Remember, Ellie's is a tiny place. You watch what you say there, because whatever you say goes in one ear, and then goes in every other ear. You hear? You be careful."

Chapter Fifteen

Ellie's bread and breakfast is in a small, one story wooden building, overlooking a pond that used to be pretty, but is now thick with brown and green algae. Crowding the front of Ellie's is an ATM, a soda machine, menus, signs, and cases of bottled water wrapped in plastic. A take-out window allows a little bit of natural light to reach the inside.

Phil and I squeeze between the small wooden tables to reach the counter where we place our order. As we sit nearby waiting for our sandwiches, Gordon Helms comes in and walks up to the counter. The woman across the counter asks, "The usual?" Gordon nods, and walks over to a table in the corner of the restaurant.

Instead of sitting with his back to the wall, he sits facing directly into the corner. Just looking at him there makes me start gulping for air. Maybe Gramma is right – it's a perfect position to overhear as much as he can without making eye contact. More likely, it's his way of avoiding people because no one would go up to him and start talking when he's sitting like that.

I have a sadistic thought, imagining Phil and I taking up seats behind him and talking loudly and endlessly about the weather, but our sandwiches are ready and we choose a table near the door. In a few minutes, Maureen Helms arrives. She looks around for her husband, but then sees me. She strides right over.

"I just think it's horrible what you did to that neighbor of yours. I feel so sorry for Amanda. I hope she sues you for every penny you've got."

"Huh?" Not the pithiest comeback, but my mouth is still full of food.

"You made up this thing about her husband and two *mystery* men coming over to harass you, and all you wanted to do was make it okay to shack up with this guy. For heaven's sake, you even called the fire department *when there was no fire*. All so you could say to your hubbie was, 'Oh, poor me, I couldn't be alone. I needed this guy to stay with me.'"

Lately, I feel like I've been thrown into some kind of assertiveness training camp, because everybody's been in my face about something. Enough. "I don't know what your problem is, Maureen, but I don't appreciate this public display of bile while I'm eating." I turn away from her, proud of myself for coming up with the word 'bile' on such short notice. "Perhaps we can talk later."

"It's Amanda you should be talking to, getting down on your knees and telling her you're sorry. I can't believe you thought you could get away with making up lies about the guy, dragging his name in the mud. For what, just to fool your husband?"

"I did not fool my husband, and those were not lies."

"Amanda says she and Terry were out shopping the whole time, and that's what she told the Rensford police this morning. The police were the ones who suggested that she should sue you for slander."

This leaves me speechless. Phil seizes the opening. "I'm sorry. I didn't get your name."

"Maureen Helms, *Ashton Bulletin*."

"Ah, well, Ms. Helms, perhaps you could allow us to finish our lunch."

"And your name is?"

"Phillip Demers, attorney to the Bingham family."

"Oh, perfect! Lover and lawyer! Create the mess and then get paid to clean it up. How do you spell your last name?"

"Do you intend to write about this?"

"Hell, yes!"

"Then I shall be very busy indeed. While I'm defending Ms. Bingham against the claim of slander, I shall be pursuing an action against the *Ashton Bulletin* for libel."

"Are you threatening me?"

"Lawyers do not threaten. They advise people to consult their own attorneys about the consequences of their actions. In this case, I am providing you with the advice, so it comes free of charge."

A boy in his early teens comes in and slams the door, and for a second, all eyes are on him. Then the motionless silence of the restaurant is broken. Everyone resumes their activity and noise, pretending that they hadn't heard a thing. Maureen and I exchange one more long stare and then she joins her husband in the corner.

Not being able to talk about what just happened, and not being able to think about anything else, I finish my sandwich in silence. Actually, I stuff the sandwich down in huge gulps, mindless of the stomach ache that I'm going to get later. I can't wait to get out of there, but I don't want to look like I've been chased off.

In the car, I let loose. "I can't believe it! Terry and Amanda conspired to make me look like a liar and a slut!"

"It doesn't surprise me. Amanda has probably extracted her pound of flesh from her husband privately. What does she gain by having the world know he was pushing himself on you? It only makes him look bad and her look like a fool."

"So, they lie and everyone in town believes them and not me."

"Like that fireman said, they've been here forever and you just moved in."

"But, how am I going to live next to them? How am I going to drive by their house everyday without hating them?"

"I don't know."

"For that matter, how am I going to go to the post office or supermarket or any place in this town, knowing what everyone is thinking about me?"

Phil sighs. "This is the point where I'm supposed to tell you not to worry so much about what people think of you."

"That would require a personality transplant."

I drive Phil back to the camp to get his car, and make plans to meet him again at the Rensford Inn for dinner at seven. For the rest of the afternoon, I need to get the house ready and the refrigerator stocked for Jack's homecoming tomorrow night. I can't face the idea of going to the supermarket in Rensford, and I drive an extra twenty minutes to go to the one in Marshfield. In a strange supermarket, it takes me an hour to find what I need, but the anonymity and the cool air slowly calm me down.

Marshfield has a correctional facility for women, and as I'm driving home I see Flo walking through the parking lot. I could recognize that woman a half a mile away, even with her clothes on, because of that platinum hair teased up into a beehive on top of her head. She's never mentioned any friends or relatives in prison, but she grew up here and it might be some old acquaintance she doesn't see very often. Is it proper to ask someone who they know in jail? What would Miss Manners say?

Feeling ridiculous, I go the long way so that I don't have to pass by Terry's house. I know Amanda works during the day, but Terry might be home and if he were, say, sitting on his front steps, I might swerve accidentally and run him over. When I drive up the other driveway entrance, I notice the point at which Terry backed into the corn. I stop and look for tire tracks that might prove my innocence, but I see none. Just flattened corn.

For the rest of the afternoon, I clean the house. Jack has always encouraged me to hire a house cleaner, but that's not how I was brought up. I can't imagine feeling comfortable while someone else takes the hair out of my bathtub, or cleans up the stovetop where I spilled something yesterday. You make a mess, you clean it up. It has something to do with karma.

Cleaning up also makes me excited about Jack coming home. The only time I do a thorough job is when Jack's coming home, and when Jack comes home, we have sex. Just like Pavlov and his dogs, I now make a close association between cleaning and sex, even if there's a day or so between the two. It may be hard to see how scrubbing the sink could feel like foreplay, but it works for me.

When Jack calls, he sounds tired but excited. He's tired because it was a hot muggy day at the site. He's excited because he just got confirmation of an invitation to testify before a Congressional military appropriations committee in Washington.

Jack has invented a mechanism for detecting the newest kind of land mines, the kind that don't contain iron and so are invisible to metal detectors. He went to the military with his invention, thinking that it would save the lives of soldiers, and was decidedly rebuffed. It turns out that the military is stock piling these new land mines and didn't want a detection method out there that they couldn't keep secret.

Jack doesn't want the technology to be kept secret because it could save the lives of so many people in places like Sudan and Afghanistan. One thing led to another and now there's a Congressional hearing scheduled for next Monday. Jack will be the star witness.

As he is winding down, he says, "One more thing before you tell me about your day. I've been thinking about last night. I think we ought to get a gun."

This takes me by surprise. "A gun? I don't want a gun in the house! I've never even held one, for Pete's sake."

"I know. I know. But it would make me feel better."

"It would make you feel better? Do you know what you're saying? You think this place is really dangerous. And you're saying that a gun would make you feel better about leaving me alone in a dangerous place."

"That's not what I mean."

"Do you think a gun is a good substitute for you? Do you think a gun would make everything okay? Picture a situation in which I would use a gun. Should I have to face that kind of situation alone in the first place?"

I don't know where this is going, but the effect of scrubbing the sink is wearing off fast. Maybe my nerves are frayed or maybe it's my new assertiveness training, but I'm suddenly tired of being alone, surrounded by all this hostility. And a gun is only going to make me feel more scared, not less.

"Catie, I'm just trying to keep you safe."

"I can think of better ways to do that than buying a gun."

"I know, like me being there all the time. But you knew when you married me that this is what I wanted to do."

"Yeah, but I didn't know how it would make me feel."

"We've been through this..."

"But this is the first time you've mentioned a gun. This is the first time you've acknowledged that there might be something wrong with leaving me alone all the time. But instead of saying, maybe I should be home more, you say, let's buy a gun."

I know I'm being unfair to him. He was probably up all night worrying about me and he thinks that having a gun around would really help. In my heart of hearts, I know he loves me and that his intentions are good. I'm not angry at him as much as I'm scared, scared that he is affirming my worst fears. *He thinks I need a gun.*

I think the worst marital advice I've ever heard was never to go to bed angry. My advice is, sleep on it. And the same goes for the phone. Don't worry – hang up. Let those emotional chemicals dissipate in your bloodstream, and then call back and start talking again. That second part is important. You have to call back.

We've gone through this routine before. Ten minutes later I call back and I tell him that I love him and that I know he loves me. He does the same, and we both mean it. We promise each other that we'll talk when he gets home.

I change out of my cleaning clothes to get ready for dinner with Phil. Those chemicals in my bloodstream are hanging around longer than usual, because I am still freaked out. Jack thinks I need a gun. I lock the house as I leave, check the lock again, and then walk around the house to make sure I didn't leave any windows open. I get in the car and then push the button to automatically lock the doors.

Getting to the Rensford Inn from my house requires a series of turns down small side streets. The same set of headlights follows me turn by turn. When I pull into the parking lot of the Rensford Inn, I look in my rear view mirror but the car has already gone past. This is ridiculous. A lot of people know the back way to the center of town.

Chapter Sixteen

I tell the waitress that I'll have wine with dinner, but I want a martini now. Phil's eyebrows go up but he's polite enough not to comment. I don't want to tell him about my fight with Jack, but I can't think of anything else at the moment.

After a minute or two, Phil asks, "What were you going to tell me at lunch? You told Roland to track down something, remember? You were going to explain at lunch?"

I'm grateful for the diversion. "Donald Thaler's cabin looks down on a ravine, called Pine Hollow. Pine Hollow is part of a sixty-acre parcel that was owned by the Gellerman family. The Gellermans sold that land at the end of June to the camp, in a quickie deal that wasn't brought before the camp for a vote."

"Wait. I thought the camp was broke."

"It is. The money was provided by the national organization, the AANR—American Association of Nude Recreation—maybe as a loan, I don't know. Anyway, it was an offer they couldn't refuse because the asking price was about 20% of what similar properties have been going for."

Phil looks skeptical. "You mean it was 20% lower."

"No, it was 80% lower,"

"But, why?"

"That's what I'm trying to find out. This morning I talked to the realtor who handled the transaction. Actually, she didn't handle anything, because the Gellermans were trying to sell it to an abutter called Mountville Trust, and Mountville insisted that everything be done in private. Looks like Mountville had one hell of a bargaining chip."

"Like what?"

"That's what I'm trying to find out. Phyllis said every time the Gellermans talked to the people from Mountville, the price went down. Then Mountville got a surprise. They pushed the Gellermans so hard that those poor people just wanted to get rid of it. When the camp gave the Gellermans a ridiculously low offer, the Gellermans jumped at it."

"Why are you so interested in this?"

The question takes me back a little. "I don't know. I just hope that the camp didn't make a bad investment."

"And why are you interested in the camp's investment strategy?"

"Well, because of my grandmother, right? It's her home. And I want the camp to survive."

"And you don't want your grandmother to come live with you."

"You got it."

"Your grandmother doesn't belong in the camp or with you. She belongs with other senior citizens, so she can make some friends, maybe even meet a nice guy."

"My grandmother can't keep her clothes on."

"I think she's trainable."

"Maybe there's a nudist deprogrammer, or Nudists Anonymous. 'Hi, my name is Eleanor, and I'm a nudist. I'd like to announce that I've been wearing clothes now for 58 days in a row, but every day is a struggle, especially when I take a shower.'"

Phil rolls his eyes. "What I'm trying to say is that you're pouring a lot of energy into taking care of your grandmother and worrying about the camp. You're a bright woman and you're wasting that brain of yours."

"You and Jack been talking? This sounds very familiar."

"No, we haven't been talking about this. Catie, anyone who spent any time with you can see that you need something to focus on. I think that's why you got so excited about the possibility of helping the police."

"You still don't believe me, do you, that they wanted my help?"

"I'm just saying that you got very excited about the possibility because you needed the stimulus."

The martini has left my feelings floating too near the surface, and my eyes are tearing up. Phil reaches a hand across the table, but I wave it away. "I'm just feeling a little sorry for myself. It'll pass."

But it doesn't pass, and in another minute I'm telling him about my fight with Jack and the matter of the gun. My voice is pleading. "I don't need a gun, do I?"

Phil takes a sip of his wine, and puts the glass down slowly. "I don't think you need a gun. I think you need to live in a place where having a gun wouldn't occur to you. Maybe you ought to leave Rensford"

"You're serious."

"Unfortunately I am serious. You and Jack can live anywhere you want. Why would you want to live in a place where you are afraid? Why would you want to live next to a guy who threatens you, and has a wife who wants to sue you for slander?"

"But Jack and I want to have kids someday. Here they won't get the wrong values about toys and video games, like they would in the suburbs."

"Here, your kids will always feel like outsiders, just like you do already."

"But that would be true in any rural town, and I don't just don't want to live in some fancy suburb where people pretend to be nice and then are cruel behind your back."

"Those cruelties are called 'slights' for a reason. They're minor."

"No cruelties are minor," I say.

"Yes they are. My wife was recently turned down for a book club that supposedly had too many members and then she heard about someone else joining. My wife felt a little sting, but she got over it."

"Are you sure she got over it? Women feel these things more than men."

"Oh, yeah? My feelings were hurt when I asked a friend to nominate me for membership at a country club. He told me he couldn't because he was allowed only two nominations and he wanted to save them."

"Ouch. Maybe you two should move to Rensford."

"And be 'first in a village, rather than second in Rome?' My point is this. Social snubs may sting but they don't lead you to think of owning a gun." Phil smiled. "Okay, maybe briefly."

There's a minute or two of silence, and I can feel my heels dig in. "Look, I got off to a bad start in this town, okay? I alienated a journalist with a bully pulpit, and a neighbor who's a respected pillar of Rensford society."

"But you did nothing wrong to alienate them." He paused. "I'm sorry. I'm overstepping my bounds here. There are no legal reasons why you should not live in Rensford, and I should limit myself to legal advice."

"No. I obviously need every possible category of advice, legal and otherwise, especially from you. You've been a little island of sanity in the past couple of days. And, believe me, that was a total surprise."

"Oh, really?"

"I thought you would be so painfully embarrassed by naked people that I wouldn't be able go near the camp for the duration of your visit. I couldn't figure out what I was going to do with you—show you the exhibit of the Junior Farmer's of America at the grange? Visit the town's historical records in the basement of the Lutheran church?"

"Either would have been fine, but I am thrilled that I got to go to the camp. It has been an experience of a lifetime. I only wish I could have taken pictures, because it's going to be hard to describe. By the way, I hope I'll get to go back tomorrow to say goodbye to your grandmother, and Flo and Roland."

"When are you planning to leave tomorrow?"

"When is Jack coming home?"

"Is this some kind of relay race with me as a baton? Jack should be home late in the afternoon. Is there any chance you could stay long enough for dinner at our house tomorrow?"

"That would be great, assuming I can get in some phone calls to clients tomorrow. If we could make it an early dinner, maybe six? That way I'll be home around ten."

"Great," I say as I push my chair back. "You want to make your calls in the morning and then we'll visit Gramma after lunch?"

From behind Phil I see the manager of the inn approaching. She hands Phil a note, saying, "I don't mean to interrupt you, Mr. Demers, but I saw this at the front desk and I wanted to catch you before you left."

Phil opens the note, shakes his head, and hands it to me. The note says, "*Sorry to bother you, but I tried to reach Catie at her house and she wasn't there. If you know where she is, could you let her know that I really need to apologize to her and I'm hoping she can stop by my office tonight. I'll be there until midnight. Thank you. Maureen Helms."*

I hand him back the note. "And your advice would be…"

"There are no legal questions at issue."

"That's helpful."

"Anytime."

Chapter Seventeen

As usual, I know what I *should* do and what I'm *going* to do, and they are not the same thing. I should go home and go to bed because I'm short on sleep and I've had wine and a martini. And of course, I'm not going to do that. I'm going to stretch the day out just a little longer, because that apology is something I really need.

Actually, I need an apology from Maureen, and my neighbors, and most of the camp, but I'll start with Maureen. Maybe this will be some sort of tipping point, and all of these people will sit back and realize how unfair they have been to me. If it can happen to Maureen, why not the others?

It is with this renewed hope that I drive into the parking lot in front of her office. I don't see Maureen's car, but maybe Gordon dropped her off. Since her office faces out the back, I can't see if there's a light on. I lock the car and go over to the door to her office, where there's a note that says, "*Be right back.*"

I look over at the drugstore which is still open. Maybe I should kill some time in there, but I don't really need anything. I just want to settle into my front seat and listen to my ipod for a while. I find a playlist, then tilt my head back and close my eyes. I'm going through various scenarios in my mind, trying to figure out the best response to Maureen's apology.

I open my eyes to the blinding headlights of a car. The car is directly facing mine, as if trying to block my exit. Since my lights aren't on, I can't see who's in the car. A person gets out and passes in front of the headlights. From the profile and the paraphernalia hanging around his ample waist, I can see that it's a Rensford policeman.

"License and registration, please."

"Sure, but I was just waiting for my friend, Maureen." My voice is sleepy, and I wonder how long I've been here. I look down at my ipod and see that the playlist is over.

"Can I ask what you're doing here, ma'am?"

"I'm waiting for my friend, Maureen Helms. That's her office over there." It's taking me a while to come up with my registration in the glove compartment. I don't get pulled enough to remember what my registration even looks like. I finally find it and hand it over to the officer, along with my license.

"Will you step out if the car for me, please?"

"Sure. But why?"

"Just step out of the car, ma'am."

"Okay." I step out.

"Do I have your permission to conduct a sobriety test?"

Adrenaline rushes through me as I remember the martini. Without thinking, I burst forth with, "Peter Piper picked a peck of pickled peppers. A,B,C,D,E,F,G…Do you want it backwards? Z…Y…X…W…" Backwards is harder than I thought. "V…U…T…"

"That's fine, thanks, really, that's all I need."

I take a deep breath. "Is there a problem, officer?"

"No. We had a tip that there might be a break-in somewhere tonight, so when Mr. Lupien over there," pointing to Lupien's Drug Store, "called in a suspicious car, we decided to check it out. How long are you planning on waiting here, Mrs. Bingham?"

"I don't know. I think I might have fallen asleep." I look at the time and realize I've been here for an hour. "I think I'll go home now."

"I think that would be a good idea."

So much for Maureen's apology. I wonder whether Maureen had been hiding somewhere nearby to see if I would come by. I have to stop and remind myself that I am no longer on a sixth grade playground. Adults do not hide in bushes and laugh at other adults. I'm pretty sure of that.

As I'm driving up my driveway, my heart leaps at the sudden, mind numbing blast of the fire station horn. Someday, that horn will no longer remind me of last night. Maybe it would help to learn the code so I know where the fire is. I pause until I hear the engine siren and listen to it fade into the opposite end of the town.

With my pajamas on, contacts out, and teeth brushed, I am in bed with a book when I see lights in the driveway. I sit on the edge of the bed with my hand on the phone. When I see that it's the Rensford police, my first reaction is relief, followed quickly by fear. Something must have happened to Jack or Gramma. That kind of news is the only reason police come to your house uninvited.

I grab my bathrobe and rush downstairs and open the door before the bell rings. "What's the matter?"

The man outside is the same gentleman I just left at the parking lot. "I'd like you to come down to the station, ma'am, to answer a few questions."

"Why? About what?"

"If you'll just come with me, ma'am."

I really, really don't like being called ma'am. "It's late officer. Is there any bad news I need to know about?"

"No, ma'am. We just want to ask you some questions."

"About what?"

"About a fire at the office of Maureen Helms."

"A fire? Is that the siren I just heard? Is she okay?"

"She wasn't in the office at the time."

I'm thinking, did you check the bushes? The relief of not hearing any bad news about Jack or Gramma is giving way to a very tired, very irritated feeling. "Look, Officer…"

"Putnam, Jim Putnam."

"Look, Officer Putnam. You can't just expect people to hop out of bed like this and go down to the station. Don't you have to have probable cause or something?"

He nods. "You were overheard threatening Mrs. Helms at Ellie's today, and you were in the vicinity prior to the fire."

"I didn't threaten to burn her office down! My lawyer threatened to sue her for libel! And as for being in the area, I was asleep, for heaven's sake. You saw that. Who falls asleep at the scene after setting a fire?"

"I understand."

"What do you mean, you understand?"

"Let's just say that Captain Larini grew up with Terry Curtis. Good friends, actually."

"Oh, I get it. Let's see now. You know and I know that I didn't do this thing. But your captain is mad about what supposedly happened last night. And he's using this as a way to get me down to the station so he can yell at me or something?"

Officer Putnam lifts his shoulders in a slight suggestion of a shrug.

I go on. "And, of course, you can't actually say that's the reason, because he's your boss."

Again, he gives a slight shrug. No other muscles seem to move on this man.

My own shoulders move down, and I sigh. "Is there any possible way that you can leave here without me?'

"No, ma'am."

"I think I should call my attorney first."

"You can do that as soon as you get to the station."

"Okay, let's get this over with. I'm not even going to change. I want him to see me in my bathrobe to remind him how he dragged me out of bed for this."

"Thank you. I appreciate it."

"But I'm not going to ride in back. Either I ride up front with you or I don't go at all."

"Fine."

Neither of us talks on the way down to the station, a single story brick building between a warehouse and an auto repair place. Inside, there is the glare of cheap fluorescent lights, with one of the tubes flickering. Officer Putnam speaks through a metal circle in a glass window and we are buzzed in. Immediately to the left is a small, windowless room, filled by one table and two chairs.

"Don't shut the door, please!" I say quickly, as Officer Putnam leads me in.

"Claustrophobia?"

"No, too little air,"

"Sure," he says, and leaves the room.

It's now eleven o'clock and I'm in my bathrobe and I just want to go home and go to bed. I feel like I've been pretty gracious about this whole thing, coming down here to allow Captain who-ever-he-is to vent his spleen at me. He's probably going to call Terry Curtis right after, and brag about how he roughed me up.

A man in his mid-forties comes in and we shake hands as he introduces himself as Captain Larini. He sits down and then gets up again as if he's forgotten something. He turns around and walks to the door and shuts it.

"Excuse me! I would prefer that the door remain open, please!" I say immediately.

"I'm afraid that is not police procedure."

"Fine. But as a personal favor."

"Like I said, police procedure, ma'am." He starts a tape recorder. "Now could you state your name and..."

"Look, I've been cooperative and haven't made a fuss. I will continue to act in such a fashion if you *open the door.*"

"Sorry." He continues. "State your name and date of birth."

"Please."

"Again, I'm sorry." And again he gives me a little smile that says he isn't sorry at all. Suddenly, the door opens and a flood of air rushes into the room. Officer Putnam is standing there, "Sir, I thought I told you that she..."

"Shut that door now!"

Officer Putnam gives me a sympathetic look and shuts the door. What is this? Are they playing good cop, bad cop? "Sir, please, I know you're a friend of Terry Curtis and that you want to yell at me and I'm perfectly willing to sit through that, even though it's an abuse of police power, but could you just do it with the door open, please?"

"No. I am not going to open the door. And, you are here under suspicion of arson, not because of any personal animosity."

My breathing is getting deep and rapid but I manage to get out, "That's ridiculous. Ask Officer Putnam."

"Officer Putnam would not have brought you down here if he didn't believe we had sufficient cause."

"He saw that I was asleep in the parking lot. There are no sleepy arsonists." I know I'm not being rational, but I'm not good at debating on limited oxygen.

"You certainly don't look sleepy right now. You look scared, and you look scared because you have been caught."

"But why would I do it?"

"Because Maureen was going to run a story that would have ruined your marriage."

I'm breathing hard but it doesn't seem to be doing any good. I'm breathing in the air that I've already breathed before. The oxygen has been used up. "So I burned her office?"

Captain Larini looks at the tape recorder and smiles. "If you say so."

My eyes are getting wider, not because of what he's saying, but because of the little exploding pinpoints I'm beginning to see. My lungs are working hard but it's not doing any good. I need to get out of this room *now.* I get up and move toward the door. "I'm going."

"No, you're not."

"I have to get out of here."

"Then I'm afraid I have to arrest you on suspicion of arson. You have the right to remain silent. Anything you say...."

I hardly hear any of this until I am out of the room and I feel the sudden expanse of air around me.

"...in a court of law."

My brain is trying to push the reset button. "Wait. I'm being arrested?"

"...to be represented by an attorney...

"Where's my cell phone?"

My cell phone is in my purse which is still in that little room. I rush in, grab my purse, and get out before anyone can shut the door again. Do I really only get one phone call? What about 411? I don't know the number of the Rensford Inn and I don't remember where I put the number of Phil's cell phone.

I dial the operator and say, "This is an emergency. I need you to connect me to the Rensford Inn, in Rensford, New Hampshire."

"Certainly. Should I alert the local police?"

"No."

Finally, I reach Phil and he answers in a groggy voice. I have no idea what time it is.

"Hi Phil. This is Catie. I'm at the Rensford police station and I've just been arrested for arson."

"Don't say anything. Do you hear me, Catie. Do not say *anything*. I will be there as fast as I can. Now hand the phone to the arresting officer."

I do as I'm told and watch Captain Larini on the phone with Phil. "We do indeed have probable cause, sir," he says. "We heard her threatening Maureen Helms, and she was in the immediate vicinity just before the fire broke out." He listens a little longer and then grunts his acceptance of something. He hands the phone back to me, saying, "It sure helps to have a hotshot lawyer for a boyfriend, don't it?"

"Catie, I heard what he just said." Phil is speaking to me slowly and deliberately now that I'm back on the phone. "Don't let them provoke you. They will be nice, and say they just want to hear your side of the story. They will say that it looks bad when you don't talk and you hide behind your lawyer. Whatever they say, you just keep your mouth shut. Do you hear me? Keep your mouth *shut.* "

"Okay, okay, okay."

"I'm sorry. Catie. I don't mean to be hard on you. Hang in there. Everything is going to be okay."

After talking to him, and getting my oxygen and carbon dioxide back in balance, I am beginning to feel better. Officer Putnam offers me a cup of coffee, and while I coldly decline, I'm wondering what to think of this man in front of me. When he picked me up, I had the impression that he knew I didn't do anything wrong. Going over the conversation we had at my front door, I try to remember what he said. I realize now that he didn't say much at all.

From past experience, I know there's one type of person I should be on guard against. Officer Putnam is that type of person. He says very little and moves even less. I mistake it all for composure, but it's really an excess of mental control. What did he say? He just let me guess at what he was thinking.

I got tricked into coming down here without a fuss, without calling Phil, who would have certainly stopped everything in its tracks before I ever got into the police car. Whatever their 'probable cause', it obviously wasn't sufficient and they needed to extract something here at the station. And they almost did, because I would have confessed to anything if I had to stay in that little room much longer.

In the other room, I hear some tapping of fingers on a keyboard. That's my arrest they're typing in. I now have a record. After about ten minutes, Captain Larini and Officer Putnam emerge from an office, pull up chairs near me, and turn the chairs so that the backs are facing me. They sit on the chairs with their arms draping in a relaxed manner over the backs of the chairs, the same way as the cops do on TV shows.

"Calling that lawyer, that was a smart thing to do," says Captain Larini. "You're a smart lady."

"A compliment! Nice opening move," I say.

"Look. he'll be here soon, and he's not going to allow you to say anything, right?"

"You betcha."

"Which means that you will leave under a cloud of suspicion."

"But every cloud has a silver lining, right?"

"And?'

"I get to leave this place. That's one hell of a silver lining."

"We're merely giving you a chance to tell your side of the story."

"Ding, ding, ding," I wave an arm in the air. "Congratulations. You have just confirmed one of my lawyer's predictions."

Captain Larini gets up to get some coffee. Officer Putnam pulls his chair a little closer. "I'm really sorry you have to go through all this, ma'am."

"What are you sorry about?"

He gives one of those tiny little shrugs. "The whole thing."

"I don't understand."

He is staring at me. I think he's a little uncertain as to how to proceed, but it's hard to tell. "I am trying to help you."

"How are you trying to help me?"

He changes course. "You're in a lot of trouble here, ma'am."

"Enough about me. I'm trying to understand how *you* feel."

He is still gazing at me calmly, but the lids of his eyes are closing in. Those tiny muscles around his eyes are apparently not under his conscious control. They show that he's not happy. "I don't think you're taking this seriously."

"Believe me, I am"

At this moment we hear the front door open and in a few moments, Phil is buzzed in. He looks at me, face-to-face with Officer Putnam, with Captain Larini nearby. In contrast to Officer Putnam, Phil Demers does not have any trouble showing anger.

"Catie! What did I tell you?! I told you specifically not to talk to these people. What are you doing? Can't you listen?"

It's the first time I've seen Phil lose it, and I'm stunned into silence. Phil turns towards the two men. He voice is menacing. "This is outrageous. You will be very, very sorry in front of the judge tomorrow."

Captain Larini gets up off the desk he's been sitting on and smiles at Phil. "Old Judge Canton is a rubber stamper. He can hardly read anything or hear anything we tell him anyway."

"Then I will contact the Inspector General," says Phil. "I also have a former classmate in the DA's office. One way or the other, I'm going to make sure this causes you more trouble than it will us. Catie, let's go."

Captain Larini has to have the last word. "I don't care how big a lawyer you are. We have her on motive and opportunity. A few rags and some paint thinner in her house and we'll have means. And if we don't find any, we'll just say she threw them out."

"Believe me, you won't even get that far. Your own …." Phil is interrupted by the buzzer of the door opening. Chief Detective George Myers of the New Hampshire State Police walks in. He looks like he's just gotten out of bed.

"George!" I say.

Phil turns to him as George introduces himself. Phil does not share my enthusiasm at seeing this new visitor. "My client and I are leaving now."

George is blocking the door and he's about twice the size of Phil. "Stay. I think you'll want to hear this."

Chapter Eighteen

I touch Phil's arm and nod to him. George walks up to Captain Larini and brazenly invades his space, standing only about a foot away from him.

"Captain Larini," says George, in a growl. "I'll make this quick so we can all go back to bed. You don't give a rat's ass about that fire. The fire marshal says it was a pitiful, half-hearted thing anyway. But, hey, opportunity knocks, right? Mrs. Bingham was seen in the area, so bingo. You got something to pin on her."

George pauses for effect and then continues. "Now, why would you want to do something like that? Why would you jump at the chance to drag her out of bed," he says as he turns toward me, "looking like that? Is it because you talked to your buddy Curtis today and heard his tale of woe? Is it because you bragged to him that you would find a way to get her?"

Phil jumps in. "Would you be willing to testify to that?"

"I would, but I won't need to. Because after you two are on your way, we boys are going to void out every trace of this arrest. Mrs. Bingham will walk out with nothing on her record. Captain Larini will enter into his records that it was all a big, stupid mistake. Because if he doesn't, I will drag both of these asses in front of a 91(a) hearing. And these guys know what that does, come promotion time."

My relief spills out of me. "George, thank you...."

"Quiet. I'm not finished." He turns back to Captain Larani.

"This whole thing smells so bad of local shenanigans that even Judge Canton will wake up and be pissed. And then someday when you catch a real criminal, Canton's going to think to himself, now what local brawl is this one about? And some bad guy is going to walk because Canton's going to think that you guys are wasting his time again."

Officer Putnam moves slightly away from his captain. "Detective…"

"Shut up. From now on, no one from Rensford PD bothers Mrs. Bingham, her husband, her lawyer, or her pet squirrel if she has one. If I so much as hear of a speeding ticket, I will put this whole sorry episode before the board. Do I make myself clear?"

Both men are silent. George nods at Phil and me. "I will escort these people out of the building and then I will come back and we will slog through the paperwork. I won't leave until the record says that you two messed up and are really, really sorry this whole thing happened." George pivots and then ushers us out the door.

Outside, Phil extends his hand and thanks George. "You just saved my client's butt, and believe me, that's not a phrase I use very often. But, how did you happen be here at the right moment?"

"Someone at Ashton recognized Catie's name when the arrest popped up on his screen. He called Kevin, and Kevin was really upset but didn't know what to do. He called me and filled me in on the Curtis-Larini connection, and I told him I'd take it from there."

"Thank you so much," I say with a sigh.

"You're welcome." says George, and then turns to Phil. "One more thing, and then I have to go back in there with the boys. I meant to call you to put your mind at ease about Catie helping us with the murder investigation. Is it alright with you if we call on her again if we need her knowledge about the camp?"

"I will recommend that she be helpful to you at every opportunity."

On the way home, Phil breaks the silence. "Catie, it's tempting to say, 'All's well that ends well'. And I understand you're too tired to talk about anything right now. But the fact remains – someone set you up for this. Someone knew that you were having dinner with me, and had that note delivered to me, so that you would show up at the parking lot."

"I know. I had the feeling someone followed me to the Rensford Inn."

"Someone out there doesn't like you, and we don't know who it is," says Phil.

"The list of people who don't like me seems to get longer every day."

"Right. So I would feel better if you would take a room at the Rensford Inn tonight."

"No. No way. For one thing, I can't wait to get home to my bed, my own bed. For another, I don't want to fuel the fires of the town gossip machine. It's firing on all four cylinders as it is. And, yeah, yeah, I know I shouldn't care, but I do."

"I don't feel comfortable leaving you by yourself tonight."

"I'll call the fire department again if I have to. Besides the evildoer probably thinks I'm still at the police station with bamboo sticks under my nails. Really, Phil, thanks, but end of discussion."

We pull up in front of my house and set up a time to meet after lunch. In the house, I pass a mirror and see my reflection with my grubby bathrobe, thick glasses and matted hair. Even after all that has happened tonight, vanity rises to the top. Thank God they didn't take a mug shot.

I wake up at ten the next morning and have an extra cup of coffee at breakfast. I wash my hair, and blow dry it while I'm hanging my head down, which is the extent of my styling ability. I'm getting excited about Jack coming home. I can hardly remember what we fought about last night. Getting arrested and unarrested provides a certain perspective on things.

I make a list for tonight's dinner and drive over to the supermarket. Gordon Helms is not outside and no one appears to be pointing any fingers at me for being an arsonist, adulterer or anything else. I stop on the way home to get the *Ashton Bulletin*, and because it's Friday, the *Rensford Villager*. It's becoming my daily routine to check on the kind of press I'm getting.

The headline of the *Ashton Bulletin* announces that the citizens of Ashton voted against building a new school. The murder has dropped to beneath the fold, where again, it's an article by Maureen Helms. The article is entitled, "Murder Victim Acknowledged Sex Addiction." The source of Maureen's information is primarily the divorce papers filed a year ago. Apparently, Donald Thaler tried to save his marriage by agreeing to get counseling for his chronic infidelity.

Below that article, in a small corner of the front page, is the following headline, "Arson Suspected". It reads as follows. "Last night a fire at the office of Maureen Helms was deemed to be of suspicious origin by Fire Marshal John Zellmer. Maureen Helms is a reporter for this newspaper. At press time, a Rensford resident, Catie Bingham, had been taken to the police station for questioning."

I'm trying to remember when I was picked up by Officer Putnam. It had to be at least ten o'clock. I look at the second page and find a phone number for the *Ashton Bulletin*. When the phone is answered, I ask, "Can you tell me, when is the latest I can submit information to the newspaper for the next day's edition?"

"Press time is ten o'clock."

"Is there any way that I can find out who submitted information for a piece in today's edition?"

"I can give you the voice mail of the reporter responsible for the story."

"There was no byline for this story."

"Then I'm afraid I can't help you."

It was probably Maureen herself who submitted the story. The fire department probably called Maureen to tell her about the fire and then Maureen called the police to find out if they had any leads. The police probably told Maureen that they were going to bring me in for questioning because I had been seen in the parking lot by Officer Putnam.

But Maureen took a chance by saying that I had already been brought in for questioning when, at that time, I might not have been picked up yet. What is her problem with me? Since I complained about that initial article she seems to have taken an intense dislike of me. Sometimes people start to hate the people they've offended.

I turn to the *Rensford Villager*. The headline there is "Murder Prompts Review of Nudist Camp." The article takes up most of the front page and talks about the murder itself and the less than sterling character of the victim. Most of this latter information appears to have been taken from Maureen's previous articles.

The majority of the article is devoted to the nudist camp and whether or not the town should take steps to close it down. I don't recognize the name of the reporter, but I can guess how he's going to vote. He flows seamlessly from a discussion of the flaws of the victim to the vote on the camp. He might as well ask outright, *'do we want these kind of people in our town, and naked no less?'*

It seems that the town counsel has already raised the possibility of putting the squeeze on the camp by increased taxation on the zoning category. He justifies this increase by saying it is necessary to cover the costs of litigation with the camp. Of course, the most likely litigation would be a challenge of the increased taxes, but either way, the town counsel is covered.

I put down the paper and do a few things ahead of time for dinner, crossing each one of them off my list. I wish I could just throw together a dinner without lists, without worrying about the simultaneous climax of everything needing to be done at the same time. I am convinced that the extraterrestrials give themselves away by being able to throw together a dinner at the last minute while simultaneously talking to people around them. No humanoid can do that.

At eleven-thirty I head over to the camp, so I can check in on Gramma before Phil arrives at one. At the trailer, I knock on the door but there's no answer. Roland yells over that Flo and my grandmother are at Buff Cuts, the salon/barber shop located in a big Airstream motor home on the other side of the camp. My grandmother goes there every week, coming out with a tightly coiled set that lasts a whole week as long as she is never without her plastic rain bonnet.

I wander over. "Hi Roland. Any luck getting information on those land holders I asked you about?"

He looks up from his computer. "I found one, but came up short on the other."

"Let me guess, you couldn't find anything on Mountville."

"Right. The only thing I got for them was a post office box in Carterton, Mass. But I'll keep digging. Mountville looks like a shell corporation hidden inside other shell corporations. As long as none of them is located off-shore, I should be able to peel back the layers, but it'll take some time. Someone out there sure went to a lot of trouble to hide who they are."

"Do you have the time? Do you mind doing this?"

"Are you kidding? I love digging up information anyway, but once I sense that someone's trying to hide something, I get that thrill of the chase. I can't let up."

"Thanks, I really appreciate it. I guess I'm the same way, because I'm not even sure why I'm pursuing this. I'm worried that there might be something wrong with the land the camp bought, but what if it's true? The deal's done already, anyway."

From the blank look on his face, I can see that he doesn't know what I'm talking about, so I fill him in on the purchase of the land and the strangely low price that the national organization was able to buy it for. While he thinks about this, he moves the mouse back and forth nervously, as if his hand can't wait for the next command.

"So Mountville knew something about that land," he says, "and whatever it was, it scared the Gellermans so bad that they almost gave away the land. And then the Gellermans turned around and sold it to the AANR, probably because $72,000 was more than Mountville offered. Do you think that the Gellermans told the AANR what was wrong with it? Did they have to?"

"I don't know," I say. "I do know that the realtor is required to disclose that kind of information, but I don't know about the owner. Phyllis, the realtor, said she was excluded from the negotiations, but she may have excluded herself once she sensed there was a problem."

Roland's mouse is now moving all over the place. "Do you mind if I look into this. I love this kind of thing, you know."

"Mind? I'd love it. By the way, what did you find out about the Gellermans?"

"They are both in their seventies, and living in a little town called Easton Center, Massachusetts. I have their address and phone number right here. Their house is currently worth $234,000, and from a satellite picture, it looks like they live in a lower middle class neighborhood. Up until a year ago, they were paying their bills promptly, but since then, some of their bills have remained unpaid for 60 or even 90 days."

"It sounds like they couldn't afford to lose the-half million dollars they were expecting to get for that land."

I thank Roland, and we promise to update each other with the information we get. Taking out my cell phone, I dial the number that Roland just gave me. I don't think the Gellermans are going to be anxious to talk to me, but I might as well try. When Mrs. Gellerman answers the phone, I explain the reason for my call.

Mrs. Gellerman speaks in a high-pitched nervous rush. "Oh, I don't think we want to talk to you. There's no reason to talk to you, really, you know, because we don't own the land anymore. They certainly can't come after us now. We have nothing to do with any of that and it wasn't our fault to begin with. Anyone can see that."

"Who do you mean 'they'?" I break in.

"The federal government," she says and then pauses and speaks to someone in the room. "Oh, hi dear! It's just another telemarketer." And then the phone is quickly hung up.

I walk back over to Roland and relate the conversation with Mrs. Gellerman. "Why would the federal government want to come after them? And for something she says wasn't their fault to begin with?"

He shrugs. Roland focuses on one thing at a time, with his

brain acting like a flashlight on his forehead. Everything else is dark to him except that single thing in front of him that his brain has lit up. And right now it's lighting up something else and he has lost interest in the Gellermans.

I look at my watch and see that I have an hour before Phil arrives. I could wait around for Gramma, or I could take a walk down to Donald Thaler's cabin. I decide to walk, thinking that at least I'll be getting some exercise. Plus, I'm curious as to whether there's still yellow tape around the cabin. When does the scene of a crime stop being a crime scene?

As I approach the cabin I can see that the yellow tape is still there. Apparently, however, they're not expecting too much more evidence to be gathered here, because there's no one guarding the place. I have a momentary temptation to go under the yellow tape, but I would die of embarrassment if someone drove up.

I continue past the cabin, turning up Sandhill Lane, named after a huge natural deposit of sand only about a hundred feet beyond Donald's cabin. The hill is half gone now, a reminder of when the camp used to use this sand as its yearly supplement to the beach. These days, it's cheaper to simply call someone up and have them deliver a truckload.

The excavation of this sandpit left a quiet amphitheater of sloping sand, with shrubs and small trees perched on the top edge. As a kid, this place felt huge and majestic to me, and I would come here and pretend I was on stage and playing to those trees on the top row. When I was a little older, I would come to sit on the slopes, thinking about some boy or the other and whether he would ask me to dance at the teenage pavilion.

I loved the sand itself, and I've always wondered if it led me into soil science. As an adult, I now know that this particular sand is called 'dirty' sand because it has a lot of clay in it. And that's what made it great, not only for sand castles, but because you could burrow into it and mold it to you. Parents, on the other hand, generally didn't like it because it was so sticky even when dry. Parents won, and now there's 'clean' sand on the beach imported from some other sandpit.

I remember George or somebody saying that there was sand in the footprints found in the foyer of Donald's cabin, and that it was similar to sand you'd find on a beach. George called it 'fine' sand, but I wonder if it had any clay in it. The clay would be easy to miss, since I would guess that the clay in this sand is white, probably kaolinite.

George is probably assuming that the sand in the cabin came from the beach. After last night, I am eternally grateful to George and I would love to do something for him. At the risk of being seen as a little too eager, I decide to take a sample of the sand here and at the beach and give it to him so that the lab can see which one matches the footprint. George will probably just say thank you and give me a little pat on the head, but that's okay.

I walk back to Gramma's to get a couple of Ziplock bags, but Gramma and Flo are back from Buff Cuts and I have to put it off. Gramma is upset. Leonard has been doing yoga in his front yard again.

"If I have to go past that ass hole one more time I'm going to plug it with something." Gramma is referring to the fact that Leonard stands on his head with his legs spread apart, thus presenting the opening to his rectum to the sky. Leonard is in excellent shape with washboard abs, broad shoulders, and a large penis and matching testicles.

Flo shakes her head. "That low life calls it his spiritual air bath. Well, la-dee-dah. All those toxins gotta *escape* into the atmosphere? I don't understand why he can't just fart like the rest of us."

"Clap trap. It ain't about his gas. It's about his dick. He just wants everybody to know how well he's hung. And in case it don't get noticed while he's on his feet, he goes and hangs it upside down."

Leonard is one of a minority of men who are here in camp for one reason, and that is, to show off their most prized possession. Most of them are happily married or partnered up, and that is the source of their problem. Monogamy means that that only one person sees their astounding piece of anatomy. Here at camp, everyone can see it and be amazed. These guys are often found on the volleyball court, or sitting at the edge of the pool with one knee up and their backs slightly arched.

"Personally" says Flo, "I think it looks like somethin' the cat drug in."

Chapter Nineteen

Phil knocks on the door a few minutes later, after the conversation has moved on. Gramma is now complaining about the steadily shrinking size of toilet paper rolls. I yell out for him to wait there, saying I'll be out in a second. I grab a couple of Ziplock bags.

"What are the bags for?" asks Flo.

"Phil and I are going to be collecting some evidence."

Gramma snorts. "Don't be ridiculous. What kind of evidence would the police let you collect?"

"Sand."

"Bullfeathers," says Gramma. "Is Phil trying to take some sort of souvenir or something?"

"No, Gramma, sand. I'll show you when we come back."

"Well, that's one stupid souvenir if you ask me. Tell Phil that when he comes back I got a better one for him."

Phil is waiting outside when I come out with the plastic baggies. He looks confused as I motion him away from the trailer. As we walk down the road, he says, "I thought I was here to say goodbye to your grandmother."

"Not when she's in one of these hissy-fits. Jack says that my grandmother has tripolar disorder – manic, depressive, and whiney. She'll be okay in half an hour. And," looking at the baggies, "I want to take a walk anyway."

I tell him about my interest in the differences in the sand from the sandpit and the sand from the beach and whether either matches the sand from the footprints. "I assume that I have your permission to provide this assistance, for whatever it's worth."

"I meant what I said last night. I want you to assist the state police wherever possible, and notice that I said state police, not local. I was truly impressed with that detective last night. I was appalled by the other two."

"I've got to say, I was floored that George would jump out of bed and come rescue me."

Phil smiles. "I'm sure part of it is that he likes you personally. But I think he also takes the justice system pretty seriously. The whole system is based on trust and if the judges start distrusting the police, bad guys are going to walk."

"Damn. You mean the entire thing wasn't about me?"

"I beg your pardon. Of course, a man needs no other motivation than a damsel in distress."

"That's better. But, now that I think about it, I never thanked you for your own knight-in-shining-armor contribution. Thank you for not only coming to my rescue, but coming to my assistance so *fast.* I am amazed that you were able to go from groggy to fully awake within seconds. Do they train you for that in law school? Do they wake you up in the middle of the night so you can practice saying, 'don't say anything?'"

"They should, in case all else fails and you're reduced to defending drunk drivers for a living."

"By the way, what did you say to Captain Larini on the phone that would make him remark on how lucky I was to have a hotshot lawyer?"

"I said that anything you had said in a small closed room would be ruled inadmissible because your claustrophobia meant that you were being coerced. I told them that your claustrophobia had been observed and recorded by the state police when you gave your statement to them on the day of the murder."

We are approaching the sandpit and I tell Phil about how it was my special hide away when I was a kid. "It's one of the few places at camp that hasn't changed that much. Of course it's not as big as I thought it was when I was a kid, but it's still just as quiet and private. It feels more like a chapel than an amphitheater now."

"I'm sure there is something lacking in my own spiritual receptivity, but I think only a soil scientist could see a chapel in an excavation pit."

I scoop up a handful of sand and throw it into the bag. "Look, it sticks like sugar to a donut."

"Now that I can relate to."

We walk up Sandhill Road toward the beach. As usual, Phil seems endlessly fascinated by everything and everyone he sees. "What do people do here in the winter? Does the place close up?" he asks.

"No, it's open all year, but it slows down quite a bit. There are some people who have winterized places, but most others come and just visit for the day. Some of the main buildings are heated in the winter."

"What do the people do?"

"They mainly come to visit with their friends. The heat is turned way up in the main building and in the winterized cabins, so everyone takes their clothes off while they're inside. And people go in the hot tub and the sauna, of course."

"There's a sauna here, too? I haven't seen that."

"It's on the other side of the tennis courts. In the winter, some of the Nordic types like to get roasted in the sauna, and then walk around naked in the cold. Supposedly, it builds character. Every once in a while, some one with a whole lot of character will punch through the ice on the pond and take a dip."

We are approaching the beach now. In the parking lot I can see two state police cars, but no one is around. I lead Phil over to the beach and scoop up a handful of sand and let it run through my fingers. "See? Nothing sticks!"

"Will wonders never cease."

"Okay, okay. Humor me." I grab a handful of sand and put it into the other bag. The two bags now look almost exactly alike. "Let's go over to the office to get something to mark these bags with."

Unfortunately, that means walking the entire length of the crowded beach. As the only people with clothes on, Phil and I get lots of cat calls and whistles. One lady says, "My, my, you two make me feel positively *naked.*" Another says, "Take those clothes off, just leave the bow tie on!" In contrast to his usual self, Phil walks quickly, staring at the ground as if absorbed in deep thought.

When we are near the office, he slows up and asks, "What was that all about?"

"Who knows? According to some unwritten rule, you're fair game for harassment if you have clothes on. I get it all the time."

We can hear voices inside the office as we approach. One of them Ellsworth, a little higher-pitched than usual. We open the screen door and Ellsworth is standing with his back to a filing cabinet, guarding it as if it contained his most precious possessions. In front of him stand Kevin and George.

George turns to me, looking tired and hot. "Catie, Phil, good to see you. We seem to be having a little problem here. I need to get the names of camp members."

"And I can't give them out," says Ellsworth.

"I am aware of the camp's policy toward releasing last

names, which is why I took the trouble to get a court order *and* an order of confidentiality so that the names would never be released to the public. It took me days to get these two pieces of paper, and I had to endure a lot of giggling and silliness from people who I thought were grownups."

"I'm sorry. I will not release the names," says Ellsworth.

"Kevin was unsuccessful in convincing Ellsworth of the serious nature of a court order. I was called and have been similarly unsuccessful."

Ellsworth turns toward me. "Catie, you know how many lives would be ruined if the names got out. There are teachers here, and bus drivers, and day care workers, and state officials, and a judge, even. I can't destroy their jobs, their families, everything. I just won't do it."

George takes his glasses off, puts his hand on his forehead, and sighs. "That is what the order of confidentiality is for. No one is ever going to find out." It sounds like he has said these same words three or four times already.

Again Ellsworth appeals to me. "But they'll put it into the computer, and everyone knows what happens then. Identity theft. That's why I don't let anyone put those names into a computer. They are safe right here in this file cabinet, which is locked every night when I leave." He says this to George, just in case George is thinking of breaking in tonight.

George turns to Phil. "Do you think you could add something here?"

Phil holds up his hands. "My client is Catie and she has no stake in this disagreement. I want to make that clear first. So any advice I give at this point would not be legal advice, but personal. And I'm only participating at all because of the enormous favor this gentleman did for my client last night," he says, gesturing toward George.

"Phil," I say with a smile, "just get on with it."

"Ellsworth, you have several options here. First, you could comply with the order and turn over the names. Second, you could say that you are not the official in charge, and you could lock the cabinet and go get the person in charge."

"But that means Bernie, and Henry, and those boys play loosey-goosey with all this information as it is. I wouldn't trust them either."

"Third, you could go to the attorney who represents the camp and ask him or her to get a judge to quash this order."

Ellsworth looks at me, "Who's the attorney for the camp?"

"I don't know."

Phil continues, "Given that neither of you even knows who the camp counsel is, it is unlikely that a motion to quash the order could be filed in a timely manner. Therefore the police would have every right to obtain the information in the interim, until such a motion could be filed."

"And what happens if I refuse?" asks Ellsworth.

"Since this is a criminal investigation, you could be charged with interfering with that investigation. What is more likely, however, is that the police would flood this camp with officers, and ask each person to show some form of identification. That is a basic right of the police even for bystanders at a minor traffic accident. It certainly is their right in a murder investigation."

I see where he is going with this. "Ellsworth, if you let the police have the list, camp members themselves would probably never find out that their names were released. But if you don't, you could have dozens of officers scaring the living daylights out of members when they are asked to show identification. Either way, the names are out. One way is discreet, the other way causes a panic."

Ellsworth looks at me and then gives a defeated nod. He

steps away from the filing cabinet. George thanks Ellsworth and then motions to Kevin to help with the files. Phil and I step out on the porch and George follows.

Phil turns to George, "Why didn't you point out to him that you could get the ID's from people without his permission?"

"I was afraid he'd call my bluff. Who's got that kind of manpower? Besides, it sounded less like bullying when it came from you. By the way, what are you two doing here?"

"I forgot!" I run back in to mark the two bags of sand. "One of these is from the sandpit near Donald's cabin, the other from the beach. If the footprints in the foyer contain both types of sand, it may mean that the perp hid in the sandpit before the murder."

George's bushy eyebrows go up. "The perp?"

"You gotta keep up, George, you gotta keep up."

As we walk back to George's car, Phil thanks George again for his help last night. "Are there any details of the fire that you can share with us?"

"It looks like someone wanted to create a lot of smelly smoke. The *perp* stuffed some oily rags under the doorway and then lit them, but the rags were crammed in so tight there wasn't enough oxygen to create a real fire. Lupien, in his drugstore, smelled it right away and called the fire department."

"So what do you make of it?" I ask.

"According to the fire marshal, this is the kind of thing that people do to their own properties when they don't want to destroy anything, but want to collect some insurance. In this case, though, it was Lupien, not Maureen, who had insurance on the door that was damaged. Somebody may have been trying to intimidate Maureen for some reason."

"Or it might have all been about Catie in the first place," says Phil.

"Come again?"

Phil relates the story of last night, about the possibility of me being followed to the Rensford Inn, about the note given to him at the table and the 'be right back' sign on the door, and about the anonymous tip to the police that there might be a robbery that night. "I know that we attorneys are accused of the thinking that everyone is out to get their clients, but in this case…"

"Do you still have the note?" George breaks in.

"It's in my room."

"Do you think you could get it, and then maybe you and Catie could come down and give a statement?"

"*No*!" I say. "Look, I'm suffering from a little bit of post traumatic stress disorder today, okay? One more small, windowless room and you're going to see little bit of foam at the corners of my mouth."

"I have to be at the Ashton barracks all afternoon," says George. "What are you doing late in the afternoon?"

"I am joining Catie and her husband Jack at their house for an early dinner. Could you stop in while I'm there? Catie, would you mind? This is serious business, and I'd feel better if it were on the record in case they try something again."

George nods. "That would be perfect because it's right on my way home. How about five-thirty?"

"You want me to cook while I'm speaking and you're taking notes? I want you all to sign a waiver saying that I am not responsible if the chicken ends up dry and hard, and the pasta turns out soft and mushy."

George looks at Phil. "How about I bring over a pizza?"

"No anchovies," says Phil.

Chapter Twenty

"Let's go say goodbye to your grandmother," Phil says. "I'll need to be at your house by five-thirty, and I still have to make a lot of calls."

The dust kicks up around us as we walk down toward my grandmother's trailer. We pass a man coming the other way wearing a billowy long sleeved tee shirt that comes down to his knees. On his feet are sandals with tall socks. Phil looks at me after he passes, and says, "Fashion statement?"

"No, probably someone who doesn't like to slather sun block over every square inch of their body several times a day. Nudism is having a hard time with the whole skin cancer thing, which is why they no longer call themselves the American Sunbathing Association. Sometimes it's easier just to cover up."

We knock on the screen door of Gramma's trailer. Without opening it, she yells through the screen, "Hey, Flo! He's here!"

Phil looks around quickly to make sure he isn't getting a surprise party of naked people. He doesn't see any, but on the other hand he doesn't sit down either. He simply holds out his hand to my grandmother. "Eleanor, I can't tell you what a pleasure it has been to meet you..."

"Sit down."

He sits. "I'm afraid I can't stay long. I have to get back to my hotel room to make a few calls."

"Relax. I ain't asking you move in. I just want to give you that souvenir I promised. Flo! Where are you?"

Flo opens the screen door. "I swear, Eleanor, you'd win the callin' prize at the fat hog show with that voice of yours."

Gramma points to the counter. "It's over there." Then she sits down next to Phil on the couch and cuddles up next to him. Flo turns around and aims a Polaroid camera at the two of them.

"Smile!"

Phil looks like his career is passing before his eyes, but he is too much of a gentleman to protest. The camera spits out a pale square.

"Now me," says Flo.

"I ain't moving," says Gramma.

Flo looks at me. "Will you take it?"

"Sure."

Gramma looks at the beginning of the image on the first picture. "Goddamn, Phil. You look like you swallowed something nasty and you don't know whether to chew it or spew it. This time, smile."

Phil does his best, sandwiched as he is between the two naked women. Flo is squirming to get just the right angle to show off her curves. Gramma is looking at her. "I could do that, too, only I got bursitis," she says to Phil.

"Wait," I say. "That's perfect. Now, a couple of extra shots and we're done. Phil, does Harvard Law have one of those where-are-they-now, alumni magazines? I know you're really busy, so why don't I take it upon myself to send this in for you?"

"I believe I can take care of it myself, thank you."

Gramma is reminiscing. "That's Andrew's Polaroid, you know. He was so excited when they invented that thing. Before that you couldn't take any pictures around here, or, if you did, you had to find some seedy place to bring the film to. And then Mr. Polaroid comes out with that camera and it changed everything. Everybody could take pictures of everybody. That's when they decided that nobody could take pictures anymore."

"I don't follow," says Phil.

I explain. "With everyone in camp walking around with a Polaroid camera, people began to worry that their pictures were going to end up in the wrong hands. So, this camp, at least, adopted a policy of requiring permission before taking someone's picture."

Gramma turns toward Phil. "You want to help me up?" He starts to get up, and she swats at him. "Don't get up, jes give me a push." Phil gingerly pushes the top of her rounded back. "Hey! What are you trying to do? Push me over on my face? Lower!"

"Gramma…" I start to get up to give her a pull, but she tells me to sit down.

"For heaven's sake, man, give that butt a shove!" says Gramma. Phil takes a deep breath, carefully puts his hands on both sides of her buttocks and gently lifts her off the couch.

Gramma turns triumphantly to Flo. "See that?"

Phil finally says goodbye and promises to come visit both of them again soon. He manages to confiscate all the Polaroid pictures and put them in his pocket without Gramma or Flo noticing. Outside the trailer, Phil agrees to be at my house before George arrives.

On the way home, I force myself to face the question I've been putting off all day. Should I call Jack and try to explain last night or should I wait until he gets home? It's complicated by our fight last night, about his being away so much. I'm worried that it's going to sound like I'm still whining – see what happens when you're not home? I get arrested for arson. I decide to wait until he comes home and let Phil tell him. This is probably yet another case of avoidance followed by rationalization, but I have become so good at it I can't tell anymore.

At home, I shower and blow dry, straighten up the house and cross off some things on my to-do list for dinner. I'm getting a little nervous because of the close timing required for everything to go correctly, not only for the dinner but for the order of arrivals. Phil must come first and explain things to Jack, so that Jack will be prepared for George's arrival. I open a bottle of Cabernet to let it breathe, and then gulp down a large glass while the wine is still gasping for air.

At four-thirty, I hear the crunch of tires on the gravel as George pulls up in front of the house. I pour another glass of wine, and take a few gulps. It's okay. It's okay. As long as Phil gets here before Jack. *Just don't forget the chicken*, I tell myself, and repeat it like a mantra as I go answer the door.

"Hi Catie. I left work early. Hope you don't mind. The missus and I are doing barbeque tonight, and I don't trust her to get the coals going without burning the house down. So I can't stay long."

"No, that's fine. Come on in. Do you want some wine? Are you allowed to have wine? I mean, you know? Driving and all that? Can you drink?"

"You okay? You're acting like you just shoved some dope under the seat cushions."

"No, it's just that I expected Phil to come, and then Jack, and then you."

"Want me to wait in the car until I get my cue to enter stage left?"

"No, no. Never mind. I'm sure it'll be okay." The wine on an empty stomach is beginning to provide the assurance I need. I invite him into the kitchen and pour him a glass of wine.

He holds the glass by the stem and takes a sip. "Nice, very nice."

I refill my glass, noting that the entire glass is already cloudy with greasy smears. I have not been holding the glass by the stem. Oh, well. Too late. I sit across from him at the kichen table. "Jack takes care of the wine in this house. Not to change the subject, but before the others come, maybe you can tell me what's been happening on the Donald Thaler thing."

"Not making too much progress. Dechesne, the son, wasn't at the camp that day and has a solid alibi. The older Dechesne was there, but his wife gives him an alibi, for what that's worth.

"What about Donald's cabin? Find anything?"

"There are footprints throughout the kitchen and living area, but the place wasn't trashed. My guess is that the guy was looking for something and either got scared off or found it right away."

"And the sandals?"

"Cheap flip flops available at the local Wal-Mart and every other Wal-Mart in the country. Probably bought them for the occasion and then dumped then somewhere. By the way, I sent your sand samples to the lab. Nice thinking."

"Thanks." I hear a car on the driveway, and recognize the motor of Jack's Ford Expedition. He's driving up the driveway slowly, careful of the equipment loaded into the SUV. The corn prevents him from seeing the state police car until he's right in front of the house. Ordinarily he would have put the car in the garage, but this time he stops suddenly and makes a run for the front door.

"Catie?" He comes into the house and pulls up short at the sight of his wife and a state policeman sitting at his kitchen table drinking wine. "Where's Phil?"

"On his way over, honey." I go over and give him a big but unsteady hug.

"What's going on here?"

"Jack, I'd like you to meet Chief Detective George Myers."

George has risen from his seat and extended his hand, "It's a pleasure to meet you, Jack."

Jack is trying to decide what to do. He shakes George's hand. "Nice to meet you, too, Detective, but I wonder whether it's right for you to be here without the presence of counsel."

George turns toward me. "Let me guess. You haven't told him about last night."

"Uh, no, actually."

George nods. "And that's why you didn't want me to arrive before Phil. In that case, why don't I wait out in the car until Phil arrives?"

"What about last night?"

"George saved my butt, didn't you, George?"

"Yes. In fact, I think those were the exact words that your attorney used."

"How?"

I smile and motion Jack over to the table. "Sit. Have some wine. We'll talk about the weather until Phil comes. We could really use some rain, huh?" I get him a glass of wine and top mine off.

Phil's car can be heard coming up the driveway. George says, "It has been dry, but it looks like the corn has sprouted another foot."

I pick up the thread as I'm moving toward the door, "I don't know where corn finds the water to grow like that…Hi, Phil!"

Phil smiles and walks past me, and puts his hand on Jack's shoulder. "Are you all right? Do I need to get a defibrillator?"

"You want to tell me what's going on here, Phil?"

"I will. But how about some of that wine?" Turning to George, he says, "Jack here is known for his wine cellar."

George reaches for the bottle to see what it is. "This one is terrific."

"I'll go down and get another one," I say.

By the time I come back up the stairs, Phil has begun telling Jack about last night, wisely starting at the end to explain the role of George and how he made it all come out alright in the end. After I describe some of what happened to me in the police station, Phil says, "And now we come to the reason George is here. It appears that Catie may have been set up for this. I don't think it was a coincidence that she was in the parking lot at that time."

Except for a few quiet exclamations, Jack has been listening in silence. "Who would want to set up Catie?"

Phil says, "That's what we're all here to figure out."

Chapter Twenty-One

"I want every detail," says George, "leading up to the point where you were picked up by Putnam." He takes out a notebook. "Let's start with the confrontation at Ellie's yesterday. Did you recognize anybody there besides Maureen?"

"Just her husband Gordon."

"Terry Curtis or his wife, what's-her-name?"

"Amanda. No. He wasn't there, but she might have been. I've only seen her a few times and her back might have been to me."

"And just what did you threaten Maureen with?"

Phil leans forward. "Catie didn't threaten anyone. I merely told Maureen that if she published her accusations, we would be forced to take action against her paper for libel"

Jack jumps in at this point. "What accusations?"

Phil leans back. "Let's see if I can get this straight. Maureen accused Catie of making up the invasion and intimidation by Terry and his friends, so that Catie could call out the cavalry, thus giving me an excuse to come sleep over, and do so without raising your suspicions."

"But I told you to stay here!"

"I am merely reporting. And by the way, if Amanda Curtis sues you, Catie, for besmirching the good name of her husband, please call me immediately. That one I'll do pro bono."

We move on to my suspicion of being followed to the Rensford Inn before dinner and the note given to Phil as we finished. Phil produces the note and hands it to George.

George looks at it and then passes it around. "Definitely a female. Catie, do you have anything that Maureen has written to you to use as a comparison?"

"I can't think of anything offhand."

"Tell us about what happened at Maureen's office."

I tell them about the note that said she'd be back in minute and then about going back to the car and falling asleep. "The next thing I know, the headlights of Officer Putnam's car are blazing straight at me."

"Did he mention that they had gotten a tip about a burglary and that the drugstore owner, Lupien, had become suspicious about your car?"

"Yes."

"I checked police records and there was an anonymous call that night warning of a drug robbery. The voice was male. He hung up before anyone could figure out if he meant a robbery of a drugstore or a drug dealer. Lupien did call that night and reported your car, but he also reported that there was a man in the store hanging around a little too long. The man left as soon as you and Officer Putnam drove off."

"Who called the fire department?" I ask.

"Lupien did. He smelled the smoke. And that call was about twenty minutes after his call to the police. How long did you talk to Putnam in the parking lot?

"No more than five minutes."

"So there was time for that guy to leave Lupiens, stuff the rags under the door, light them up and leave."

Jack shakes his head. "So, in the end, we don't know who tried to frame Catie?"

George shrugs. "We know that Maureen and Amanda Helms were both mad at Catie, and both could have had some help from husbands or male friends. But neither really makes sense. Maureen really wanted to run with that libelous stuff, and Amanda wanted her to run it, too. So what was the point of trying to burn Maureen's office down?"

"BURN!" I jump up. Everyone stares. "The chicken. I was supposed to take it out twenty minutes ago."

With the story of the arrest and all that had led up to it, we have been talking for almost forty-five minutes. George looks at his watch and announces that his wife is going to kill him. Phil looks at his watch, and asks if he can take a rain check on dinner so he can get home before his kids go to bed. I'm half expecting Jack to look at his watch and leave, too.

Wine and conversation are two things I must avoid if I ever want to cook for anyone. And, in this case, I had a lot of wine, and the conversation was riveting because it was about me. I take the chicken breasts out of the oven and try to stick a knife into one. No liquid comes out, clear pink or otherwise. A dry shadow of its former self.

George comes over to the stove top. "Whoa! Weapons-grade chicken! Capable of causing blunt force trauma!"

"Thanks, George. Didn't you say your wife is going to kill you? Or was that just wishful thinking on my part?"

"I'll be fine. But if I'm going to have my men working with you on this case, I'll have to issue chicken proof vests."

"I have a few extra upstairs," says Jack.

I stab a fork into one of the breasts and hold it up threateningly. Unfortunately, it falls off.

"She never could hold her chicken," says Jack with a sigh.

"Enough!" Phil comes around to my side. "You are causing my client undue suffering, I will not stand idly by and watch you peck at her with chicken jokes."

"Get out of here, all of you, right now!"

Before opening the door, George reaches into his pocket, takes out his wallet and gives Jack a card. "Here's my card with my home phone number and my cell phone number and a number that goes directly to my car. Don't hesitate to use it. And I advise you to stick pretty close to her side until we figure this thing out, okay?"

"Got it," says Jack. "And I'm sorry for being a jerk when I first came in."

"No problem."

"And thanks for your help last night."

George gives a wave and is out the door. Jack closes it and shakes his head. "I can't believe how wrong I was."

"You were wrong about him and his group," says Phil. "But your instincts were correct when it came to the Rensford police."

I go back to the kitchen and clean up the floor where the piece of chicken dropped. "George might have been the knight in shining armor last night, but let's not overlook Phil's help in all this. Without him, I might have been back in that little room confessing to who knows what. If I had confessed, I don't think even George could have straightened things out."

"I owe you, Phil."

"Only temporarily. You tend to pay more promptly than most of my clients."

"No, really. Thank you."

"You're welcome. And now I'll be saying goodbye."

"But you have to show Jack your souvenir from the camp!"

Phil pulls out one of the Polaroids and shows it to Jack.

"This is great!"

Phil shrugs. "All in a day's work."

After Phil leaves, Jack gets on the phone and orders a pizza with absolutely everything, on the theory that all those sources of vitamins and protein make pizza a health food. While we're waiting, we cuddle on the couch and catch up on the news on CNN.

The pizza arrives and we open up some beer and sit at the table talking about his week and what he found at the site. He talks about Monday and what he's going to say at the Congressional hearing on land mines. Later we make love, and as I fall asleep, I make a mental note to buy a lamp that doesn't get knocked over so easily.

Chapter Twenty-Two

In the morning, the lamp gets knocked over again and then we go downstairs for breakfast. I tell him about my ten o'clock appointment with a realtor.

Jack looks pained. "Wait. First of all, you are doing nothing by yourself, per order of the state police. We operate as a dynamic duo until further notice. Second, what on earth are we going to see a realtor for?"

I explain about the land that the camp just bought, and my suspicion that there might be something really wrong with it. "And if there turns out to be nothing wrong with it, then I think the Gellermans got hosed by Mountville, which makes me mad."

"And I know how you get when you get mad. Who, or what, is Mountville?"

"Mountville Trust. I've got Roland working on that now." I fill him in on the information we have so far.

"Does the realtor know what's wrong with it?"

"Phyllis claims she knows nothing about anything."

"So we're going to go rough her up? Force her to tell what she knows?"

"No, we're going to sweet talk her into thinking we are interested in buying land in that area, but we're concerned that there might be something wrong with it."

"There *is* something wrong with it. It's too near your grandmother."

"Just for that, I think we might have to drop in and check on Gramma this afternoon. Still want to be the dynamic duo?"

"Egad. You can drop me off at the gate and pick me up later. The camp's a pretty safe place, right?"

"Just one teeny tiny lil' ole murder, as Flo would say."

"Okay, okay. Just make it so that I'm always facing you, or, of course, Flo."

"Phil was great at the camp."

"Look where it got him, squeezed between the naked flesh of Gramma and Flo."

"And then Gramma insisted that he grab her by the butt and push her up."

Jack closes his eyes and shakes his head, as if he's trying erase the image before him. "I think that's called hazardous duty and entitles him to a bonus. I'll give him a little extra."

On the way there, we stop and pick up the *Ashton Bulletin*. There is no mention of me today. I tell Jack about the inclusion of a short statement about the fire and the fact that I had been brought to the police station for questioning.

"I forgot to tell George that I called up the paper and found out that they must have had that information before Officer Putnam arrived at my house. It was probably Maureen, calling the police for their leads, but still, she must have had to hustle to get that information in on time."

I glance through the rest of the paper and find Maureen's byline has dropped to page three. It is an article about the lack of access to Donald Thaler's medical records, and restates her previous allegations of his sex addiction, and the stalking of local high school girls. It does everything but accuse Donald Thaler of infecting the entire town with sexually transmitted diseases.

My cell phone rings. "Hi Gramma! What's up?"

"I can always tell when your lover boy is home," she says. "Instead of 'Hi Gramma, how ya doing, how ya feeling' it's more like 'Hi Gramma, what's the problem?'"

"Hi Gramma! How are you on this fine summer day?"

"Cut the crap. My sink is plugged up."

"We'll be there somewhere between one and five."

"We? Lover boy comin', too?"

"Yup."

"Why?"

"Does he need a reason?"

"Come on. You know I tell everybody here that you got a tight ass prude for a husband, and he won't let you take your clothes off. If he starts hanging around here, looking too comfortable...."

"There's no chance he's going to start hanging around there, and I can guarantee he's not going to look comfortable."

"So why's he coming?"

"He wants to see the crime scene."

"Okay. That's good. Everyone will understand that."

We say goodbye and arrange to meet at her place between one and two this afternoon. "Got that?" I say to Jack. "You're going there to see the crime scene."

"As long as there aren't a lot of naked, out-of-shape, fitness-challenged people at the crime scene, I'll be happy to spend the afternoon there."

"They can't all look like you." I say. Jack has a tall, naturally lean body, the kind that looks fantastic in a well tailored suit. He's also got deep set, blue eyes and reddish brown hair, the color of a rich sandy loam with a lot of iron in it.

When we arrive at Phyllis's, she is pleasantly surprised to see the two of us, presuming that it means a serious intent to buy something. We get into Phyllis's exceptionally clean SUV and drive toward the northeast part of town. I ride in the back, with my bodyguard riding shot gun in the front seat.

I lean forward and put my hand on the back of Jack's seat. "I was telling Jack about the low price that the Gellerman land went for."

Jack plays his part. "Yeah, what was that all about? The other parcels of that size are listed at $500,000 or more. Think they'll come way down in price, too?"

"Absolutely not. Like I told Catie yesterday, the Gellerman sale was not at all typical, and I expect that these other sellers will get close to their asking price."

"Why wasn't the Gellerman sale typical?" asks Jack. I thought that Jack would just come along for the ride, but obviously he's enjoying his new role as probing investigator.

"Well, this is a bit awkward. I know Catie's association with the nudist camp and all, but the original appraisals that the Gellermans got said that nudist camp as a neighbor reduced the land's value by half."

"Half?" I ask.

"Yes. They had two appraisals done and both said that no developer would touch it. Nobody would want to buy a house that backed up to the nudist camp."

Jack feigns innocence. "Why not?"

Phyllis pauses, obviously trying to avoid insulting me. "Well, you know how mothers can be these days. They worry about everything when their children go outdoors to play."

"And they would be worried about the type of people who might be wandering around?" I'm picturing my grandmother getting lost and then knocking on the back door of one of these houses.

"No, no," Phyllis says quickly. "But what if the camp expanded and they had to look out on naked people. Not that there's anything wrong with naked people."

Jack takes pity on her. "That only accounts for half of the reduction. What was the original asking price?"

"The Gellermans were asking $575,000 but I think they would have been happy with $500,000. They had bought this as a retirement investment, and they had figured out that half a million was what they needed."

I thought of my conversation with Mrs. Gellerman. From the sound of her voice, I would guess that the land had been a big part of their financial future. "Okay, so the Gellermans find out that the nudist camp lowers the value to about $250,000. Then what?"

"Then an agent from the people who own the property on the other side of the Gellermans, Mountville Trust, called them and expressed interest."

"An agent? A realtor?" asks Jack.

"No, just some sort of representative of the company. I never met the guy, because he wanted to meet privately with the Gellermans."

"And that was okay with you?" asks Jack.

"I had the promise of a full commission, so I figured why not?"

"And with the neighboring nudist camp, maybe you figured that the less you knew the better?" asks Jack.

Phyllis stiffens. "I disclosed everything I knew to Mountville Trust."

Jack continues. "When the Gellermans sold the land to the nudist camp, did you get a commission?"

"A small one, yes."

Jack is doing a very subtle Perry Mason imitation. "And did you disclose everything you knew to the camp?"

Phyllis is silent, and her hands tighten on the steering wheel. "Look, are you people interested in buying land or not? I didn't do anything wrong on that Gellerman deal and I resent the implication that I did."

"We don't mean to...." I start to apologize.

"I told you that the negotiations between the Gellermans and Mountville were private. The guy flew in, talked with the Gellermans in a meeting room at the Best Western, and then he left. This happened maybe three or four times. In the end, the Gellermans turned around and sold it to the camp for that ridiculous price. End of story."

Jack is on a roll. "Did you advise your client that they shouldn't settle for such a low price?"

"Of course I did."

"And what did they say?"

Phyllis pulls the car over and stares out the front windshield for a moment. She starts to turn the car around.

"Phyllis, wait," says Jack. "We're not here to get you in trouble. Nobody is going to sue you or report you to the state board or whatever. You properly disclosed what you knew to the party you thought would buy the land. When the Gellermans finally sold the land, you probably didn't know anything for certain, maybe just some bits and pieces from your conversations with them, right?"

"Exactly. I didn't know anything for sure."

I lean farther forward and put my hand on the back of her seat. "We just want to get a better idea about the Gellerman land so that we know whether to invest in the properties nearby. Anybody in our place would be doing the same."

"And you're not here to get information for the camp, so they can sue me?"

"No, absolutely not," I say.

"Okay. All I know is that every time I talked to the Gellermans, she was more and more hysterical and he was more and more tight-lipped. In the end, she actually said that Mountville was offering to take it off their hands for nothing and that maybe that they should do that."

"You mean, give it away for free, for zero dollars?" I ask.

"Yes. I couldn't believe it myself. I told them to stop talking to Mountville, and I tracked down the president of your camp and talked to him, Bernie, I think his name was. I told him that the Gellermans needed to sell very quickly, and would take whatever they could come up with."

"And what did he say?" I ask.

He just laughed and said that the camp was totally broke, but he would see what he could come up with. He called back and said that the national organization would only give them $72,000 for it. He was stunned when I told him that I thought the Gellermans would take it."

"Did he ask why they needed to sell so fast?"

"Yes. And I made up something about a fiscal deadline of June 30th. It was a total lie, but I wasn't doing it for the commission. I couldn't stand to see the Gellermans talked into giving away the land for nothing. It was bad enough to only get $72,000, but nothing?"

Jack turns toward Phyllis. "So we need a drum roll here. What was so bad about that land that they were about to give it away for free?"

"I swear. I honestly don't know for sure. Every time Mrs. Gellerman opened her mouth, Mr. Gellerman would tell her to shut up. All I know is that the EPA kept coming up, you know, the federal environmental agency. And another thing she kept saying was, 'we're not a PRP', whatever that means."

Jack suddenly leans back in his seat. "Are you sure she said PRP?"

"Yes. What does that stand for?"

"Principal Responsible Party."

"Responsible for what?" asks Phyllis.

"You don't want to know."

"You're right. But am *I* in trouble with the EPA?"

"No. But the camp is going to have some trouble with them."

"Why?" I ask.

"Because now the camp is the Principal Responsible Party."

I slump back in my seat. "What is this, a game of hot potato?"

"Yup."

Chapter Twenty-Three

As soon as we are back in our car, I close my door and say, "Principle Responsible Party. What does it mean? Responsible for what?"

"It's kind of complicated. Let's get something to eat." He drives to the local gas station and we pick out some subs to eat on the picnic table in back of the gas station.

"Responsible for what?" I ask again as we sit down.

"Responsible for cleaning up a toxic waste site," he says, trying not to talk with his mouth full and not succeeding.

My sympathy for the Gellermans evaporates. "The camp bought a toxic waste site?"

"Yeah. Technically, they bought a superfund site."

"Like Love Canal? Will you put down that sub and talk to me? This is serious."

"Maybe serious and maybe not. It depends on who bought the property, the camp or the national organization."

"According to the town hall, the national organization bought it."

"Okay. Then it's serious, because EPA only tries to collect if there are some deep pockets to dig into. The camp is so broke, it would be like trying to get blood from a stone."

"But why should the camp or the AANR be responsible for cleaning up stuff that they didn't put there?"

"Because the law says that EPA can go after two Principal Responsible Parties, the one that did the dumping, and the one that owns the land now. And since, most of these old dumps can't be traced back to the original people involved, it all falls on the current owner."

"That's not fair."

"The law was written that way to prevent someone from buying up a contaminated property at a bargain rate and then selling it at a high price after it had been cleaned up at taxpayer expense."

"But what if they didn't know it was contaminated?"

"In order to be off the hook, the buyer has to show that he tried his damndest to find out whether or not it was contaminated. Like checking EPA's website, asking at the town hall, and things like that."

"Who thinks to check EPA's website when they're buying property?"

"Maybe someone should, if they're paying $72,000 for land that's worth a half a million." Jack puts his hands on both sides of his sandwich and leans forward. "Can I eat now?"

We eat in silence. I can't figure out where to direct the anger that's beginning to build up. At the Gellermans? At Phyllis? Why didn't someone at the camp try to figure out why they were getting the land so cheap?

"But wait," I say. "Why were the Gellermans so scared? They didn't have deep pockets."

"They probably learned they were on the list from Mountville. And it was in Mountville's interest to scare the living daylights out of the Gellermans so they would want to just hand over the property free of charge. When you read the law it sounds really threatening, so it would have been easy to scare the Gellermans."

"Why would Mountville want to take on the cost of clean up?"

"Maybe they knew what was in the dump, and they had already found out the clean up costs would be low."

"How do you know so much about this anyway?"

Jack looks at me. "Haven't you been listening to *anything* that I've been saying in the last two years? Or do you just grunt and nod at the right times while I talk?"

"Hey, don't knock it. Proper timing of grunts, along with proper inflection, is a skill that comes only after considerable practice. Fortunately, every female gets in a lot of practice while dating."

Jack grunts and nods.

"Forget it. You need two X chromosomes."

"I know so much about this because my job is to go out to these sites and see if there are any metal drums or other things buried below the surface which might indicate a lot of toxic waste. And there are hundreds of these sites in rural areas and farm country in New England."

"Why so many?"

"Because people used to make a few extra bucks by allowing their land to be used as a trash dump. Sometimes it was construction material, sometimes it was old cars, but sometimes it was some real nasty stuff from a local manufacturing plant. People would think, hey, I could fill up that low area, get rid of all the mosquitoes, sit back and get paid for it."

"So people filled wetlands with toxic waste."

"Back then it was 'clean fill,' and it was being put in 'swamps.' "

When we get back in the car, Jack takes the passenger side because we are going from here right to the camp. As I drive through the camp, Jack will pretend to be reading something on his lap. He will raise his head when we get near my grandmothers place. We've done these visits three or four times before, and I know the routine.

Jack has a kind of physical aversion to being around people at the camp, and it's not because he's a prude. He and I are very comfortable walking around the house without clothes. It's hard for me to understand since I'm so used to being around nude people, but I think he's feeling an acute embarrassment *for* these people. He says he feels like going up to every one of them and whispering, 'For God's sake, put on some clothes!'

As we get near Gramma's trailer, I slow the car and Jack looks up. Ahead of us is Roland, waving madly and Jack looks down again. Roland comes around to my side and Jack looks up again.

"Everything okay?" I ask.

"Yes. Well I guess so." He looks over at Jack. "Maybe not."

I sigh. "What has my grandmother done?"

"It's not her fault. It's my Flo. She heard that Jack was coming and she spread it all over camp, and now there's a whole bunch of people in your grandmother's trailer."

Jacks head sinks down again, along with his shoulders. I reach over and pat his back. "What are they all doing there?" I say quietly.

"They want to have an intervention."

"An intervention?"

"Yeah, you know, like when all your friends and family come together to confront your drug use?"

"We do not use drugs." I look over at Jack and think, at least not until today.

"I know. This is an intervention to confront Jack about his inhibitions."

Jack's elbows are now on his knees and his fingers are interlocked around the back of his head.

"And they want to release him of his inhibitions?" I ask.

"I heard Alice say that if they don't get Jack to take his

clothes off, they will at least get him to allow you to take yours off. Alice says it's a feminist issue."

"Are you telling us this so we have a chance to turn around before they see us?"

"No, I have a message from your grandmother. She says if you don't play along, she's going to sell the trailer and move in with you. She's been telling everybody that Jack wouldn't let you take your clothes off, and now you've got to back her up."

"My grandmother is never moving in with us. In fact she'll never set foot on our property again after this. I'll put up an electric fence if I have to."

"It's not her fault. If my Flo hadn't gone around blabbing this never would have happened. She and I feel really bad about this, so we cooked up a little plan. Jack, do you have your cell phone?"

Jack looks up with a defeated sigh. "Yeah, why?"

"Give me your cell phone. I'll say I took it so that you wouldn't be disturbed during this important session. After fifteen minutes, I'll run over saying that you got an emergency call from your mother saying that she needs you. It goes without saying that all of the women in that room will expect you to take that call. Then you run over to our place and hide there until they give up on you."

"Think you can handle fifteen minutes, Jack?" I ask.

Roland jumps in before Jack can answer. "It won't be hard at all. Ever been to one of these things? They happen at the high school all the time. I've been to dozens of them. Everybody in the room has a turn at saying how rotten you are. But you don't have to say anything until the end and you'll be out of there long before that."

I'm beginning to see how this might be possible. "And since Jack's problem is that he's too inhibited, he could just sit there looking at the floor with his eyes closed. He could pretend to be listening, but be totally somewhere else."

"Which is where I'd like to be right now," says Jack. He takes out his cell phone and gives it to Roland. "Fifteen minutes, man, you got that?"

"I got it."

Chapter Twenty-Four

When I walk into the trailer, I can see that its occupancy limit has been exceeded. Normally, the living area of the trailer has room for five people, three on the sofa and two on the kitchen chairs. When Jack and I walk in, there are already six people in the room, all piled on the sofa. The plastic chairs have obviously been reserved for Jack and me.

The mound of bodies on the sofa looks like a photograph in some art museum. Reading from the left, Flo is perched uncomfortably on the arm of the sofa, leaning in toward Charlie, who has his wife Debbie on his lap. On his other side, Charlie has his huge arm at the top of the sofa, and squeezed under his armpit is Gramma.

Gramma, in turn, has her shoulder hunched because she is being squeezed against Charlie by Alice, on her other side. Alice is not a small woman and she is feeling the pinch because Janis is using the other arm of the couch as a back rest, as she sits on the floor with her knees up to make room for me to pass by.

This heap of flesh against flesh is a tough way to begin an intervention on overcoming inhibitions. Jack walks right over to the sink and says, "Is this the one that's plugged up?"

"It's nice of you to worry about Eleanor's little problems, Jack," says Alice, "but we're not here to talk about that."

I pull up one of the plastic chairs and put it directly in front of Alice. "What are we here to talk about?"

"We're here to support you, Catie, by talking to Jack about his control issues."

"Wait a minute," says Charlie, already trying to shift his wife's considerable weight. "I thought we were going to stay away from that marriage stuff. I'm a man and men don't talk about control issues. I just want a chance to tell him how wonderful it is to walk around, you know, with it all hanging out."

"No, Charlie. Alice is right," says Janis, trying to turn to face Charlie but lacking the room despite her thin frame. "We want to empower Catie. She needs to be able to decide for herself if she wants to be nude or not. We don't need to talk Jack into taking his clothes off. That is definitely not the point here."

Debbie sticks up for her husband as she tries to find a more comfortable position on his lap. She has a boney butt despite her heft. "Charlie's right, you guys. We need to stay positive. Jack, did you know that in a nudist camp you don't worry about being rich or poor because no one can tell?"

Gramma snorts. "He's rich, remember?"

"Well, you know what I mean. We're all equal here, like God meant us to be in the beginning. Naked, and all."

Janis cuts her off. "Well maybe God meant us to be equal in marriage, too. Doesn't that count? Shouldn't Catie have an equal say in whether she takes her clothes off?"

"Exactly!" says Alice, shaking her finger at Jack. "You are being irrational, and you are imposing your irrationality on Catie."

"Irrational?" Flo asks in a little whisper. Dolly Parton is apparently too intimidated by this crowd to make an appearance.

"Modesty is irrational," says Alice. "Modesty is the stamp of approval that society puts on shame."

Jack has moved away from his intense study of the sink and taken his seat in the other plastic chair. He is leaning back with his arms crossed, staring out the window. I know he's trying not to look at his watch.

Charlies shifts his position again. "Look, Alice. No offense, but that's a lot of you-know-what. We're not here to get all philosophical on the guy." He shifts again. "Honey, sweetie," he groans. "My legs."

"You asked me to sit here, dear."

"I know. But I can't feel my legs."

"But there's no where else for me to sit, dear."

"Allow me!" Jack is up out of his chair. "I would much rather stand anyway. Please, sit here. I'm sorry. I didn't get your name." He smiles and reaches out to help her up while Charlie assists from the back end.

"Debbie," she says. "And I already know your name."

"Of course you do!" says Jack as if he's congratulating her on her quick intelligence. "There, are you comfortable?"

"Yes, thank you."

Charlie beams as the blood reaches his feet again. "See, this is the kind of guy we need around here. Someone with a good heart and manners to go with it."

There is a knock on the door, and Roland comes in. He looks around the room and gets nervous, which means a speech is coming. "As you know," he begins, "I suggested that Jack's cell phone should be commandeered in order to remove the possibility of distraction. Jack, I must say, gave up his cell phone without protest. I kept that phone with me in case..."

"Roland," my grandmother growls.

Roland speeds up. "Yes, well it's a good thing I kept it by my side because it rang and it's his mother and she needs to talk to him right away and I left the phone across the street so Jack has to come with me right now."

Flo and Gramma and I all speak at once about the proper duties of a son. Jack is out the door before we finish. I stand up and stretch and say how helpful this has all been.

"Sit down," says Alice. "I'm glad he's left for a while because now you can speak freely without intimidation. First of all, I am assuming that you *do* want to take your clothes off when you're here, right?"

I am aching to tell this bully to mind her own damn business, but I catch Gramma's eye and she is pleading silently. "Yes," I say.

"So why don't you?" she asks.

"Because a good marriage requires compromise."

Debbie sits up straight. "I believe that, too!"

"Thank you, Debbie. I appreciate your support."

Charlie smiles. "You married ladies need to stick together! Am I right or am I right?"

"You're right, Charlie," I say with a smile.

Still stuck under Charlie's armpit, Gramma says, "It's stuffy in here."

Taking her cue, Flo says, "My butt hurts from sittin' on this little arm rest here. I think I'll go see what my Roland is up to." She walks over to Gramma and pulls her up.

Charlie is finally able to put his arm down, and he rubs his shoulder. Alice arches her back to stretch out a kink or two. Janis uses the arm of the couch to hoist herself up stiffly. Standing around awkwardly, no one seems to know what to say. In the end, the group breaks up early, simply because too many people tried to fit into too small of a place.

I go across the street to Flo's place and walk up to Jack. "I'm sorry, honey. I had to give in. I had no choice." I start to unbutton my blouse.

"A girl's gotta do what a girl's gotta do," he says, and starts unbuttoning the bottom part of my blouse.

I slap his hand. "I thought you were the guy with manners."

Chapter Twenty-Five

Making sure the coast is clear, we sneak past Gramma's trailer and head down Pine Hollow Road to the crime scene. It's the middle of the afternoon on a Saturday in August, so a lot of people pass us going toward the beach and pool. Jack keeps his head down, looking like someone who dropped his keys on the road somewhere, and is searching the gravel with great care.

After a few minutes, we are alone on the road. I start to thank him for putting up with the crowd on the couch, but he interrupts me.

"Forget that. I found out something interesting on Roland's computer while I was over there. The Gellerman land is not, and never was, on EPA's list of superfund sites."

"What do you mean? There's no dump there? There must have been something there, or the Gellermans wouldn't have dropped their price."

Jack shrugs. "Maybe the Mountville people found something on the land, or maybe some old timer told them about stuff that was buried there long ago."

"How did you find this out so fast?" I ask.

"Takes two seconds. You go on EPA's website and click on 'superfund'. A couple of clicks from there, you put in a zip code or town name and it pops right up. Rensford comes up clean. There's one site in Ashton, but it's been cleaned up already. "

"Does this mean that the camp, or the national organization, is off the hook?"

"Not if Mountville reports it and it gets onto the list."

"I wish we knew who these Mountville people were."

"Roland said he's still checking it out. He's got nothing yet but he's going to keep at it."

Ahead of us, we can see the yellow tape still around the cabin, six days after the murder. There is no one around and the only sound is the piercing, high-pitched cry of a red-shouldered hawk, momentarily drowning out the equally high-pitched staccato of hundreds of crickets. We can hear some voices on Sandhill Lane, but they're barely audible.

Jack is staring at the cabin. "I don't know what I was expecting, but this doesn't look like a crime scene. It looks like a small log cabin with yellow tape around it."

"It would feel different if you had been here the day it happened. Just think. Six days ago, someone was standing at that front porch, with a gun hidden in a tote bag, ready to end the life of the guy who opened the door. And Donald was thinking of something else, maybe irritated by the interruption. He opens the door and that was the last moment of his life."

Jack just stares and shakes his head. "What's going to happen to this place?"

"I don't know. It's one of the nicer pieces of property in camp, although it turns out that it's the one closest to the property line. Well, at least it was before the AANR bought the Gellerman land."

"And the Gellerman land is where?"

"Right behind you." I say. "That ravine down there, Pine Hollow, is part of the Gellerman piece."

"So Donald's beautiful view might actually have been a view of a toxic waste site."

"You think the dump is down there in Pine Hollow?"

Jack walks over to the top of the steep slope across from

Donald's cabin. "It's always in a low area. But there might be other low areas on the property with easier access. That looks like a tough place to get in and out of with a truck."

Instead of walking back toward my grandmother's trailer, we round the corner and go up Sandhill Lane. The voices get louder, and eventually we see a state police car and more yellow tape, this time blocking the entrance to the sandpit. Beyond the yellow tape, George and Bruce are talking and looking up at the amphitheater of sand. At its peak, it's about twice as high as the two men.

When I yell out, they turn around and George waves us in. "Look who's here!" he says. "Our genius!"

"Who me?"

"The very one," says George as he approaches.

"Hey, if genius is 99% perspiration, maybe so," I say, shaking the shoulders of my blouse to fan myself. "To what do I owe this tribute?"

"The lab analyzed your samples of this sand and the beach sand. Turns out that there was no beach sand in the footprints, only this sand."

"What does that mean?" asks Jack.

"It means that the killer was here before he committed the murder."

"And he didn't go on the beach?"

"He didn't go on the beach before the murder with those sandals on."

"Find any of that wavy pattern here?" I ask.

"We got a partial print over there. Looks like he was pretty careful to scuff up most of it."

"Why? Why would he be willing to leave footprints in the cabin but not here?"

George shakes his head. "Don't know. Could be he was just

in too much of a hurry at the cabin. Could be that there's something special about this place."

"Like maybe it's where he hid the gun?" I ask.

George smiles. "Like minds think alike."

"That's why you called me a genius, right?"

"Takes one to know one."

We walk over to Bruce who is still staring at the wall of sand. "I can't see any disturbance," he says to George.

Bruce is introduced to Jack, who says, "But this place could have been disturbed ten minutes ago and you wouldn't be able to tell. The sand would flow down and over the disturbance and go back to its usual surface. But, hey, I shouldn't be telling you when you've got a genius of a soil scientist standing here."

"I hate to ever admit that my husband is right about anything, but, yes, you wouldn't be able to see a disturbance in sand because it so readily assumes its angle of repose."

"Its what?" asks George.

"Isn't that a lovely term? If you pile up sand, or any other granular material, the angle of repose is the slope of the sides of that pile. I love sand. The particles slide right by each other, so easy going," I sigh. "They bounce back from any disturbance and fall right back into place."

"Ooookaay," says George, with a glance at Jack.

Jack nods. "You should hear how she feels about clay."

"Moving on," says George. "We've called for the guy with the fancy metal detector. He should be here in about half an hour."

"George, do you know what my husband does to keep himself busy?"

"Indeed I do. Geophysical prospection. I read all about it on his website. He's got a bunch of sophisticated gadgets that detect things underground. So, Jack, when the metal detector comes, do you want to take a spin with it?"

"Please. I wouldn't be caught dead with one of those things."

"Jack considers himself too advanced for a metal detector," I say.

"Well, don't say that in front of Fred when he comes with his precious detector. He practically sleeps with the thing."

"I'll be sure to admire his technique and fawn over his equipment," says Jack.

"Which is exactly what I do for Jack," I say.

"Please. That's more than I need to know," says George.

Jack and I decide to go to Gramma's trailer to deal with her blocked drain and then come back to watch Fred survey the sandpit. We walk slowly up Sandhill Lane. Both Jack and I are in pretty good shape, but the air around us is almost dripping with humidity. Whenever there's an opening in the trees, we can see a haze that looks like a thin smog. We need the relief of a thunderstorm.

Jack puts his arm around my shoulder as we walk. "I've got an apology to make."

"Okay, what did you do wrong this time?"

"I doubted your ability to help the police. I was condescending and dismissive when you told me on Monday that the police had asked you to help them out."

"I don't blame you. It sounded silly even to me."

"And now you've given them a real jump on things by leading them to the sandpit. That was a really great idea, giving them those two samples. And the reason you thought of it is that you knew enough to notice the difference in the two types of sand."

"Well, thanks."

"You could be a forensic soil scientist."

I smile. "And you could be a forensic geophysical prospector."

"What would we call ourselves, the Bad Ass Binghams?'

"I like it. It's got the ring of truth to it," I say.

Chapter Twenty-Six

"They're gone now. You can come in," Gramma says when she sees us coming back from sandpit.

I can hear a tiny bit of guilt in her voice. "Are you sure?" I ask. "Because it looks like the trailer is still tipping a little toward that end."

She shakes her head. "Bunch of crazy people, especially that Alice. She's a piece of work."

"Why do you let her push you around?"

She waves her hand in disgust. "Somebody like that, it's easier to let them push you around than to push back."

We enter the trailer and Jack uncoils the auger and starts to work on the drain in the kitchen sink. Gramma has made coffee, and she tries to maneuver around Jack to get some cups and milk out of the refrigerator. The drain auger is a long unwieldy metal snake and Jack has to watch both the end in the drain and the end hanging down so it doesn't hit my grandmother.

"Do you think you two could go visit with Flo for a bit?" he asks.

My grandmother puts the cup down on the table with a bang. She tries to hide her face but I can see she's taken offence. "Gramma, for heaven's sake, he's just trying to make some room for himself to get the job done."

"Sure. Right. He loves to come see me."

"Eleanor...," Jack looks up from the sink but doesn't know what to say.

"You two have been in Rensford more than a year, and he's come to visit me, what, maybe three times?"

"Eleanor, I would love to see you more often, but..."

"But what?"

"Damn it Eleanor. You are standing three feet away from me and you're buck naked. Every part of you, right there for me to see."

"If you don't like what I look like, you don't have to look at me."

"That's not what I mean and you know it. Look, you're the one who kept turning Catie down every time she asked you to come over. You said you didn't want to have to put your clothes on. So after a while, she stopped asking."

"I would have put clothes on to go to your house, but she said I'd have to keep them on while I was there."

"Yes, that's right. Because that's the rule in our house – guests can't walk around naked – and you have to respect the rules when you're at our house."

"Well, what about the rules of this house? What if I said that my guests can't walk around with clothes on? What about respecting my rules?"

I don't like where this is leading, since I doubt that Jack is going to want to fix her sink if he has to do it in the nude. "I have an idea. Why don't we go to neutral territory? Why don't we take you out to dinner somewhere tonight?" I look at Jack and he nods with some hesitation.

"That's not fair," says Gramma. "They got the same rules you have."

"Eleanor, after what I went through for you this afternoon, you could at least do me the favor of putting some clothes on for a few hours. You owe me that."

"You did put up with a lot from that crew."

"Damn right I did."

Gramma sighs. "Okay. You can take me out to dinner tonight. Nothing fancy, though."

I help my grandmother down the trailer steps and Roland waves at us to come over. He is sitting on a lounge chair reading, while Flo is stretched out on the lounge chair next to him, toasting her back. Two beers and a bowl of pretzels are between them on a white plastic table.

Roland gets a couple of chairs for us, while Flo gets up off her stomach and puts the back of her chair up. "Jack kick you out of the trailer?" she asks.

"He just needed room to work with the auger," I say before Gramma can get started. "What are you reading?" I ask Roland.

"A book about meta tags." When he gets a blank look from me, he says, "The links that get a website noticed by a search engine."

"Speaking of searches," I say. "Any information on Mountville yet?"

"I found out that Mountville is a Massachusetts corporation owned by a Vermont corporation called Newbury, which again, only has a post office box. Papers for both corporations were filed in early May."

"So Newbury didn't go out and buy Mountville. They were both created at the same time for…"

"Obfuscation," Roland finishes.

"To make it harder to find out who the real owners are."

"Right. One other thing—the post office box in Massachusetts and the post office box in Vermont are each about an hour's drive from here."

Gramma shifts in her seat to look at Flo, and says, "I have to go to a restaurant tonight."

"Well that sounds like fun, darlin'!"

"I don't like wearing clothes."

"Who does? But you can't have a rainbow without a little rain, can you?"

"Is that from Dolly?"

"Direct from her scarlet red lips, it sure is," says Flo.

"Well, she don't know nothing."

"She does, too. To get that teeny-tiny, little-bitty waist of hers, she's got to be wearin' some mighty uncomfortable clothes."

"She gets paid to look like that."

"Just think of all that free food tonight as bein' paid to wear clothes."

"I guess so," says Gramma, but she sounds a little doubtful.

A golf cart bumps down the rough gravel road and stops in front of us. A husky guy gets out with a few catalogs and a letter. "Sorry I'm running a little late. I went and got the mail for the camp, but then I stopped at Ellie's and got to talking." He hands the mail to Flo. "Now, why would a nice girl like you be getting a letter from," he reads from the envelope, "the Marshfield Correctional Facility for Women?"

Flo leaps up from her chair and takes the mail into the cabin without a word. As the mailman drives off, Roland sighs and shakes his head. I know Gramma is dying to ask Roland what the letter is about, but I suggest that it's time to go see how Jack is doing. At that moment Jack appears at the door of the trailer and waves the auger in triumph. "All clear," he says.

I escort Gramma back to the trailer, and tell her that we'll pick her up at six for dinner. She protests that six is too late, but I tell her to eat something to tide her over until then. Walking back to the sandpit, I relay the results of Roland's search to Jack. He is most interested in the fact that both post office boxes are within an easy drive of Rensford.

"So Mountville or Newbury could actually be somebody local. Maybe even somebody here in the camp," he says.

"I can think of one person in the camp who had the financial know-how to set something up quickly like this."

"Had?"

"Yeah. I'm thinking it might have been Donald Thaler."

As we approach the sandpit, I can hear the intermittent nasal beep of the metal detector. "They found something."

Jack smiles. "Keep your pants on, Catie. They're going to find more than they want to."

"What do you mean?"

"In order to find a gun they are going to have to set the detector to find anything and everything. These detectors are usually set to ignore iron, so they don't start beeping over every nail or bit of old barbed wire. But a gun is steel and steel is iron, so that thing is going to be beeping constantly."

"Do they have to dig up everything or can the detector tell the difference between a piece of barbed wire and a gun?"

"It can tell you whether the object is iron or not, and the better ones can tell how deep the object is, but they can't tell you what it is."

"How deep does it detect?"

"Maybe two to three feet if it's something big, like an old cast iron sink or something, but there's not that much iron in a gun. So the gun would have to be no more than one to two feet down for them to detect it. Since it's pretty hard to dig a two-foot hole in loose sand, the metal detector should be able to find it if it's here."

George and Bruce are watching Fred work, along with a small group of naked onlookers. I look over at them, wondering if the murderer is among them. How could he resist the temptation to watch the police try and uncover his gun? How could he resist smiling if they were on the wrong track, or showing anxiety if they were on the right one?

"Find anything?" I ask George.

"Lots of junk, so far." He motions toward a laundry basket where someone is putting small bits of things in plastic bags with numbers. "We've been at this for fifteen minutes and already we have an aluminum can, a piece of tin foil, the nozzle of a hose, a couple of nails, a metal toy car, and fifteen bottle caps."

"And you have to save everything you find?"

"Thanks to you, we know the guy was here. That means everything that's here has to be labeled and stored as possible evidence."

"Let's hope then," says Jack, "that you don't find any old fenders or tractor parts, because they'll fill up your office fast. I once found a 1931 Desoto, with its chrome still beautiful."

"What do you use, since I know you are too sophisticated to use a puny little metal detector?" asks George.

"Mostly ground-penetrating radar and magnetometry."

"I know what ground-penetrating radar is, because we use it to find dead bodies. What's the other one?"

Jack points to the metal detector. "See that puny little thing there? It creates a magnetic field and then detects any pull on the field from metal as it passes over it. That's why you have to keep a metal detector moving so it can sense the metal creating a little drag on the puny little magnetic field."

"Now you've got him started," I say to George.

"With a magnetometer, you can measure the disruption of the *earth's* magnetic field from, say, a gun buried seven or eight feet deep."

"A single gun, buried that deep, disrupts the earth's magnetic field?" asks George.

"It creates a tiny, localized disturbance, and the magnetometer can pick up a change as tiny as a hundred-thousandth of a difference in the earth's magnetic field."

"How much does one of these things cost?"

"Top of the line, about twenty grand."

"I thought for a second that I would buy one for the department," says George. "You willing to volunteer yours?"

"Only if no one touches it but me."

"Jack sleeps with the thing," I say.

"You serious about that offer?" asks George.

"I owe you. You rescued my wife from the clutches of the Rensford police. So, yeah, anytime."

After about a half an hour, the basket is filling up with lots of little things like a piece of a broken mirror, a couple of keys, and an old fork. Up until now, Fred has been standing on solid ground and lifting the metal detector, passing it over the slope of the sand. Now he climbs to the top of the sandpit and lowers the detector in front of him so he can survey the top part of the slope.

As he steps in the loose sand, a lot of it comes streaming down the slope and lands on the ground. I find myself staring at the pebbles on the ground and watching them get buried under the falling sand. The more Fred walks on the sand, the more sand comes down and the deeper the pebbles get buried.

I turn to Jack. "We're going to need the magnetometer."

"Where? When?"

"Here and now."

"Okay, I'll bite. Why?" asks Jack.

"You know how we were saying back there that it's hard to dig a deep hole in loose sand and so the metal detector would be all that's needed?"

"Yeah."

"Well, most people know about metal detectors, right? Lot's of people have them. Assuming that the murderer has half a brain, he wouldn't dig a shallow hole for a gun when it could easily be detected by a metal detector. If it's here at all, it's really deep."

"But how did he dig a deep hole?"

"He didn't dig at all." I go over to a part of the sandpit that Fred has completed. "Watch that pebble. Watch how deep I can bury that pebble in a matter of seconds." I climb up above the pebble and start walking in the sand, which tumbles down and covers the pebble. As I continue walking, more and more sand falls until the pebble is covered by about three feet of sand.

George nods. "So he could just put the gun on the ground at the edge of the sand and then walk around above it."

"And since sand falls back into its angle of repose so easily, you can't tell where he walked," I say.

"With my trusty magnetometer," says Jack, "I could walk around the sandpit and see the gun even if it were covered up by a ton of sand. Actually, it would be a little tricky to use it while I'm sinking into the sand, but I'm up for it. It'll have to be tomorrow though, because it takes a bit of time to calibrate."

"And he's got to dress up like a surgeon," I say.

"A surgeon wears an outfit that has no metal in it," Jack explains. "In the operating room, you don't want to have a spark explode all those gases they use to put you under."

"You can't wear metal when you're using a magnetometer?" asks George.

"The magnetometer would give me a reading that there was a disturbance in the earth's atmosphere and it would be detecting the zipper in my pants."

By the end of the afternoon, the basket is filled with everything but a gun. We make arrangements to meet back at the sandpit at one o'clock tomorrow with the magnetometer, and head home to clean up and change our clothes. Then we turn around and head right back into camp to pick up my grandmother. Jack has grown silent.

"Have courage," I say.

Chapter Twenty-Seven

"I was hungry" Gramma says, as I walk into the trailer and see her standing near a plate of fried liver, and mashed potatoes.

"You were supposed to have something just to tide you over."

"I eat at five every day, so I get hungry at five every day. Ever hear of those dogs that drool at the sound of the dinner bell? That's me. Besides, its five-thirty now, and it's going to take a long time to drive there and park the car and get a table...."

"Okay, okay, never mind," I say as I help her clean up. "By the way, you look very nice."

My grandmother is wearing bright blue pants with a matching bright blue and neon pink blouse. She's put on pink clip-on earrings in the shape of daisies, and brown open-toed shoes that reveal some pink polish on her toes. She looks thinner and more erect than she usually does.

"I'm sweating like a pig."

Outside, I get in the back, and Jack helps Gramma with her seatbelt in the passenger seat.

"How far does this seat go back?" she asks, as soon as we're on our way.

"Here, I'll help you," I say as I move the lever on the side of the seat. "Tell me when."

Gramma says nothing as the back of the seat reclines. When I stop, she says, "Keep going. I want to lie down."

"Why?"

"I can't very well sit up when my girdle cuts me in half, can I?"

"You're wearing a girdle?"

"How do you think I fit into these pants? I haven't worn these pants for years."

"Why did you wear them?"

"It's this or my fat pants, and I don't like my fat pants. They make me feel like a frump."

"How are you going to sit up at the restaurant?" asks Jack.

"I can sit up if I have to. But if I can lay down on the way over, why shouldn't I?"

"Be my guest," says Jack.

Twenty minutes later we are seated at a booth at the Riverside Restaurant and Bar. Jack and I have worked out the seating arrangement beforehand – he and Gramma will sit on one side while I sit on the other. That way, Gramma and I will be facing each other and we can do most of the talking. Jack can chime in when he wants to.

Jack and I order wine and my grandmother orders a Manhattan with ice. When it comes, she lifts it up and drinks the entire thing before setting it down, making a face and shuddering. Jack and I have seen this before. Gramma feels that it's silly to spend money on two or three drinks, when one will get you just as drunk if you can get it down fast enough.

"I think I ate too much before I got here," says Gramma holding her stomach. "I have to go to the bathroom."

"Want me to come with you?" I ask.

"No," she says. I watch her wind her way through the crowded restaurant. I turn to Jack, who is staring out the window at the parking lot. After a while, I stare out at the parking lot, too.

"Nice cars," I say.

"Actually there is a nice one over there. Looks like a Fiat Spider from the seventies. Wires in that little thing are like spaghetti. All over the place."

Jack loves sports cars, especially the old ones. Our barn houses four of them, all under custom made covers, and I have a feeling that more are in our future. Personally, I don't like riding around so low to the ground. It feels like I'm in a speeding go cart.

"How about we take one of your babies out for a ride tonight?" I ask. "It's a beautiful night and we'll probably be out of here by eight."

"You feeling guilty about dragging me here?"

"Not guilty. Appreciative."

I see Gramma coming towards the table. She is holding her purse in front of her abdomen in an unsuccessful attempt to hide her white underwear, now visible because she can no longer zip up her pants. Something beige is stuffed into her purse. At a nearby table, a little girl puts her hand over her mouth as she stares wide eyed at my grandmother going by.

"There. Now I feel better," says Gramma taking her seat. "Now I can breathe."

"You took your girdle off," I say.

"Had to. That thing felt like a boa constrictor. Couldn't even get air down there, never mind food."

Sitting down opens up the zipper even more, showing a greater area of white nylon underwear. Gramma tries to drape her blouse over it, but there isn't enough material to cover it all. Jack offers to change places with her, so that he can be on the outside. Gramma says no, because she might have to pee in a hurry.

To change the topic of conversation, I ask Gramma, "Did you find out why Flo got that letter from the prison?"

"No, but I saw her crying."

"Really? When?"

"Right after you guys left. She came out to get her stuff from her chair and I could see she was crying."

"Why such a big secret? Flo is one of the most open people I know. I mean, she talks about everything and everybody."

Gramma nods. "Not exactly tight-lipped."

"You two are making too big of a deal about this. She probably has a friend who's locked up there. Maybe even a relative. She came from a pretty tough area, right? Someone she knows probably took a wrong turn somewhere, and Flo is nice enough to keep in touch."

"Believe me," says Gramma. "If she was being that nice to someone, she'd be telling it to the world."

"But this mystery person probably asked her to keep it a secret."

Gramma waves her wrist and shakes her head. "Flo can't keep a secret."

"She's been keeping this one for a while," says Jack.

When our food arrives, it's obvious that my grandmother will be asking for a doggy bag. She seems happy enough to see the huge cheeseburger and heap of fries, but she only chews on the ice left from her Manhattan. I ask her if she's feeling alright.

"Actually, I think I have to go to the bathroom again. A bit of the collywobbles, I think."

Jack looks at me after she's left. "Collywobbles?"

"Diarrhea."

"Oh, terrific," he says. "My upholstery."

"It'll be okay. Let's think of better things. What car are we going to tool around in tonight?'

"I was thinking maybe the XKE."

"And where would you like to go?" I ask.

"I don't know. Where would you like to go?"

"Let me see. I think I'd like to try my hand at competitive skillet throwing."

"Last night you were threatening to throw a piece of chicken. Now skillets?"

"The 4-H club is having a fundraiser tonight, and the highlights are the Women's Skillet Toss and the Powder Puff Ox Pull. I figure you could watch the oxen while I toss a few frying pans."

"Are you kidding? I'm going to be right there with you. Knowing how far your wife can throw a frying pan is one of the secrets to a long and healthy life."

Gramma is walking back to the table holding something that is neatly folded and white. From across the room, I can tell that the white thing is her bra. The bra had lifted her breasts and given them some shape, but now her breasts must be hanging flat against her. Her chest looks concave.

I sigh and turn towards Jack. "Here she comes, this time without her bra."

"No bra?"

"Don't worry. Her nipples point down, remember?"

"Unfortunately, I do."

"Thank God I'm free of that thing," she says as she hands me the bra to put in my purse. "I was trussed up like a turkey."

"How are your collywobbles?" asks Jack.

"False alarm. I'm cramping up, but I think my underwear is too tight. See?"

Gramma hoists herself out of the booth. Facing me, she lifts up her blouse to show me the top elastic of her underwear. "It's killing me."

Jacks eyes are boring into me, mentally projecting the desperate hope that I will take charge of this situation.

"Gramma, why don't you sit …"

While I'm saying this, she pulls her blouse higher so she can see better, and then pulls down her underwear a little. "See? It's leaving a mark."

Jack closes his eyes, and leans against the back of his seat.

"Gramma, you need to…"

"I got it. If I pull it down like this," she says, lowering the top elastic so that it sits under her belly, "that way I got that low slung look."

Gramma is now standing there with much of her front exposed. Jack's head drops down and he's got both palms on his forehead.

"Catie," he moans.

"What's the matter with him? I'm not showing anything important." She pulls her blouse up further and looks down. "Am I?"

Conversation around us has stopped. The waitress is approaching rapidly.

"Can I get you anything else?" she asks, trying not to look at Gramma.

I look up at the waitress. "Just the check, please."

Chapter Twenty-Eight

The 1965 Jaguar XKE may be a beautiful car, but to me it looks like a fish. The oval grill in front looks like the half open mouth of a fish, and the headlights look like fish eyeballs set into the slope of the fish face. In lieu of a bumper, there are two tiny little nubs on the front that look like little whiskers on either side of the fish mouth. It doesn't look like a jaguar, it looks like a catfish.

The engine takes up most of this car, making the cabin look like an afterthought. The seats in this car are so low that my chin can rest on the window sill while I get a lovely view of the tires of most other vehicles on the road. Of course, I don't share these feeling with Jack, especially the fish part.

Right now, Jack has one hand resting loosely on the polished wooden steering wheel, and the other hand making a quick smooth shift into third gear. Driving this car makes him forget all about Gramma and her undergarments. Jack was very gracious when we dropped her of, when she said it hadn't been as bad as she thought it was going to be.

Jack looks up at his rearview mirror. "I think we're being followed."

"You're kidding!"

"Nope. This guy was behind us near our house and he's stayed with us, even though I've slowed down and given him a chance to pass."

I look in the side mirror and make out a dark pickup truck in the shadow of some overhanging trees. "Can you see who it is?"

"No. The only thing I can see is that it's a Ford and I think it's a dark red."

"It could just be going to the 4-H camp."

"We'll see in a few minutes."

As we approach the dirt road leading into the 4-H fairgrounds, Jack slows down, forcing the truck to pull up directly behind us. I can see a man with a dark moustache. His head is tilted because he has a finger in his ear and he appears to be lost in thought. When we turn in, he continues on.

"False alarm," I say. "He was cleaning out an ear, and that's not what spies do on the job."

When we reach the lawn which is being used as a parking lot, the teenager in charge lets us park near the entrance so that he can keep an eye on the XKE. As we walk up the hill, I turn to look at the bright red car, and see a few guys around it already. From the side, it looks quite beautiful, not at all fishy.

After paying our twenty-dollar donation at the entrance, we pass the maze that has attracted a lot of the little kids. The walls are made of hay, two bales high. This means that the toddlers can get lost in the maze but still see their mothers over the tops of the walls, providing the perfect mix of thrill seeking and safety.

The skillet toss turns out to be behind the restrooms in a long alley of grass. When we get there, we find that someone has forgotten to bring the red spray paint needed for a line on the grass that the contestants must aim for when throwing the frying pan. The event has, therefore, been postponed for half an hour.

The 4-H club is offering three forms of refreshment: barbequed chicken, cotton candy, and freshly-squeezed lemonade. We opt for the lemonade. As we move away from the counter, we hear our names being called. It's Phyllis, the realtor, and she gets up from her table of friends and beckons us over to another table where we can talk privately.

"I found out where the dump is on the Gellerman land," she says in a stage whisper. I wonder if Phyllis has added something extra to her lemonade.

"Where is it?"

"In a place called Pine Hollow."

I shake my head. "But I've seen Pine Hollow from the nudist camp," I say, "and there doesn't look like there's any possible access to it for trucks to dump anything."

"Yes, but that ravine goes on and on. I knew there was an old colonial road that goes in there, so this afternoon I drove down it and sure enough, I looked over the edge and saw some rusty barrels and an icky, you know, oil slick."

"Do you think you could show it to us?" asks Jack.

She shakes her head. "I have friends staying at my place and I'm up to my ears with stuff to do."

"Is there any way we can find out where it is?" I ask.

"Yeah, you could go to the town hall. I've seen the old maps there, the ones that used to show all that stuff, like old cart paths and logging roads."

Phyllis's friends are calling her back from the table to answer a question for them. When she gets up to go, Jack puts a hand on her arm. "Guess what? It turns out that there is no record of any EPA involvement in the Gellerman land. That dump is not on any superfund list and the Gellermans were never a target of any collection effort for clean-up costs."

Phyllis sits back down with a thud. "You mean to say that Mountville made the whole thing up?"

Jack shrugs. "They probably knew about the dump, and maybe they thought it would be reported to the EPA eventually, but I think they probably doctored some EPA forms to look like it was already on the list."

Phyllis is aghast. "The Gellermans had already cut their price in half because of the proximity to the nudist camp. And then Mountville gets so greedy that they tried to scare the Gellermans over *nothing?*"

I shake my head. "I just hope the camp doesn't suffer a lot of clean-up costs. And it stands to reason that Mountville will be so pissed about this whole thing that they are going to contact EPA right away."

"I don't think so," says Jack. "They're not going to want to advertise the fact that their new development is right next to a superfund site."

"So if Mountville doesn't mention it, and the camp doesn't mention it, EPA's probably not going to find out about it," I say. "The bad news is that it's not going to be cleaned up, the good news is that EPA may never come after the camp."

Phyllis shakes her head. "The camp comes out okay, but what about the Gellermans? They got shafted. And all their eggs were in that one basket."

I turn to Jack. "Do you think they have some legal recourse against Mountville?"

"Maybe. But it might get sticky for Phyllis, and the camp might end up paying more for the land."

"I don't care," says Phyllis, dramatically banging her fist against the picnic table. "My conscience is telling me I should call the Gellermans about this." She bangs the table again. "The Gellermans were my clients after all, right?"

Jack and I look across the table at each other, since it's obvious that the additives to Phyllis's lemonade are getting into her bloodstream. When her friends yell over to her to rejoin them, Jack has to help her up off the bench. I have my doubts about her whether her commitment to the Gellermans will last until tomorrow.

The skillet toss is about to get started, so Jack and I head back to what is called Fry Pan Alley. Before signing up, we are given the chance to lift the skillet, which is much heavier than I expected. I wonder whether there are sports medicine people who specialize in injuries from skillet tossing.

We are given instructions by someone who looks like she could have been a past champion. We are each to be given two throws which will be averaged for our score. Since accuracy matters, if the skillet does not fall on the line, the distance away from the line will be subtracted from the overall distance. Jack's eyes are already starting to cross from the tedium.

"I thought this was going to be a fun event with women hurling frying pans everywhere."

"Are you kidding? There is a big prize at stake."

"Which is?"

"Ten dollars and that tee shirt," I say, pointing to a tee shirt that says: *There are never too many cooks in MY kitchen*.

First up is a girl of about eight who swings the frying pan back and forth about twenty times before letting it go. After precise measurements that would shame a surveyor, it is determined that her first throw has gone fifteen feet and three inches after incorporating the distance from the line. This first throw has taken five minutes, so multiplying that by two throws each, and the twenty-two participants signed up, this event should take three hours and forty minutes.

Luckily the order is alphabetical, so I hope I won't have to wait long. Jack, on the other hand, is beside himself with boredom after the first two contestants. He mutters quiet encouragements to the contestants to just throw the thing already.

I pat him on the knee. "You don't have to stay here, you know. You can go do something else."

"I'm not supposed to leave your side. I have to stay here."

"It's lovely to think that when you're with me, it's because duty calls."

"Believe me, I should get time and a half for being with you at a skillet toss."

At that moment, there is a loud roar and sputter of an engine from the other side of the fair. Jacks eyes light up.

"That's a race car! Sounds like a lead car!"

"That's a car that needs a muffler."

Jack turns to one of the few men among the bystanders. "What's a race car doing here? There's no track in a 4-H camp."

"They just trot it out before they do the tire burn," the man says.

"There's going to be a tire burn?!"

"Yup. Should begin any minute now."

Jack turns toward me, nearly jumping out of his skin with excitement but wanting to do his duty. "Maybe it will still be going on after this has ended."

"Are you kidding?" the man says. "This thing goes on forever."

"Go already, will you?" I say. "Just tell me. What's a tire burn?"

"It's hard to explain. Just come over when you're done here. It will be easy to find because there will be huge columns of smoke."

"Okay, let's see. I go from the frying pan to the fire, right?"

Jack groans. "I'm outta here."

About twenty minutes later, I stand at the painted line, and throw my very first frying pan, without dislocating my shoulder. It goes a respectable 22 feet, after adjustments. I'm swinging the pan for my second throw, when I see the man who was following us in his truck. He's standing at the end of the line, smiling at me under a thick moustache, as if he's daring me to hit him with the skillet. He's short, with dark hair pulled back from his receding hairline into a low pony tail. I swing the pan go, let it go, and it clunks to the ground about six feet from me.

Chapter Twenty-Nine

Two women rush over to take the measurement, and there is a general expression of sympathy and an offer of a do-over. By the time I look up, the man is gone. Refusing their offers, I tell them that I need to go and join my husband at the tire burn. No one urges me to come back in case I've won a prize.

Walking toward the sound of the engines, I keep an eye out for man I just saw. Unfortunately, there are a lot of short men with ponytails and thick dark moustaches. In a line up, I'd have to ask all these men to stick a finger in their ears to see if I had the right one. I'm not even sure now whether the guy at the skillet toss was the same man we saw following us.

Jack is behind a chain link fence that surrounds the paved parking lot of the 4-H camp. An old black Corvette is approaching the center of the parking lot where two men with hoses are standing. The Corvette comes to a stop between them.

Jack motions me over. "Quick! Wait till you see this!"

The Corvette has two very wide tires in the back. As the driver guns the engine, the car stays still, while the back tires start spinning faster and faster until they are smoking. As they spin even faster, the smoke starts forming a cloud around the car. With the pedal to the floor, the smoke billows up twenty or thirty feet in the air and drifts over the cheering crowd.

"This has got to be the most idiotic thing I've ever seen," I say, with my cardigan pulled across my nose and mouth. The smoke, after all, smells like burning tires.

"This from a woman who's been throwing skillets?"

"Hey, at least that required some talent. These people just sit in the car and push the gas pedal."

"It used to require a lot of finesse with the clutch. But now everyone has to have a line lock which immobilizes the front wheels."

"Why take the fun out of it?"

"Because those back wheels are doing a hundred miles an hour and if the driver was less than competent, the car would shoot out into the crowd at that speed."

"Just the kind of thing you want to bring your whole family to."

"Of course, one or two guys try to slip into the competition without a line lock, usually the old timers who think they don't need one." Jack says. "And I bet that third one in line is one of them." He points to a thin older man with long stringy white hair, smoking a cigarette in a rusted Mustang convertible.

"Looks like he's inhaled a little too much smoke."

"Of every variety."

Sure enough, when the Mustang gets to center stage, the smoke starts rising, but at the same time the car starts bucking, lurching forward and side to side like the wild horse after which it was named. The car is immediately surrounded by officials with heavy pipes, who threaten to bang on the car if the guy doesn't shut it off immediately. Nothing is more effective at getting the attention of these guys than the threat of body damage to their car.

After a bit of arguing, they convince the old timer to leave, and by this time, I'm ready to leave, too. Jack is reluctant until I remind him that we don't want to leave his baby in the parking lot too long. After all, there is the possibility of body damage to his car if someone bumps into it. Jack pulls himself away from the fence and we head back to the car.

On the way back, I stop suddenly and pull at his arm. Coming toward us is Ralph, one of the guys that came over with Terry Curtis on that awful night. I explain who he is to Jack, and then I'm sorry I did. I don't want any kind of scene. I just want to go home.

Jack strides up to Ralph, who looks startled and tries to go around. Jack steps in front of him again. Ralph is taller than Jack, and he's got a swagger built into every motion.

"What's your problem, man?" asks Ralph.

"Do you see this woman here? She's my wife."

"Well, lucky you."

"If you ever go near her again, I'll kick the shit out of you."

"I'm scared."

Approaching Ralph from behind is a short thin woman who stops and looks at me closely. Then she goes up to Ralph and swings her purse, hitting him hard in the kidneys. Ralph presses his arm against his side and bends over.

"Tracey," says Ralph, drawing her name out into long whining syllables. "What did you go and do that for?"

"Because I could tell you weren't apologizing to her. And I told you, the next time you saw that girl you were going to get down on your knees and ask forgiveness."

I smile at her. "Thanks. I appreciate it."

Tracey turns toward me with a sigh. "I'm sorry to say that I have this mouth-breathing, knuckle-dragger for a husband. It's terrible how he bothered you. You must have been frightened half out of your wits."

I nod. "I was pretty scared."

Tracey takes a piece of paper and a pen out of her purse and writes down a phone number. "Here's my cell phone number. If he ever so much as comes near you again, you call me. I may not be as fast as the fire department, but I know where to find him."

As Jack and I walk to the car, I try and lighten the mood. "We have just witnessed the power of the purse." I say. Jack groans.

We walk to the XKE, which has managed to survive without a scratch under the watchful and adoring eye of the attendant. I feel strangely disoriented by the encounter with Tracey and Ralph. It's been a while since I've felt welcomed by this community.

As if reading my thoughts, Jack says, "At least one person around here seems to be on your side."

I sigh. "What pleasure does it give, to be rid of one thorn out of many?"

"Let me guess. Your friend Horace, right?"

"My friend Horace."

On our way home, the soft black leather seat wraps around my back in a semicircle of a hug. I lean back and look out the window and watch the shades of gray in the overhanging branches. Then Jack brakes hard, and I am pulled forward.

"What was that?" I ask, thinking it was probably a squirrel. Jack would rather wreck his car than run over something.

"A pickup truck just pulled out in front of me from that street back there. There was no one behind me so you think he might have been waited just a few seconds longer."

I sit up to look at the truck ahead of us. "Well, at least we know he isn't following us." I tell Jack about my apparition at the skillet toss.

"You should have told me about that, Catie. Remember, I'm supposed to be keeping an eye out for you."

"And make you miss that macho generation of toxic gas that you enjoyed so much?"

"You have to have a Y chromosome, I guess."

The truck in front of us is being driven erratically. Jack has to watch carefully because the truck seems to slow down and speed up for no reason. At one point we find ourselves about ten feet behind him because he has slowed down to twenty miles an hour. Jack is constantly looking for a way to pass him.

Each time we approach the truck, I am reminded again of how low this car is compared to a pickup truck. Staring ahead, my eyes are about level with the bottom of the truck bed. Involuntarily, I press my head back against the seat each time we approach the back of the truck.

We go over the top of a steep hill and discover that the truck has come to a dead stop half way down the hill. There is someone coming up the hill in the other lane. Jack presses his foot on the brake but we just skid down hill. As the brakes try and grab the pavement, the front of our car tilts down. We are headed right under the truck.

At the last second, the truck moves ahead about twenty feet barely allowing our car to come to a stop with its nose just under the back of the truck bed. Another six feet and we would have been decapitated. Jack and I sit frozen in stunned silence. A man gets out of the truck and comes toward us. It is the same man who was following us, the same man I saw at the skillet toss.

Jack rolls down his window. "You almost killed us!"

"It was a deer," the man says in a monotone, staring at Jack. "A deer ran across in front of me."

"I didn't see anything."

The man nods. "It was a deer, all right." He turns and walks back to the truck.

The truck turns off at the next intersection and we continue on. I reach out and touch Jack's hand. We almost died a few moments ago. Right now, nothing seems important except the feel of his hand.

Chapter Thirty

Bracing for impact apparently involves a set of muscles that don't get used very often, because the next morning we are both stiff and sore. Last night we went to sleep without even talking, just spooning our bodies tightly against each other. This morning, we make small talk in the kitchen until we can't avoid the topic anymore.

"There was no deer," says Jack.

"It might have disappeared before we came over the top of the hill."

"No, there was no deer. He was just sitting there waiting for us to come over the top of the hill."

"But then he pulled ahead just a little so we didn't crash," I say.

"Which means he wasn't trying to kill us, just scare the hell out of us."

"Which he did."

"So the question is, why did he want to scare us?" asks Jack.

"He could be a friend of Terry Curtis."

Jack shakes his head. "If Ralph's wife is defending you in public like she did last night, then everyone must know the truth about what really happened."

"So what else could it be? Helping the police on the murder?"

"That doesn't make sense, either. If we were scared off, the police would continue to do just fine without us."

"But they wouldn't have someone doing the magnetometry today."

"Now that's pretty scary to think about because there were only a handful of people who overheard us talking about that."

I putter around, cleaning up the breakfast dishes. "Maybe we should tell George he should get someone else to do the magnetometry."

"We'll have police protection while we're doing it, and after that, there will no longer be any point in scaring us."

"You just really want to do that survey."

"I have to admit, looking for a gun is a hell of a lot more exciting than looking for a 50-gallon drum of solvent."

"I just wish I remembered who was standing nearby when we were talking about it."

I get dressed, then go out to gas up the car and get the Sunday paper. Today we will be using the Ford Explorer, not only because it's capable of holding the equipment, but because it's the least likely to slide under a pickup truck. I have a feeling that the XKE is going to stay in the barn for a long time.

There is only one gas station in Rensford, and I usually see someone I know there. This time it's Maureen Helms. Her back is turned at one of the pumps as I slip in to get the paper. I'm hoping I can hide in there until she goes, because I can't face another confrontation right now, especially after last night.

When I don't see her for a while, I figure it's time to stop lurking in the back of the store, and I go up to the counter to pay for the paper. Maureen walks in with large sunglasses. Even with the glasses I can see that her eyes are swollen like a puffer fish. I smile to myself. One swollen eye could mean spousal abuse. Two swollen eyes mean she got her eye lids lifted.

Well, well, well. As one of the more vocal feminists I have met, Maureen must be feeling very, very insecure about her looks to opt for plastic surgery. There is something very satisfying about seeing insecurity in your enemy. It makes me feel wonderfully catty.

The lead article of the *Ashton Bulletin* is about the nudist camp. A poll was taken of 374 likely voters in the upcoming referendum, and 57% would like to get rid of the camp if legal measures could be found to do so. Thirty nine percent would vote to keep it, and four percent were undecided. Of those voting against the camp, most said that the recent murder had influenced their opinion.

I notice that there is no mention of me for the second day in a row. The next thing I notice is that there is no mention of Maureen, either. She did not write the lead article about the nudist camp, or any other article. She usually has a piece in the Sunday edition called the Hospital Report, but there is only a statement saying that Maureen Helms is on vacation this week.

Back at the house, Jack asks, "Can you give me some help?"

In the room that Jack uses for his office, he has the pieces of the magnetometer laid out. I check things off while he goes through all the parts of the equipment to make sure everything is clean and charged up.

I can't get my mind off of last night's close call. "Do you think that guy last night was trying scare us off of the Gellerman business?"

"Maybe. But the guilty party in that case only faked some federal documents, and those documents probably aren't around anymore."

"I'd still like to find out who these Mountville people are. I hope Roland has come up with something."

"But what would you do if you found out who they were?" he asks.

"I don't know. Report them or something. Even if nothing could be proven, I'd still like to see them sweat a little. What they did to the Gellermans was despicable."

"My guess is that the Gellermans were too cheap to hire a lawyer. A lawyer would have known enough to check out what Mountville was saying."

"I suppose."

"And now the camp has purchased some contaminated land. Sometime in the future they may have to pay for clean up."

"If there is a camp some time in the future." Neither of us wants to pursue that topic because it raises the question of Gramma's future living arrangements.

After lunch, we put everything in the car and head over to the camp. On the way down to the trailer, we meet Roland coming up the hill. He's got a towel over his arm, a thick book and some sunscreen. Roland is not the type to socialize on the beach, and it's hard to find somewhere to be by your self in this place.

I roll down the window when we're next to him. "Hi, Roland. Off to the beach?"

"Gotta go somewhere."

"What's the matter?"

"Flo. She's a mess, and it's getting on my nerves."

"What's the matter with her?'

He closes his eyes and shakes his head. "It's ridiculous. I'll let her tell you."

"Find out anything about Mountville?"

"Haven't been able to give it a thought."

"Okay. Well, maybe we'll catch you later."

"Sure."

We continue on our way, and Jack says, "Not a happy camper."

"I want to talk to Flo. I can't have her interfering with the help."

"Try not to phrase it that way," says Jack.

We pull up in front of the trailer, and find my grandmother across the street sitting in one the chairs at Flo and Roland's place. We join her, and ask where Flo is.

Gramma leans forward and says, "She's gone in to take a dump, and I hope she's blocked up for days."

"What's going on?" I ask.

"Apparently she's been pulling a fast one on the government and she got caught. The state of New Hampshire is no longer going to provide all that plastic surgery."

"How did she ever get the state to do it?" asks Jack.

"Prisoners get free plastic surgery, and she has a friend in the Marshfield prison who's a secretary or something. Anyway, this friend kept slipping in Flo's name as a prisoner whenever there was an opportunity for free surgery."

"Since when do prisoners get free plastic surgery?"

Gramma shrugs. "Those students gotta practice on somebody, I guess."

"Flo was being operated on by students?"

"She says that real doctors were always there in case somebody messed up."

Jack and I look at each other, each of us probably thinking the same thing. Flo is one lucky lady if she had all those surgeries by trainees and nothing went wrong. Getting caught may have saved her life.

"So is she in trouble? Is that why she's so upset?" I ask.

"No, that's the thing. That's why Roland is so pissed at her. She's not in any trouble at all, even her friend is going to be okay."

"So why is she so upset?"

"Because, heaven forbid, she might end up looking like me."

"You?"

"She sits here and whines and cries about her future, about the wrinkles and the sagging, and the liver spots, and the hanging this and the hanging that. And all the time, she's describing me. I've learned to love my inner self and all that garbage, but I can't take much more of this."

I hear the toilet flush. "Jack, why don't you take Gramma over to the trailer, and I'll try talking to Flo."

When Flo comes out, she plops down on the chair next to me. "Oh, great," she says. "Now I get to sit next to someone younger than me. At least with Eleanor, I *felt* young."

"Gramma told me about your volunteering for practice surgery. I think you're pretty lucky to have escaped without some sort of disfiguration or worse."

"But, funny thing is, I haven't escaped without *disfiguation*, now have I? I'm going to get old. And don't launch into a lecture about how we all get old and how wrinkles make your face more interesting and all that crapola."

"Okay, but try this. Think of when you were really little. One of the faces that you truly loved to see was the wrinkled face of your grandmother. You had a grandmother, right?"

"Yeah."

"And did you love her?"

"Yeah, a lot."

"And you weren't bothered by her wrinkles and the way her arms were floppy and her stomach bagged out and all that, were you?'

"No."

"That's because you were reacting to the love she had for you, the way her face lit up when she saw you, right?

"I guess."

"There are old people out there whose faces are always lit up, who have animated, charming faces that are always looking for the good side of life, or at least the funny side. And they have more friends around them than anybody with smooth skin and perky boobs."

Flo sighs. "I think it's easier to get the smooth skin and the perky boobs."

"Hey, even Dolly is going to get old some day. If she can do it, so can you."

Chapter Thirty-One

Jack emerges from the trailer dressed in a light blue v-neck cotton top with short sleeves, and matching light blue pants. If he tied a light blue hat over his hair, he'd look ready for surgery, except for his shoes. He is wearing white shoes that are too big for him, so he flops a little like a clown when he walks. He has to wear special shoes that contain no metal, and he left his regular pair at a hotel a while ago and has been making do with this pair he meant to return.

We drive to the sandpit and start unloading and assembling. The sensors of the magnetometer are so sensitive that they have to be held several feet away from Jack's body even though he's not wearing metal. They are located on the end of a long plastic tube that has a strap that goes around Jack's neck. A counterbalancing weight is on the other end of the plastic tube to help him keep the tube level. He looks like he's playing a very long, funny-looking guitar.

At the center of the plastic tube is the data logger, which Jack will watch as he's doing the survey to make sure everything is working. The reason why magnetometry is so incredibly boring is that it takes hours to gather the data, while walking in endless parallel lines over the site, without knowing what the machine is sensing. You don't find that out until you load the data into a computer. It'll take a couple of hours of surveying before the computer maps out the results at the very end.

George drives up and joins us. "Whoa, I don't know what I

was expecting, but it didn't look like that. Are you sure you brought the $20,000 one and not the $20 one? That looks like something you put together in your basement."

Jack laughs. "Everybody reacts like that. It looks cheap, first, because so much of it is plastic, and second, because most of what you are seeing is just a contraption for holding those two wicked expensive sensors there," pointing to the two small cylindrical objects, each about six inches long. "If I turned those babies on now they'd have a meltdown standing so close to you."

"Don't they all," says George.

"He was referring to your gun and all those other contraptions that hang around your waist."

"Of course."

"As a matter of fact, George, you will need to resist the impulse to come give me a hug while I'm doing this," says Jack.

"I'll try."

George and I move the cars back about thirty feet, and Jack is ready to start. Since it's easier to walk down the sand then up it, the plan is to have Jack circle around and up the side of the sandpit, and walk in a straight line down the sand. For each pass, he will circle around and up again, and walk down in a line parallel to the previous line.

I will be stationed at the top of the sandpit, marking off one meter segments so that the lines are equally spaced apart. I'm eager to take my position because I want to be able to look down on the little crowd that is gathering to see us work. I don't expect to see last night's man with the moustache and the ponytail, but there may be someone in the camp who's in contact with him.

The problem, of course, is that there would be no way to recognize such a person. He or she wouldn't exactly be wearing a tee shirt that said 'Friend of Local Terrorizer'. He or she wouldn't even be wearing a tee shirt for that matter. One of the problems in a nudist camp is that it's very hard to get a sense of someone when they're not wearing clothes.

I assume my position on one side of the top of the sandpit and survey the people assembled: a man and a woman with small children, a gay couple, and one man standing alone off to the side. The man by himself doesn't seem like he'd be the friend of the guy with the moustache. His posture is too good, and he seems too openly curious about the process.

At the top of the sandpit, Jack turns on the data logger and makes his first traverse down across the slope of the sandpit. The going is not easy because he sinks in the sand a little. I mark the point at which he started, and then measure out one meter for his next starting point, placing a little numbered flag at the start of each traverse.

While I wait for him to come around again, I see that the camp's bird watching club has discovered us as they walk down the road near the entrance to the sandpit. When Jack comes up to me again, he looks out at the naked people all pointing their binoculars at us. "That is one strange sight."

"Kodak moment," I say, as I wave to the group. They all wave merrily back. "Of course they're saying the same thing about us."

"That woman with the family down there. Why does she have shorts on?"

"Heavy period," I say.

"Sorry I asked."

"Oh, grow up."

He positions the sensors over the point I've marked and starts down again, maintaining an almost perfectly parallel line with his previous track. Jack has had a lot of practice, so he's comfortable with the unwieldy instrument even in the unevenness of the sand. It's hard work, and by the time he's done, he will have climbed the hill and walked down the sand about forty or fifty times.

About twenty minutes into the survey, I watch a man come up the driveway to the sandpit, and walk directly over to George and start talking. He points to the end of the driveway while he's talking. George is apparently interested in what he has to say, because he pulls out a notebook and starts taking notes. Then the two of them walk back to the police car where George makes a phone call. They shake hands, and then the man walks down the driveway.

A half hour later, we take a break and I go directly to George. "What did that guy have to say, if you don't mind me asking?"

"Some guy, Doug, only comes on Sundays and he said last Sunday he saw a van that caught his attention. He usually doesn't see any workers around on a Sunday, so when he saw the van and these two guys wearing clothes, he thought it was odd."

"Where did he see them?"

"They were coming up Sandhill Lane, away from Donald's cabin, and probably drove right past this sandpit. They were driving slowly and this guy, Doug, thought they were going to stop and ask him for directions but they didn't."

"Does he remember anything about them or the van?"

"He said he didn't get a good look at the guys, but he remembered that the van was white and didn't have any writing on it."

"So what do you think?"

"I don't know. I've called Kevin and asked him to come over here and find out if someone was having some work done on Sunday, or if anyone else saw the van."

"Kevin should also go to the office and find out who was on gate duty last Sunday, because these guys would have had to say who they wanted to see. The gate person is supposed to call and confirm that the visitor is expected, but sometimes they don't bother."

"I'll tell Kevin. Did you know that Kevin is thinking of joining this place?"

"What?"

"Yeah, he's talked to his wife and she's getting up the courage to come visit. Kevin says that it would be a great bargain for his family, like joining a country club for less than half the cost."

"Has he taken the plunge?"

"And walked around in his birthday suit? No, he's only been here when he's on duty, and we discourage that sort of conduct in our officers. He's waiting until he comes here with his wife so they can give each other moral support."

"Just think, last week you and Bruce had him convinced that he had to walk around with in a big overcoat so he wouldn't embarrass himself."

"Then after a short ride with you he steps out of the car like he owns the place. Bruce and I would love to have heard *that* conversation."

I give him a big smile. "I think my break is over now. I'd love to chat, but I really must go back to work."

During the break, Jack has been at the tailgate of his Explorer, booting up the laptop and making sure it will be ready for the moment when the data is downloaded. He motions that he's ready to start again and I climb the hill, ready to be bored for another half hour or so. We are more than halfway through, but it's getting hotter and more humid by the minute. I keep thinking that we are going to have a thunderstorm to break the heat, but day after day, there hasn't been a rumble.

I think back to the last thunderstorm, exactly a week ago, that passed through just before we disposed of Grampa's ashes. It was the remaining winds of that storm that blew the ashes all over me. Those clothes are now on the floor of my closet. I don't want to throw them out, but I don't trust any dry cleaners to get every bit of my grandfather out of every seam.

I'm trying to maneuver around some shrubs overhanging the side of the sandpit, pressing a marker into a patch of grass near a shrub. Next to the marker is a clump of dried mud. The mud is dark, about an inch long with sharp corners running down each side. It is the shape of a piece of dried mud that has been dropped from the deep tread of a work boot.

Jack is coming across the top of the sandpit, ready to start down again. I measure out a meter, thinking about that cute little piece of mud that is about to get trampled by his feet. Suddenly, it doesn't seem like such a good idea.

"STOP!" I say, just as he is about to put his foot down.

Jack jumps back like I have seen a snake or something. George looks up in alarm from down below. Everybody is staring at me, and my mind is trying to figure out how best to explain why this piece of mud is so important to me.

"George, can you come up here and bring one of those evidence baggies?" I soon as I say it, I realize how dumb it is. Just touching that thing is going to cause it to crumble. Still, I guess it's better than telling everyone to stop come see this great piece of dried mud.

"On second thought," I yell down to George, "bring up your camera."

George turns around and goes back to his car, giving me a look that says that this better be worth it. With some effort, he tromps up around the edge of the sandpit and takes a look at what I'm pointing to. "What? I don't get it. It's a little clump of dirt."

"It's dried mud, looks like a dark silty clay, the kind of stuff you find in wetlands, you know, swamps and marshes."

George looks impatient, "I know what a wetland is, Catie. Skip the soil science and cut to the chase, will you?"

"Okay, okay. See, this is the kind of clump that forms in the deep tread of work boots. Most people in camp don't wear work boots."

"True."

"And there aren't any wetlands in the camp because a long time ago the camp filled in its wet areas to try and get rid of the mosquitoes, which didn't work by the way. Besides, it takes a really low area to stay wet in August, and the only area I know of like that is right down there."

"Where?"

"Pine Hollow, the ravine that Donald's cabin looks down over."

"But how do you know this was recent?" asks Jack.

"Because it hasn't rained since last Sunday. This little clump wouldn't last for five minutes if it rained."

George makes a grunt of appreciation and nods. "So this little clump tells us that sometime in the last seven days, someone wearing heavy work boots may have been here after walking through Pine Hollow."

"Hey, I know I'm reading a lot into this," I say, starting to talk fast in an effort not to sound silly, "but what if someone walked through Pine Hollow wearing heavy work boots and then took off his clothes and his boots somewhere right around here. He might have put on the flip flops, and walked out of the sandpit looking like any other nudist with a tote bag."

Jack jumps in. "What was the weather like on Monday?"

"Hot and sunny," says George.

"So during the time that this guy might have been at Donald's cabin," continues Jack, "the mud on his boot might have dried enough so that when he picked them up to put them back on, he knocked a little clump off."

I'm starting to get excited. "So, after we're done here, let's go down into Pine Hollow and see if we can find some tracks."

"I think I'll call Ruby," says George.

"Who's she?"

"Our sniffer dog."

Chapter Thirty-Two

About twenty minutes later, Jack walks his last traverse, and it's time to load the data into the computer. He takes the magnetometer and attaches it with a cord to the laptop. After a few clicks a screen of white and black dots appears, looking like snow on a TV. Five darker dots appear on top of this background.

Jack is smiling broadly. "Oh, this is great."

I can see that George is underwhelmed by the results so I suggest that Jack superimpose the grid showing the lines that he walked. Once that comes up, Jack points out three dots that are of interest. "See, these three perturbations are close to the ends of the lines. That means they are at the bottom edge of the pit."

I turn to George. "We're still working on the premise that the gun was dropped on the ground and covered up. So, for now, we can dismiss the black dots at the top of the screen because they would indicate stuff buried near the top of the sand."

Jack turns to me. "Number 12, number 33, and number 37."

I go up to the top of the hill and find those flags, and Jack marks the end of each of these lines. When I come back, he is explaining to George that the first object is two feet in and about one foot to the left of the end of line number twelve. From the back of the car, I slide out the pointed flat boards that we'll pound into the sand in a V-shape behind the target, to divert the falling sand as we uncover the object.

Once the boards are in place, Jack gets to do the fun part.

He starts scooping the sand with his hands and pushing it away from the front of the posts. Ten minutes later the object is revealed and it is a horse shoe. Jack's enthusiasm doesn't wane. "One down, two to go!"

The second one is a little deeper and it takes about twenty minutes to get near the bottom. As he gets about six inches from the ground, a strap appears, made of plastic and printed with a camouflage pattern resembling dried leaves.

"Oh, my God." I say quietly.

George leans forward. "Don't touch it!"

Jack looks up, startled. No one has told him about the fragments of plasticized canvas found at the crime scene. "Why? What is it?"

I explain what it is as George goes to his car to retrieve his evidence collection kit. With latex gloves on, he brushes the sand away from the zipped up tote bag as if he were uncovering an archaeological treasure. He gently lifts the bag and peers into the blown out hole, and then turns the bag so each of us can take a look. Inside is a revolver with a long silencer, laying on its side.

Instead of feeling elated, I feel queasy and anxious, as if I just watched someone bag a venomous snake. I've never even been close to any gun, never mind one that had been used to kill someone. It feels like I've seen something evil, even more frightening because it's disguised as an inanimate object.

Jack also looks unsettled and turns to me. "What should we do now?"

"I don't know."

George takes the bag and the gun to the car, and then comes back with a bounce in his step and a smile on his face. "I can't tell you how happy this makes me. We were all beginning to worry about this case, because usually if you don't get a break in the first few days, you're generally out of luck. This is just great. What's the matter with you two?"

Both of us hesitate. "Neither of us has seen, you know, a murder weapon before," says Jack.

"Oh, For heaven's sake. Come on, let's get going on the third object."

"Why?" I say. "We already found the gun."

"Now that we know he really was here, we're going to tear this place apart. Starting with that third object."

"Hey, what do you mean 'now that we know he was really here.' You didn't believe me?"

"Let's just say I have a new respect for dirt forensics."

On the computer screen, the third object appears to be about three feet from the end of line 37. We pound in the boards behind our target and Jack begins to scoop out the sand. This time, George leans over Jack from the beginning, telling him to go slowly. I hope it's not another horse shoe.

When we are only a few inches from the floor of the sandpit, Jack stops. "I think I just felt something."

"Okay, let me take it from here," says George. After Jack gets up, George drops to his knees with his gloves on and begins feeling around. He begins to smooth the sand away from a beige colored canvas.

"I think we got us another tote bag," says George.

"This is probably the tote bag that held the other one with the gun," I say.

Jack shakes his head. "This has got to be more than an empty tote bag. It's got to contain a lot of iron."

Finally, George lifts the bag out of the sand and pulls open the straps. Inside are two objects, a small, silvery digital camera, and a large gray and black laptop. Both of them look like they have been smashed repeatedly with a hammer or a rock.

"Well, well, well," says George. "Something tells me we may have uncovered a clue or two."

"But they're all smashed up," I say.

George smiles. "Vee have vays of making zem talk."

Jack pats me on the shoulder. "The magic of data retrieval."

George nods, still smiling. "By the end of the day tomorrow, we'll know what's in both of them."

Jack and I are packing up the magnetometer when Kevin drives up. He jumps out of his car, and tries not to skip when he is walking over to George. He is clearly bursting with something.

"You know that van, and those guys?" he says to George. "They were going to see Donald! I asked at the office and then tracked down Dave-of-Dave-and-Marilyn, and he said that he had been at the gate when these guys drove up and said they were here to visit Donald. He said he actually called Donald because these two guys didn't look like Donald's type. And Donald said it was okay, send them down."

"Did you ask him what he meant by 'not Donald's type?'" asks George.

"Yes. I did," says Kevin, standing up straight. "He said that the van didn't look like it was in great shape, and that the guys weren't well dressed. Dave thinks of Donald as someone who was rich and classy."

"Did they say what they were there for?"

"No," says Kevin, looking down at a small pad of paper that he has in his hand. "Dave said, 'I thought they were there to fix something, you know, but the van had no lettering on it and it was Sunday.'"

"Can Dave describe these guys?"

"Just the driver. He said he was small and thin with glasses and a baseball cap."

"And the other guy?"

"'Kind of on the short side,' is the only thing Dave could remember."

George compliments Kevin on a job well done and then proceeds to tell Kevin about what we found in the sandpit. Although he's excited by the news, Kevin is also a little deflated. Up to that moment, he thought that he was contributing the most important news of the day.

I change the subject. "Is it true that you might be joining the camp?"

"Yeah, if the camp is still here by the time my wife makes up her mind."

"What do you mean?"

"Did you see the *Ashton Bulletin* this morning? The referendum is going to give it a thumbs down. And, as I understand it, the camp doesn't have enough money to fight a legal battle against the town."

"What does your wife think about this place?"

"She's not too keen on it right now. But I think she'd change her mind if she would just come visit. Unfortunately, some old boyfriend took her to a 'clothing-optional' beach one time and she hated it. Most of the people were naked, but some of the people were there just to ogle and giggle."

"If you want me to talk to her, I will," I offer.

"But you don't take your clothes off."

"What can I say. I was born with a gene for modesty, that's all. I don't have anything against the camp, and I can certainly explain to her the difference between clothing-optional and nudist."

Jack comes over and puts his arm around me. "Isn't she impressive? How many people know the difference between clothing-optional and nudist?"

"Many are called, but few are chosen," I say.

At that moment, a state police SUV drives up with CANINE UNIT on the side. A man gets out looking steadfastly at the ground. Both Kevin and Jack recognize that panicked look.

Kevin yells over to him, "Isn't the gravel in a nudist camp absolutely fascinating?" Then he turns to George. "Wait a minute. What are Ruby and Ted doing here?"

George tells him about the clump of mud I found. Kevin turns toward me. "Way to go, Catie! George just gets to stand back and watch you and Jack solve the case. Are you guys for hire?"

"We're thinking of calling ourselves the Bad Ass Binghams," I say.

George shakes his head. "Hard to put that on a requisition form."

"How about Nine Feet Under, Inc." says Jack. "That's how far I can go down."

George smiles. "Doesn't have a lot of life to it, but it'll do for now."

Ted is probably a little older than Kevin, and a little younger than George, and says about as much as Bruce. He's got blonde hair and blue eyes, and a small frame, and his entire focus is on Ruby. Ruby is a German shepherd that acts like an extremely well-behaved child – eager and happy while she sits and waits for instructions.

George leads Ted and Ruby up to the spot where I found the mud, and Ruby sniffs around. At the instruction of Kevin, we hang back so that Ruby can have a better chance of picking up the correct scent. At first Ruby starts down the sand, but Ted tells her to come back and she plunges down into the scrub and woods on the side of the sandpit.

Trying to keep up, Kevin and Jack and I follow on a parallel path down the slope. We are definitely headed down toward the ravine in Pine Hollow. The undergrowth is thick and we are forced to walk several feet apart so that the branches don't snap back and hit the person behind. Ted is holding one arm in front of his face as Ruby leads him down the slope.

With the smell of late August decay, the beds of black mud appear before us. In the spring and early summer, the mud was probably covered with a foot or more of water. But now all that water has gone, evaporated or seeped down into the cracks of New England bedrock. Ruby plunges right into the black mud.

We hear Ted say, "Ruby, stop."

By the time we reach them, George is already on his phone calling for someone to come with a casting kit. In front of Ruby is a clear, deep print of a deeply treaded sole pointing toward the sandpit. It looks like someone tried to cross the mud by jumping from one hummock to another and didn't make it. Kevin is instructed to go back to the sandpit and wait for the officer who will make a plaster cast of the footprint.

We all fan out, but no one can find another footprint. Ruby, on the other hand, still has her scent and is eager to cross the mud and continue. A little further downstream, we all cross the mud, some of us more successfully than others, and then we go back to pick up the scent again. It leads us diagonally up the other side of the ravine and through an area that has been logged recently.

Abruptly, Ruby stops at a logging road and moves back and forth, over and over. After a few moments, Ted pulls up on the leash and tells Ruby to sit. Both dog and master are panting, one from pulling forward, and the other from trying not to be pulled forward too fast.

"Looks like he got into a vehicle here," says Ted.

George shrugs. "Or got out of a vehicle here. Someone

could have dropped him off." He and Ted look around, searching for a tire track and discovering a few possibilities. He looks down the road, which is just a path through the woods where the trees have been cut to the ground. "Anybody know where this logging road comes out?"

Nobody knows. George continues, "Anyone know who owns this land?"

"As of about a month and a half ago," I say, "the AANR. The American Association of Nude Recreation." I turn to Jack. "This is the Gellerman land."

Chapter Thirty-Three

George looks at me and then at Jack. "The way you guys are looking at each other makes me think I should be hearing cymbals crashing or something. Want to tell me about it?"

Jack looks at me. "Just because the guy walked through the Gellerman land doesn't mean the Gellerman deal has anything to do with Donald."

"I repeat," says George. "Want to tell me about it?"

On the way back to the sandpit, we tell George about Mountville and the Gellermans. George agrees with Jack. "It's a stretch, but I guess it's worth looking into in case there is a connection."

For some reason, I feel slightly put down by this reaction. Maybe I've gotten a big head from my recent successes. After all, I led them to the sandpit and then deduced a lot from my little clump of mud. I feel my budding reputation as a sleuth is being challenged. On the other hand, I can't even convince myself that there's a connection. It's more of a feeling.

After Jack and I are back in the car, I suggest that we stop at the beach to see if Bernie, the president, is there. Since he was part of the negotiations with the Gellermans, he might be able to give us a new perspective. Bernie is up for reelection in a few weeks, so I'm sure he'll be out there, pressing the flesh, so to speak.

Jack tells me that he'd rather boil in oil than step over a lot of nude bodies on the beach in pursuit of Bernie, but that he'd be willing to sit for a half an hour in the parking lot, playing with the data from the sandpit. Agreeing to be back within the allotted time, I wander down to the beach, and ask around for Bernie. It turns out that he's in the office, answering emails from his constituents.

"Catie!" says Bernie, as I walk into the office. "Am I glad to see you!"

"Why?" I ask.

Bernie smiles. "Because you are not a voting member of this place. That means I don't have to address your complaints, nor do I have to promise you things which I have no hope of delivering."

"Am I detecting a little campaign burnout?"

"Burnt to a crisp. Having a hard time answering these emails respectfully."

"It's hard not to write satire."

"Exactly! Did you just make that up?"

"No. Juvenal, a Roman, made it up."

"I'd like to see him take on this towel issue. You've been in and out this place for decades, Catie. It never gets resolved, does it?"

"The oppressors versus the libertarians. Nope, it doesn't."

"Which side are you on?"

"I'm an oppressor. I remember how my mother would yell at me to wait before I sat down so she could put a towel down first. She was ready to kill adults for not using a towel, so I was brought up believing there should be a fine for the offense. What side are you on?"

"That entirely depends on who I'm talking to."

"That's why you're president, Bernie. Speaking of which, as president you recently negotiated a deal to buy some land, right?"

"Now, don't start on that. It was a good deal, and besides, it wasn't the camp's money. It was AANR's."

"Hey, remember, I'm not a voter. A couple of days ago I was in here, and Ellsworth said you got it for $72,000. That's amazing."

"I know. I know. The sellers said they had some pressure to get rid of the land because of some tax reasons, some deadline of June 30th and the end of the fiscal year. And since it was the last week in June already," Bernie puts his palms up and shrugs. "Anyway, I went for it."

"Is there any chance that Donald was involved in the transaction?"

"Ah, now I see your interest. I heard you were helping the police out in their investigation."

"But this is not the police asking. It's just me."

"No. Donald wasn't involved in the transaction. It was just me and the Gellermans, the owners, and an AANR guy that flew in to check it out."

He can see that I'm disappointed. "Sorry, Catie. The only involvement that Donald had in the whole thing was a couple of weeks before the deal went down. I was a little uneasy about this tax-break thing, so when I bumped into Donald, I asked him about it. I figured he had the financial background to tell me if it was a lot of bunk. He said he'd look into it, but when I asked him later, he said he didn't have the time."

We talk a little more, but he needs to get back to the towel issue and I need to get back to the parking lot. Wishing him luck with his campaign, I say goodbye and walk back across the crowded beach. The conversations I'm overhearing on the beach aren't about the upcoming vote for camp president. They are about the upcoming vote in Rensford that will determine whether the camp will continue to exist.

As we drive out of the camp, I tell Jack about my conversation with Bernie. "It's not much, but it's a connection," I say. "Do you think we should tell George?"

Jack shakes his head and sighs. "You said one time that you've built up such a high tolerance for embarrassment that you don't even notice it anymore. So it's my job to tell you if you're embarrassing yourself." He reaches over and puts a hand on my shoulder while he drives with his left hand. "You impressed the hell out of everybody, including me by the way, with your detective abilities the last few days, but quit while you're ahead."

I'm silent for a few minutes, and Jack says, "You mad at me?"

"No. I don't know. I'm just feeling this huge letdown."

"Tell you what. Let me go home and get out of these scrubs and we'll go to the Courthouse. Okay?"

"Okay."

The Courthouse is our favorite bar in Marshfield, named for the county courthouse which used to occupy the building. When we walk in, five flat screen TVs are showing the Red Sox losing to the Yankees. The place is noisy and unpretentious.

Legal kitsch is everywhere. We sit in a booth and open a menu that's called the Docket. We order martinis from a page called Liquidated Damages and choose sandwiches from a page called the Wrap Sheet. I love small towns in New England.

Jack takes a sip of his huge martini and carefully puts it down. "Okay," he says. "Now talk to me. What going on with you?"

God, I love this man. I reach out and touch his hand in gratitude and then sit back and rest the back of my head against the back of the booth. "I guess I was feeling important and appreciated for a while, and I wish I could keep it going. I forgot how much I missed that feeling. Makes me think I should go back to work."

"I agree. You should go back to work. For me."

I laugh. "Yeah, like that'll ever happen."

"Maybe I said that wrong. I meant *with* me. Wrong preposition."

"That's a very important preposition."

"Okay, I know, but hear me out. I really loved doing that sandpit today because looking for a gun is so much more thrilling than looking for a 50-gallon drum. But that was only part of it. I loved working with you. We make a great team."

"Right." I say. "You do all the surveying, then you download the data, use the software, and come up with the results. I sit there and mark off meters and put little flags in the ground. What a team."

"Two things wrong with that picture. One, we were there because of your brainwork – your ideas and hypotheses were directing the whole show. I loved that idea of how the guy could have buried the gun so fast. And, two, you have this area of expertise that I could really use."

"What do you mean?"

"Your soil science background. I haven't really needed it so far because any jerk can detect a huge metal drum. But if I'm going to get into anything more advanced, I'm going to need someone who can do soil corings and figure out what's down there, like the type of iron in the soil, the water content, and the layers of different kinds of soil."

"That stuff's easy."

"See? I knew it. All those lines I walked today – all that time I was thinking how silly it was for me not to be taking advantage of you."

"You've got to work on your phraseology."

"How silly of me not to be using all that brain power and expertise."

"Aw, shucks."

"Be serious. We could do great things together."

"Besides sex, what kind of thing are you talking about?"

"This forensic stuff is kind of fun. Weird maybe, but fun. Do you realize how easy it would be for me to find a body buried in concrete?"

"Lot's of soil science there."

"Okay, bad example. Bodies in soil, then. It's a little harder to do that, but we could do it if we worked together."

"What about all your EPA stuff?"

"We could do that, too. I'd cut out the drudgery of my usual stuff – they can get anybody to do that – and just take on projects that are more interesting that we could do as a team."

"So I wouldn't be home alone so much."

"And I wouldn't be stuck by myself in hotels."

"And I wouldn't be working *for* you, we'd be working *together*."

"It can be Catie Bingham, Inc., and I'll work for you."

"Now we're getting somewhere."

"Speaking of being home by yourself, what about tomorrow? Do you think I ought to contact the people in Washington to tell them I'll have to come and testify another time?"

"Are you kidding? No way."

"Think you can lock the door and stay inside for one day, or should I call Phil to send up someone to be with you?"

"I'll be fine. But thanks."

Phyllis gives a big sloppy wave from the end of the bar, and I wave back. "Our favorite realtor is here. And it looks like she might be coming over to talk to us." I watch as Phyllis makes a sudden lurch to the left. "Unsteady as she goes."

Phyllis puts a hand on Jack's side of the booth for stability. "Hi guys! How's things?"

"Just great, Phyllis. How are things with you?" I ask.

"You wanna know what I did?"

"What did you do?"

"I did something," she pauses to get the right word, "noble."

Jack smiles. "Way to go Phyllis. I admire nobility in a realtor."

Phyllis waves a finger at Jack. "Now don't you go and make fun of me, young man."

"What did you do, Phyllis?" I ask.

"I reported Mountville to the Better Business Bureau, that's what I did. They didn't treat the Gellermans right. Not one bit. I didn't like what they did."

I nod. "That was a good thing to do."

"Those Gellermans are good people and they got shafted. Big time."

"You're right."

"I even called the Gellermans and said I wanted to come over and talk about it, you know. I told them that I let them down. I did, you know. Big time. Big time."

"And what did they say?"

"They said no. Said I should stay out of it, for my own good."

"For your own good?"

"Yeah. They said the last time someone came to talk to them, he got…," here she drops her voice to a whisper, "murdered."

"What?"

"Yeah, it turns out that your nudist friend, what's his name, was over there and talked to them, and then he got shot."

"Donald Thaler?"

"Yeah, you know, the one that's been in the paper a lot."

Chapter Thirty-Four

Phyllis's friend yells over to her and she makes her way back to the bar. Jack and I stare at each other for a bit, then Jack shakes his head.

"Easy, girl. Don't jump to conclusions, here," he says.

"But what the hell was Donald doing at the Gellermans, after he told Bernie that he was too busy to look into it?"

"I don't know."

"And he must have put some real time into it, to track down the Gellermans and actually go to their house. Why wouldn't he report back to Bernie?"

Jack thinks for a minute. "Because maybe he was starting to get interested in the land for himself."

"You mean, if he found out that the land was a good investment, he wouldn't have conveyed that to Bernie. He would have grabbed the deal for himself."

"Sounds like he was that kind of guy," says Jack.

"But then why didn't he buy it?"

"Wasn't that about the same time that everything was crashing down around him? You know, the divorce, the collapse of his business, his SEC troubles. Sounds like a guy who's paying out hundreds of thousands of dollars in legal bills. He probably didn't have the $72,000 and couldn't get any bank to loan it to him either."

After a while, Jack continues. "In order for him to know that it was a good deal, he must have found out that there wasn't a superfund site on the land, despite what the Gellermans must have told him."

"But, scumbag that he was, he obviously didn't tell the Gellermans, because they *still* believe it's there. He knew that the low price depended on scaring the Gellermans into the thinking the EPA was going to go after everything they had. Those poor Gellermans. First the people from Mountville scare them and then Donald comes along and probably makes it worse."

We eat for a while in silence. "I don't want to *embarrass* myself," I say, "but don't you think we ought to tell George about this?

"You tell him. That way you can be the one to look silly if there's nothing to it."

I throw my napkin at him. "When I talk to him I'm going to tell him that you insisted I call."

Later that night, we talk about his big day tomorrow in Washington. It's nice to think about something bigger and more important than the camp and Mountville and the murder. Tomorrow Jack will have the opportunity to do something that might save the lives on a global scale.

The next morning, Jack gets dressed in his best three-piece suit. He's got a nine o'clock flight out of Manchester, which will get him into Washington with plenty of time to prepare for his testimony. He's scheduled to appear before the committee right after lunch. Then he's got a five-thirty flight out of Washington, getting him home no later than eight tonight. I reassure him for the umpteenth time that I will be fine.

As soon as he's out the door, I call George. "As it turns out, George, you and Jack are wrong again, and I am right. Donald was involved in the sale of the Gellerman land to the camp."

George shakes his head. "Wait a minute, here. I do not recall any previous occasion in which Jack and I were wrong and you were right. But I will let that pass for now. How was he involved?

"It looks like he was trying to snap up the land as an investment before the camp bought it, but Jack and I think he was short on cash."

"You got that right," says George. "By the time he died, he was frantic about money. He had already run up almost a million dollars in legal bills and creditors were hounding him. People think he was hiding from the press in the nudist camp, but he may have been hiding from the repo guys."

I shake my head. "But if he was *that* broke, he would have known from the start that he couldn't come up with the money. And he put a lot of time into this, even going to the Gellermans to talk to them. Why would he do that?"

"I don't know. It sounds fishy."

"Fishy?"

"In my professional opinion."

We arrange to meet at the sandpit in the camp to talk further. When I ask him what came out of the camera and the laptop, he says that both are en route to the computer forensics people in Manchester. The results should be back later today.

After I hang up with George, Gramma calls and says that she needs laundry soap. Although the canteen in the camp sells a number of basic necessities, there isn't a big demand for laundry soap. It's one of the things I keep her supplied with. Her voice sounds almost pleasant.

"How come you're so happy?" I ask.

"What? A person can't look on the bright side once in a while without her granddaughter getting suspicious?"

"No."

"Well, if you must know, I can finally hold my head up

around here. Instead of my granddaughter being known as the one who thumbs her nose at us by wearing clothes, you're now known as the one who found the gun. I got my bragging rights back."

"Word got around fast."

"Next time, though, would you please tell me first? I didn't like hearing it from Norm-of-Norm-and-Joyce."

"Okay, next time I find a gun in a sandpit, I'll tell you first."

"Enough with the smart mouth. And don't get me expensive detergent. Whatever's on sale."

After I hang up, I rush around trying to clean up the kitchen and get out of the house. Before I meet with George, I have a lot to do. I want to get a paper, and go to the town hall to see if there is a map of the Gellerman place showing the logging road or any other paths. Now I have to stop for detergent.

I look out the window and see Amanda Curtis coming up my driveway. She's holding something out in front of her that looks like a pie, but I would feel better if I had a bomb sniffing dog on the premises. The last thing I want to do is get pinned down in conversation with this woman, so I grab my purse and my keys and head out the front door.

Putting the pie in one hand, she waves. "I can see you're going out so I won't keep you. I just wanted to come over and give you this."

It's important to be polite to people who have recently threatened to sue you. "Not at all," I say. "Have a seat," motioning to one of the Adirondack chairs on the porch.

Before sitting, she hands me the pie. "This is my own invention. I call it 'Amanda's yellow squash quiche.'"

"Looks yummy," I say, glad I'm not yet under oath.

"Really, I came to say I'm sorry. I did an awful thing to you last week when I accused you of making that whole horrible incident up, but I was just so humiliated. I didn't want people to think that my Terry could have been involved in anything like that."

"Thank you. It's nice of you to come here to say that."

"Saturday night, Tracey, you know, Ralphie's wife? She called me and said that she had run into you at the 4-H thing and that she had apologized to you and that it made her feel good. See, when I lied and said it didn't happen, then Tracey had to lie and say that it didn't happen, too, or else she would be calling me a liar."

What a tangled web we weave. But I nod supportively and say, "I see."

"And she felt guilty, and she was mad at me for putting her in a place where she either had to be mean to me or mean to you. And in church the next morning, I realized I had made a choice, too. I had decided to be mean to you, rather than be mean to myself. And I made the wrong choice, and I'm sorry."

I haven't quite followed all this, but I say, "Thanks. I've already thought of a way that you can make it up to me."

"Anything. You name it."

"No more corn."

"What?"

"Next year, we plant something else here on our land. Hay, maybe? How do you plant hay? Is there such a thing as hay seed?"

Amanda laughs. "No. Hay is a just grass or alfalfa or whatever that you can use to feed animals. This place would look wonderful with," she turns in her chair, "maybe alfalfa in the back—you'll love the sea of purple flowers—and maybe timothy and orchard grass in front here. You know that 'amber waves of grass' thing? It's really true. It's beautiful when the wind makes waves in the grass."

"So no more corn?"

"Terry will be disappointed because that's the best feed for the cows."

"Tough."

Amanda laughs again and nods. "Tough."

When she's ready to leave, I offer her a ride back to her house, but she tells me there's a short cut that connects the two houses through the field. "I didn't want to use it this time because it felt more polite to come up your driveway. But the path is really a quick way between us. I'll show it to you sometime."

She waves as she literally disappears into the corn. One of those rows must lead to a path that I've never noticed. The corn has now reached about eight or nine feet in height, as if every stalk is trying to elbow out the ones around it in a desperate reach for sunlight. I'll be glad to see it gone.

At the local food mart attached to the gas station, I pick up a copy of the *Ashton Bulletin* and a jug of laundry detergent. They only have one brand but I will tell my grandmother that I picked out the one that was on sale. In the parking lot, I quickly go through the paper.

On the third page is an article about Jack and me assisting the local police in finding the suspected murder weapon in a sandpit in the camp. Whoever gave the information to the paper must have been standing there watching, because the account is detailed and accurate. The article also mentions that a damaged camera and laptop were found. I can't help but wonder if the murderer reads the *Ashton Bulletin* and is now a lot more nervous that he was yesterday.

At the town hall, I am led into the map room which is lined with black books so large that they are laying on their side on a shelf that runs the entire length of the room The same people who were wary of me last week when I was here with Phil, now seem almost friendly. The key to popularity must be ditching your lawyer.

The town secretary helps me find an old map of the Gellerman land, explaining that the new maps on the computer don't show the old cart paths and colonial roads. The maps are too big to bring over to a copier, but she gives me a piece of tracing paper and a pencil and warns me not to press down too hard. This is a low-tech town.

The map shows a dotted line coming off a state highway into the Gellerman land. Along the dotted line is the name, "Two Rod Road". I ask the town secretary what that means.

"A rod is a British measurement that the colonials used. It's equal to about 16.5 feet, so a two rod road was thirty-three feet wide, a major highway back then."

"Why would they need a road so wide?"

"To allow two carriages to pass safely."

"How come something that wide is just a little dotted line on the map?"

"Because it's probably only about eight or ten feet wide now. There was nothing to stop the trees from growing back once the road was abandoned. I hike on that trail a lot. It's beautiful, especially in the spring when you're so hungry for the color green that the skunk cabbage looks beautiful."

"Why does the dotted line stop in the middle of the Gellerman land? It would seem like an old colonial road like that would continue on for a long distance."

"When the state highway was built it backed up a lot of water onto the Gellerman land, so a lot of Two Rod Road was flooded. The road starts up again in Ashton."

"Have you ever seen a dump on the Gellerman land, maybe in one of those low areas?"

“There are dumps all over this town. Every farm had its own dump.”

“I mean like a toxic waste dump.”

“No, I don’t know of anything like that in town. I think there’s one in Ashton that EPA was doing something with. But nothing in Rensford, as far as I know.”

I thank her for her help, and then get in the car and head on over to the camp. I drive straight to the sandpit, where I see four state police cars. I see one man and one woman at the top of the sandpit on their knees poking around the vegetation. The rest of them must be on the path leading down to Pine Hollow.

Spreading the maps I’ve brought onto the hood of George’s car, I show him the land that the AANR bought from the Gellermans, and the land currently held by Mountville Trust. “The Gellerman land formed a buffer between the camp and the Mountville Land. The Mountville people tried to buy it to preserve that buffer.”

George nods. “NIMBY. Nudists in my back yard. An understandable reaction.”

“The Gellermans had already gotten the bad news that having naked people next door reduced their property value by one half, although I don’t know how valid that appraisal was.”

“Was it their appraisal or someone else’s?”

“Don’t know. Anyway, Mountville wasn’t content to buy it at half price. They tried to talk the Gellermans into *giving* it to them by convincing those poor senior citizens that there was a superfund site on their land. They told them that EPA was going to make them pay to clean it up at a cost of hundreds of thousand of dollars or even millions.”

“Did the Gellermans dump toxic stuff on their land?”

At this point, I have to stop and explain the superfund laws and the provision about the Principle Responsible Party. "But here's the kicker," I say. "There isn't any superfund site on the Gellerman land. Jack checked on EPA's website and I just checked at the town hall. So the Mountville people made it up and the Gellermans believed it."

"Wouldn't they have checked? For that matter wouldn't they know already?"

"They were elderly when they bought it, and I doubt they trudged through that underbrush to make sure there was no dump on the land. And they probably didn't know how to check EPA's website."

"Even so, they must have required some proof."

"I think the Mountville people doctored some EPA forms."

"Okay, now" says George. "That's more like it. I was stifling a big yawn there a second ago, but now we got a possible felony."

"Nice to know that I'm occasionally interesting."

"So Mountville gave the Gellermans some fake forms, and the Gellermans get scared," says George. "And so Mountville agreed to do a good deed and take the land off their hands for nothing."

" Then Phyllis stepped in and asked the camp if they would pay *anything* for it and the camp came up with $72,000."

"So, after all that work and a possible felony, Mountville got a little too greedy and lost the land. Fine. This a wonderful little morality play," says George. "But now let's connect this to Donald Thaler."

"Okay. Here's my theory. And don't you dare yawn because I'm very proud of my theory. It's really, really good."

"Can't wait."

"Quiet," I say. "Bernie, the camp president, asked Donald to look into why the land was so cheap. Donald told Bernie that he didn't have time, but later we find out that he spent a lot of time tracking down the Gellermans and going to their house. Why would he do that if he knew he didn't have the money to buy the land?"

"Because he smelled a rat."

"Exactly. And, like you say, it takes one to know one. Why would someone desperate for cash like Donald take the time to track down criminal behavior on the part of a fellow rat?"

"Tell me," says George.

"Donald was hoping that the Mountville family had some cash on hand. He was hoping that they might be willing to give him some of that cash in exchange for nondisclosure of their felonious behavior."

"Blackmail."

"And what might be on that laptop and camera?"

"The goods he had on Mountville."

"Georgie gets a star!"

He wags a finger at me. "Nobody, but nobody, calls me Georgie. It doesn't fit my macho, take-no-prisoner image."

"Are you sure that's your image?"

"Can it," he says with a smile. "Okay, so, the best thing he could have against the Mountville people would be the falsified EPA document. And he would have gotten that at the Gellermans'."

"How can we find out if the Gellermans gave it to Donald?"

He shrugs. "We'll call the Gellermans, right now."

"They're very skittish. They think that EPA officials are lurking under their windows ready to accuse them of unloading a Love Canal onto the nudist camp."

"Then we may have to send a uniform over there to explain the situation."

"While you're doing that, I have to go deliver some laundry detergent to my grandmother."

"Laundry detergent? No don't tell me. I don't want to know," says George. "Any idea whether Mountville is local?"

"I don't think so because Phyllis said that, on several occasions, someone from Mountville flew in to meet with the Gellermans in a meeting room at the Best Western in Ashton. But it could be local. Maybe they drove to Rensford from someplace nearby. Anyway, I've got a friend who's a whiz with search engines trying to find out who the Mountvilles are."

"You're already on that, are you?"

"For days. Nothing yet."

"Step aside. Here comes the cavalry. We'll find out for you."

Chapter Thirty-Five

"That kind is never on sale, and you know it," says Gramma, when I hand her the laundry detergent.

"I was just trying to save some time," I say, irritated at her lack of gratitude.

"Who cares about saving time? I wanted to save you money – I don't care about time. And now I owe you. If you got the one on sale I would of felt okay, but then you went and got the expensive one." Gramma sighs. "So how much do I owe you?"

I really don't remember, so I make something up. "Three twenty nine."

"For that little thing? I'm not going to pay that kind of money for a little thing of laundry detergent!"

"Then give it back."

"Okay, okay. Don't get your underwear all knotted up about it. I'll just have to make you a pie or something."

"That would be great."

"But not now. I got to call Lucinda now."

"Who's Lucinda?"

"She's a nice girl with a dog. You'll like her."

Gramma dials a number and says into the phone. "Hi Lucinda. It's Eleanor. She's here. You can come over now."

"You want to tell me who she is before she gets here?"

"She's your age and she looks like you, only naked. She and her husband, whats-his-face, just joined, and they have a big yellow dog that's by her side all the time, like it's her baby."

"And she's coming to see me?"

"Yeah, she wants to give you something or show you something. I don't know."

Ten minutes later, we hear some steps and a female voice calling my grandmother's name. "Eleanor, is it okay if I tie up Baby out here?"

"Lord, she even calls the thing Baby." Gramma mutters. "Sure. Keep it away from the flowers, though."

Lucinda opens the screen door, and says, "Oh, Baby doesn't eat flowers." Her body is lean and athletic. She sits gracefully on the low couch, something you can only do with strong thigh muscles.

She hands me a plastic shopping bag, and says, "For you, from Baby."

Inside the bag are two large flip flops, each with a wavy surf pattern on the sole. I stare at the contents without a word.

Gramma pokes me. "What do you say?"

"Thank you." I sit down next to Lucinda on the couch. "Where did you get these?"

"At the sandpit. Sam and I got up here on Friday, and we drove right to the sandpit because, well, you know, it's one place where I don't have to pick up after Baby, if you know what I mean. Anyway, Sam and I were talking in the car watching Baby and suddenly she starts digging and comes up with one of these flip flops. She brought it over to us, and then she went back for the other one."

"How come you didn't turn it over to the police when they were at the sandpit on Saturday?

"We just stopped by on Friday to drop some things off and then went up to see some friends on Lake Winnipesaukee. We just got back last night."

"But the police are here today. Why bring it to me?"

"I've never actually, you know, talked to a cop. Whenever I even get near one I get nervous and start thinking of everything I've ever done wrong in my life. And to be naked when I walk up to them? I don't think so. Maybe if they took their clothes off."

While she is saying this, I can hear a car coming to a stop in front of the trailer and in a moment, George is at the door. He knocks and says, "I have come to meet the beautiful Eleanor, of whom I have heard so many wonderful things. Can I come in?"

"I don't know who you are, but I like you already. Come on in."

When George walks in, Gramma and I look at Lucinda and laugh. When George looks at me, I say, "Lucinda, here, would rather talk to a naked police officer."

George looks like he's about to say something and then stops himself, saying only, "I see."

"Imagine that. George is speechless!" I say.

He looks at me. "I am merely holding back because I am in the presence of ladies."

"Shit, yes," says Gramma. "And don't you forget it."

I make the introductions and then show him what Lucinda brought. George is as stunned as I was. "Thank you *very* much," he says. "I'm not used to getting my evidence handed to me on a platter like this."

"Speaking of a platter, I've got some cookies here," says Gramma. "Anyone want coffee?"

"I'll have to take a rain check on the coffee, ma'am. But I'll have a cookie."

"You can have a cookie if you don't call me ma'am anymore. Makes me feel old."

"Thank you, Eleanor," he says, as he takes one.

We fill George in on the way the flip flops were found, and

George asks Lucinda if she'll show him where exactly Baby made his discovery. I quickly tell her that George and I are going to talk to Roland a bit and we'll join her later at the sandpit. I also mention that the sandpit is clothing-optional.

George catches on. "Some of my best friends wear clothes, you know."

"Not all of them, I hope!" says Gramma, who seems to be a bit smitten by George.

Outside the trailer, George makes a big fuss over Baby and promises to deputize him. Lucinda beams like a proud parent as she unties the dog and walks off down the road. George watches her go.

As George and I walk across the road, we can see Flo almost upright on her lounge chair. In her right hand she is holding a thin paperback book out in front of her. Her left hand is on her forehead, pulling her eyebrows up, while her mouth is open and her lips are pulled tightly over her teeth and into her mouth. She looks like a woman who is horrified because she forgot to put her teeth in that morning. Drawing nearer, we can see that the title of the book is *Lift That Face!*

"Flo?" I ask gently.

She drops the book and smiles, and then her smile fades quickly. "I can't smile too long. If I do then I'll get lines from my nose to my mouth. I'm supposed to smile using my zygomatic major muscles," pointing to her cheek bones. "But when I try, Roland says I look like I'm sneering at him. I looked it up and found out I'm using my zygomatic minors. This is hard stuff."

"Flo?" I ask again.

"On top of that, I have to meditate using the mantra 'I don't have to frown' seven times a day. And at night, I have to use tape all over my forehead, to keep me from frowning at night."

"Flo, I'd like you to meet Chief Detective George Myers of the state police."

She puts her book down and extends her hand, giving him a brief smile. "Howdy."

"Why are you doing this, Flo?"

"I'm going natural. No more of that surgery stuff for m, That was cheating. Now I'm gonna *earn* it. Facial fitness, body fitness. Gravity has met its match."

"If Sir Isaac had been sitting under that tree with you," says George with a smile, "no one would have ever heard of gravity."

"Darn tootin'," says Flo.

"Is Roland inside? We want to ask him a few questions," says George.

Flo looks at him and then me. "That don't sound so good, comin' from a cop. Has Roland done something, Catie?"

"No. Don't worry about it. Roland's fine."

"Okay. ROWWLAAND! Come on out here."

Chapter Thirty-Six

"I'm coming, for Chrisake! You don't need to yell. I'm right here."

"Roland, this is Chief Detective George Myers," I say. "I've been telling him how helpful you've been." Actually, I'm trying to remember if I ever mentioned Roland's name to George.

George plays along as he shakes Roland's hand. "Yes, thanks so much for all your help."

"What help?" he says blandly. Roland is immune to flattery.

George looks at me and I explain, "For helping to track down Mountville."

"But I didn't. I got the two post office boxes and then the trail ends in the Cook Islands."

George's shoulders sag, "Cook Islands? Then don't waste any more time on this."

"Why?" I ask.

"I've seen this before. First, the two post office boxes are used as an alert system. Mountville knows someone is on their tail if something ends up in both boxes. But they don't have to worry because in the end, the trail will lead to the Cook Islands."

"And that means what?

"All I know is that even the FBI has a hard time getting information out of there. Once you hear Cook Islands, you might as well give up."

I turn to Roland. "Do you have landline inside that has a speaker phone?"

"Sure."

"Then let's go in and call Phil Demers. If anyone can figure it out, he can."

The three of us crowd into the camper with Roland getting visibly nervous. I forgot that he might have some marijuana somewhere. Gramma has complained before about some funny smells coming across the road.

George picks up Roland's nervousness, too. "Relax, Roland."

I take out Phil's card from my wallet, and we call his office. After our call is tossed from one person to the next, we finally connect with Phil.

Phil's first words are, "Are you okay? Do I need to come up?"

"No, Phil, everything's okay. I'm here with George Myers and Roland, and we want to know why it's so hard to get information out of the Cook Islands. It looks like that's where Mountville established its trust."

"Then you are up the creek without the proverbial paddle."

"Why?"

"Because the Cook Islands have laws which allow lawyers and bankers to keep secrets. Of course, they don't come out and say it that way. If you ask for information, as one of my partners did, they say that you have to show up in person at their office. And if you do that, as this partner did after flying almost to New Zealand, they say sorry, their government doesn't allow them to divulge that information."

"Did Mountville have to go to the Cook Islands to set up the trust?" I ask.

"No, there are people who specialize in this kind of thing. They're called asset protection lawyers and they know who to call in the Cook Islands to set the whole thing up."

"So legally, Mountville is owned by person X, but the only people who know that are his asset protection lawyer, someone in the Cook Islands, and himself," I say.

"Right."

"And there's no way we can find out," I say flatly.

"Not unless you can prove that Mountville is a terrorist organization."

We thank Phil for his time. Phil says that his stories of the camp have made him the center of attention at lunch in his law firm. Volunteers are lining up to rescue me again, should the need arise.

I tell George that I'll meet him at the sandpit, and I go back across to Gramma. She has been watching from behind the screen door. For some reason, Gramma thinks that a screen door actually screens her from view.

"So that's the chief muckity-muck, huh? He's a hunk."

"You go for the grey hair and the hanging gut?"

"I think it's the uniform. I like guys in uniform."

I generally do all my grandmother's food shopping, and buying laundry detergent has reminded me of how long it's been since I filled her refrigerator. We make a list, and I promise to get it all by tomorrow.

Driving up to the sandpit, I can see George and Lucinda talking. She is dressed in a tank top, shorts and running shoes. Her clothes make her look even more athletic.

As I approach them, I see Lucinda throw her head back and laugh. She sees me and says, "George was just telling me about the dinner party without the dinner last Friday night. We are birds of a feather, Catie."

"I really can cook, you know, if I'm all alone and the TV is turned off."

"Let's let someone else do the cooking. How about if I call you when we're in the vicinity and we'll go have lunch somewhere, okay?"

A girl needs a friend, and since Maureen can no longer play the part, it's nice to think that I might have another friend in Lucinda. "I'd really like that."

"This chief detective is not as scary as I thought," she says, looking at George.

"He tries to be scary, but he just can't make it happen."

The three of us are facing the sand, watching two detectives move their hands slowly over one area near the base of the sand. Wearing latex gloves, they gently move sand down and out onto the base of the pit. After about five minutes, one of the men yells to the chief and the three of us walk over.

One of the men is holding up a garden glove. It has a dark blue, rubber like surface on the inner palm and a lighter blue cotton material on the back of the hand. The cuff of the glove has both color blues running in stripes around the wrist.

"Well, this might be why we didn't find any prints on the gun," says George. "Let's see if we can find the other one."

Bruce drives up and comes over to us. George introduces Lucinda and Bruce nods at her. Turning to George, he says, "Another helper?"

"Yup," says George.

"Not gonna look good at trial," says Bruce.

"What? Because I had to rely on one woman and her dog, and another woman and her husband to solve this one?"

"Can't wait to watch you on the stand, explaining your methodology."

"I have a three step methodology. Step one, ask the good citizens of this state to step forward and assist the police. Step two, sit on my butt. Step three, make up something about how I single-handedly solved this case."

"Same old, same old."

At this point the other glove is found and bagged as evidence. George gives Lucinda his card and asks her to call the state police barracks so that she and her husband can be fingerprinted. Lucinda looks startled until George explains that it will be necessary to eliminate their prints when analyzing the flip flops.

As everyone starts to leave, I go over to George and say, "As a good citizen of this state, I would like to impart some further information which may assist the police in their investigation. Something that happened to Jack and me this weekend."

George looks at me warily. "Just spit it out."

"I'm sick of working for free. Buy me dinner."

"Nothing is worth that much paperwork."

I shrug. "Okay, okay. How about we meet at the new pizza place in Marshfield at six?"

"How about six thirty? I've got a lot to do this afternoon."

"May I inquire as to the subject of your activity?"

"No, you may not. But I'll throw you a bone. I'm going to go over to the Best Western and to see who's been coming and staying for only one night."

Bruce smiles. "You're going to make a list of one-night-stands?"

"Only those that also requested a meeting room."

"Hey, could be some kinky people around here," says Bruce.

Bruce and George drive off, and I get in my car to go food shopping. I'm glad to see that Gordon Helms is not there on his soap box, lecturing on the evils of nudism and its effect on property values. But in a small town, with only one food market, there's always someone there that you know. This time it's Phyllis again. First the 4-H fair, then the Courthouse, now here. This is getting strange.

"I've got more," she says with excitement. "I've been spending some time on my computer, what with the slow real estate market and all. Nothing's moving since the murder. Anyway, I decided to find out who was the broker on the original sale of land to the Mountville people. Took me a while to track her down because she's retired now, but she had an office in Ashton for years."

"Did she ever meet the Mountville people? Does she know who they are?"

"That's the weird thing. She says she never met them, she only dealt with their lawyer."

"Who was their lawyer?"

"She didn't remember. She's pushing eighty and losing it a little. But here's the kicker. She said something like. 'Lord, I should remember his name, because he was involved in that toxic waste site in Ashton, and he died in that nasty car accident.'"

Phyllis writes the name of the realtor on her card and gives it to me. After saying goodbye, I hurry through the aisles and get Gramma's groceries. Gramma knows the price of every brand of every item. To avoid an argument, I will have to tell her that everything I'm throwing in the shopping cart was on sale.

When I arrive at the trailer, Roland tells me that Flo has taken Gramma up to the hot tub. That is no easy task, since Flo will have to arrange for several strong men to lower Gramma into the tub, and lift her out later. No one likes the sight of Gramma on wet steps.

When I go over to tell Roland what Phyllis told me, he says, "Now it makes sense."

"Now *what* makes sense?"

"What I couldn't understand was how the Mountville people knew so much about the EPA's superfund laws that they would know what documents to forge. There might be a lot of environmentalists that know that stuff, but how many *also* know about hiding things in the Cook Islands? Most environmentalists don't have that kind of money."

"But, how does this explain it?"

"Okay, say I'm this local lawyer, whoever he is, and I've seen what the EPA can do when it goes after a landowner for money to clean up a dump – a dump the owner might not even have known about. When the next client comes in the door and says I want to buy a piece of land in the area, what is this lawyer going to say?"

"I'd advise you to protect your assets?"

"Exactly. He might be overreacting because of what he's just been through, but he's going to warn this new client that it could happen to them, too. And he's going to explain it all to them, enough so they might understand all that stuff about responsible parties. Down the road, they would know enough to find the right forms and say the right words to scare the Gellermans."

"And would this lawyer also know how to hide stuff in the Cook Islands?"

"Maybe him, or somebody he knew that specialized in asset protection."

I'm silent for a moment, but then I look at Roland. "This guy was a local lawyer."

"Yeah, a small town lawyer whose clients were probably local."

"Which means that Mountville is probably local."

"Yeah."

Chapter Thirty-Seven

Starting tomorrow, Jack will be home. Therefore, if I'm going to do something that he wouldn't approve of, I have to do it now. He would not approve of me trying to find the dump. But after I leave Roland and drive out of camp, that's where I'm headed.

It's not easy to find Two Rod Road, and I drive back and forth a few times before I find the opening, obscured by thick underbrush on either side. I pull my car off the shoulder of the road, and walk over to the opening. Although it's wide enough for my car, there's a good chance that there wouldn't be room to turn around. To get out, I'd have to back up the entire way, resulting in considerable damage to both trees and my car.

On the other hand, I don't want to leave the car by the road, as an announcement to the world that Catie Bingham can be found on Two Rod Road. I compromise by driving the car a hundred feet or so up the road and leaving it there. Even *I* can back up a hundred feet.

As I walk down the road, I keep my eyes on the tree branches on either side of the road because that's where mountain lions rest. Nobody believed that there was a mountain lion in Rensford, until it attacked a horse. The horse survived but only because the owner heard it scream. She didn't see the mountain lion, but the claw marks on the horse showed that a large cat had maneuvered under the belly of the horse and hung on while it tried to rip the horse's neck open.

But it's hard to stay scared and vigilant for very long if nothing happens. Eventually, I stop looking at the branches above me and my eyes drift back down to the path ahead of me. The vegetation in the middle of the path is lush and green, just like the weeds on the side of the path. But where car wheels would have traveled, there is a lot of dead vegetation.

Phyllis told me that she drove down this road to see the dump sometime in the last few days. Plants are pretty tough, though, and they die only if a car crushes them over and over. I bend down to look at the shriveled brown weeds. There has been some heavy traffic on this path.

There's not much left of the dead plants, but I'm able to tease out a few intact ones. Among them, I can't find any seeds, even early stages of seeds. They died an early death, probably in late spring or early summer. That means the heavy traffic was around that time.

I remember that the secretary at the town hall said that she liked to hike on this road in the early spring, and that she hadn't seen any dump. But Phyllis said that she had driven down this road recently and she had seen the dump site. It sounded like the dump was pretty obvious.

As I hurry on, I see no forks or turnoffs that could have led the two women to different places. There is a small rise ahead. I get to the top and look down at the end of the road, now covered with water since the state highway was built.

I see a dump containing a variety of rusted material surrounded by an oil slick, some grayish brown goop that clings to hummocks and old tree roots. I walk down the hill with a big smile on my face. The camp will not face any big clean up charges, nor will this site ever make it onto EPA's superfund list.

Someone has created this dump according to what they thought a superfund site looked like. Someone piled up a few rusted bed springs, an intact roll of rusted barbed wire, a rusted piece of an ancient tractor, and a few beat up tires—the kind of objects that could be found on old farms throughout New England.

The 'oozy' and 'oily' liquids that Phyllis saw appear to be paint and motor oil. Hopping from hummock to hummock, I find some plastic containers of 10-W40 that account for the oil slick. Several empty paint cans formerly held paint that someone thought would look like the colors of toxic waste. I even see one lid that with a sticker that says 'military grey' mixed at a local home improvement store here in Rensford.

I shouldn't be so happy to see a polluted wetland, but I can't help myself. It is such a silly, amateurish job, meant to scare the Gellermans who had probably never seen any kind of toxic waste site, never mind a superfund site. And this will be easy to clean up. With the rusty materials removed, the paint ands oil can be soaked up with variety of absorbent materials that Jack can easily get.

I can't wait for Jack to come home so he can see this. If he weren't in Washington, I'd call him right now so I could describe every detail. But I have to tell somebody, and unfortunately, George said he would be busy all afternoon. I settle on Roland. I hurry back up Two Rod Road.

Reaching for the handle of my car door, I see that there is something on my seat. I open the door slowly. A large knife has been thrust into the leather, pinning a piece of paper. Although the paper is bent upwards by the knife, I can see the words, "Back off."

I don't want to touch it. Seeing it plunged deep into my front seat makes me want to run. Even if I pull it out, I don't want to sit on the slashed leather. I take out my cell phone and find that there's no service in this area. At least I can take a picture.

Standing there and closing my eyes, I tell myself I have to do what I don't want to do. I find a plastic bag and a discarded napkin on the floor in the back seat. Using the napkin, I grab the knife by the base of the blade and rock it back and forth until it comes out. I put the knife and the note into the bag and place it on the front passenger seat, and then force myself to get in and drive. I drive to the camp, not for the pleasure of telling Roland about my discovery, but for the safety of being around people I love.

In the camp, I find Gramma sitting outside with Flo and Roland.

"Hi, Gramma!" I try and make my voice sound normal.

"What's wrong?"

"What do you mean, what's wrong?"

"When you're lying, you voice is high like this," and she does an imitation of me saying 'Hi Gramma!' in a sing-song voice.

"How can I be lying when I just said, 'Hi, Gramma'?"

"Because you were trying to say, 'Hi-Gramma-isn't-everything-just-peachy-keen?' It's the peachy-keen part you're lying about."

I don't want Gramma to freak out about the knife and start yelling at me because I went to see the dump by myself. "I'm just tired."

"If you were tired, you'd sound tired. Out with it."

"Okay. I'm feeling a little paranoid. I'm a little worried that I'm being followed."

"Followed?" says Flo, glancing down the gravel road. "Who's following you?"

"I don't know. It's just a feeling." My grandmother is has her eyes fixed on me, like she's zeroing in on my innermost thoughts. "I just came by to tell you about the fake superfund site I found."

I begin an account of my adventure on Two Rod Road, when Gramma interrupts. "Where's Jack?"

"He's in Washington, giving testimony before Congress, but he'll be home tonight."

"What time?"

"Around nine."

"He leaves you alone too much."

"I know. But this thing in Washington is a big deal. Besides, we had a long talk and he agreed to be away less often."

"He should be here with you."

I change the subject back to what I found on Two Rod Road. From there, the topic changes to the possibility that the town might take the camp by eminent domain. All the while, Gramma has been giving me a stare that's somewhere between concern and anger. I think it's concern for me and anger toward Jack. A little after five, my phone rings. I look at Gramma and say, "It's Jack. He's probably coming home early."

"Hi, Sweetheart, how are you?" says Jack, in the same-sing inflection that Gramma caught me using.

"Where are you?"

"Well, that's the thing. I'm still in Washington. The committee was running late all day and they didn't get to my testimony. I'm on for nine o'clock tomorrow morning. There's a five-thirty flight tomorrow morning that would get me here on time but I'd have to leave the house at four AM." His words are coming out in a rush. "Would you mind being alone one more night?"

I *do* mind. But is it worth all that flying back and forth and getting up so early in the morning, just so he can be by my side for a few hours tonight? "No problem. I'll be fine," I say, trying to turn away from Gramma's eyes.

"Are you sure? Because I could come home. It's no big deal."

"I'll stay with Gramma tonight, okay?"

At this point, Gramma tries to break in. "Let me talk to him." I wave her away. "I want to talk to him," she says again, raising her voice.

"Who's that in the background?"

"It's just Gramma. She wants to know how you are."

"That's a first."

"Jack!" yells Gramma.

Jack is silent for a moment. "Catie, is everything all right up there?"

"JACK!"

"Put your grandmother on the phone, please."

"Really, I'm…"

"Now."

"Okay, okay, okay." I hand the phone to Gramma.

"Jack, you miserable weasel of a husband, get your ass up here this instant." She listens to Jack a minute, and says, "I don't know. All I know is that she's scared of something. She says that someone's following her, but you know how she under-exaggerates things." After a moment, she hands the phone back to me with a smile, and says, "He'd like to speak with you."

"Catie, I'm coming home."

"But what about the testimony?"

"I'll just have to do it another time. I'm going to explain the situation and then leave. I'll be home nine, nine-thirty at the latest. You stay with your grandmother and I'll come there."

"I'm supposed to have dinner with George and Bruce."

"Then have them pick you up at the camp and bring you back there."

"Okay."

"Now, do you want to tell me what's going on?"

"I can't."

"Because it will scare the hell out of your grandmother?"

"Yes."

"And you were going to let me stay in Washington?"

My voice is small, like a child. "I don't know. I guess whenever you say 'would you mind,' it's hard for me to say "yes, I would mind.'"

Jack pauses. "We'll work on our marital communication skills later. Right now, why don't you go somewhere out of earshot so you can tell me what's going on. Hang up and call me right back, okay?"

"Okay." I hang up and say to Gramma, "I'm going to go in back of the trailer. Jack and I have to talk."

"It's about time," she says.

I go around in back of the trailer to the little stream that Gramma loves to tend. I call Jack and tell him about the knife in the front seat. There are a few strangled twists in my voice that show how close I am to tears.

Jack's voice is firm but gentle. "When I get to camp tonight, we'll leave your car there and go right to the Rensford Inn. We'll stay there as long as we need to. Okay?"

"Okay."

"Catie, I love you so much. You're the most important thing in my life."

"I love you, too." My throat is aching and the tears are welling up as I say goodbye.

For a while, I sit by the stream and let the tears flow. I pick up a stick and poke at the leaves, opening up channels to let the water flow faster. Pretty soon, I'm sobbing as quietly as I can.

This is hormones, just hormones. In all the chaos of the last week, I forgot to pick up this month's birth control pills. For days, I've been scrounging a few leftover pills from previous months, but now it's been two days without a pill and I'm plunging back into premenstrual craziness. Another hormonal overreaction, that's all this is.

Chapter Thirty-Eight

Gramma finds me. She's not an affectionate sort of person so I know she'll just stand there, waiting for me to come to her if I want to. I stand up, and walk over to her and put my arms around her. She's so small and bent over now that she can no longer make me feel comforted physically. But her heart is still big enough to hold me when I need to be held.

I tell her I need to go for a walk, and she agrees, as long as I don't go by myself. "Go with Roland," she says. "That way people will leave you alone."

So, Roland and I start walking. We both walk in silence, with our heads down, which discourages even the most ardent socializers. At most, we get a few waves, and a few brief hellos. After a while, Roland breaks the silence.

"You want to tell me what's got you so freaked out?" he asks. "It's okay if you don't. We can just walk, if you want."

I tell him about the note and the knife, and all he says is, "Jesus." Then we fall silent again.

At the top of the hill we see a Rensford police car in the parking lot, and Captain Larini is leaning against it with his arms folded. My hormones ricochet, and I go from being afraid, to being really pissed. Larini has this smirk on his face that I personally want to wipe off.

"So, Captain," I say as we approach his car. "Here to protect and defend in the name of justice?"

"I am."

"And how are you upholding justice this time?"

"I'm here to protect the appraiser. He's going to come up with a number. And, soon, the town will pay you that money and we get rid of you."

"He needs protection? Afraid we're going to rip his clothes off?"

"No. Your dear friend Chief Detective George Myers says this is a very dangerous place. But I don't have to tell you that, do I? Being as how you're his best buddy."

"George never gave me any indication that the camp wasn't safe."

"What? Could it be that Catie is out of the loop? Maybe, just maybe, your friend Myers isn't telling you everything he knows?"

"He doesn't have to tell me anything, if he doesn't want to."

"And from now on, he won't want to tell you anything."

"Why?"

"Because his boss told him not to. Turns out that Myers was a bad boy for bringing a civilian into the investigation."

"What? I suggest some leads and he can't follow them up because I'm not a cop?"

"He's supposed to listen to you, but not talk to you. But maybe Myers makes an exception for pretty girls."

Roland comes to my defense. "Catie has been a huge help and George knows it."

"So everyone is on a first name basis with the chief around here?" Larini's smirk almost turns into a smile. "As much as I hate to, let me give you a little helpful advice. Don't trust Myers. If he has the chance to make an arrest and have it stick in court, he doesn't care who gets chewed up and spit out along the way."

"How come you said you're here to protect the appraiser?

Do you think there's a murderer running around here?" asks Roland.

"I'm standing here, aren't I?"

I touch Roland's arm to indicate that it's time to go. I can't stand Captain Larini, and if I remain in his presence, I might say or do something that lands me back in his police station. Roland, however, is annoyed. He likes precise and direct statements, not innuendo.

"That doesn't make sense. You're saying that there might be a murderer in this camp, and you're here to protect the *appraiser?* What are you, his personal hired gun?"

I grab his arm. "Time to go, Roland."

Captain Larini gives a little wave, while I physically turn Roland around and get him headed back to the trailer. I need to get going if I'm going to meet George and Bruce at the pizza place in Marshfield. If they show up at all. I check my phone, but there are no messages from either George or Bruce.

Roland sputters a bit about idiots on the police force, but I quiet him down before we get back to his place. I ask him to keep Gramma in sight at all times, not because I think Donald's murderer is in the camp, but because whoever's following me might slip into the place. Maybe by walking through the woods and then taking his clothes off.

At six-thirty I drive into the parking lot of the new pizza place in Marshfield. George and Bruce are in separate police cars, parked next to each other but facing in different directions so that they can roll down their windows and talk to each other. It looks like the cars are in some sort of courtship position, preparing to make baby police cars. Okay, now I know I'm really losing it.

At the sight of me, George pulls his car ahead so that both he and Bruce can open their doors to get out. Neither of them is smiling. I'm glad I have already been prepared for this by Captain Larini, or else I would have been confused and hurt by this reception. Even, now, I'm upset. I feel like I really *need* these two people right now.

I think George feels bad, too. "Catie, I'm really sorry, but I'm afraid we really won't be able…"

"Can it," I say, feeling like I am somehow channeling my grandmother.

"Excuse me?" George can't help but smile a little in surprise.

"I heard you had a little slap down from your boss about talking to me." I'm doing my best to sound like a tough guy from a gangster movie, in order to hide the fact that I feel like a scared little kid on the verge of tears.

"Who'd you hear that from?" asks George.

"Captain Larini."

"Oh, great. Now the whole world knows."

He's worried about his image? This makes me angry, which is a good thing because it means I am less likely to cry. "So we're going to make this an official information exchange. I have some information that will be useful to you, and I'm going to swap it for information that will be useful to me."

"What do you mean, useful to you?"

"I am interested in having as much information as I can about who is behind this murder, not," I say, holding up my hands before they can protest, "not because I am some sort of amateur sleuth, but because I am interested in staying alive."

"Staying alive?" says Bruce, a little warily.

"Yes. Now, I would prefer to exchange that information while eating pizza because I'm hungry. If walking into a pizza place would pose too much risk to your career, I will go in there myself and order take-out so that we can eat it in the parking lot."

"Catie, you're taking this too personally. It has nothing to do with you. We just have to follow the proper protocol," says George.

"Yes, I am taking it personally, and no, I do not agree that it has nothing to do with me. Now are you going to be brave enough to walk in that pizza place with me? I guarantee that it will be worth your while."

George looks at Bruce with a little smile and a questioning look. Clearly, Bruce is here to try and help George keep to proper protocol. But, in the end rank outweighs caution, and Bruce says, "Whatever you say, boss."

We go into the restaurant and place our order and then walk over to a corner booth in the empty restaurant. George and Bruce squeeze into one side and I have the other side to myself. Apparently, their bravery does not extend to sitting next to me.

Bruce leans back into the corner. "Okay, you go first."

"Today I walked down Two Rod Road and found out that the dump site that started this whole thing is fake."

"What do you mean, fake?" asks George.

"In late spring, someone made repeated trips down the road and brought various large rusty items, placed them in a wetland, and then poured motor oil and paint in the water in order to make it look like toxic waste. One item at the site is a lid from a paint can showing that it was mixed and purchased at a Home Depot. That lid may have fingerprints, and may also lead you to a credit card purchase."

They both are quiet. I think it's because this is good information and they are each trying to fit it in with what they already know.

"How do you know it was late spring?" asks Bruce.

I cross my arms and shake my head. "My turn. I'm assuming

that any data you were able to retrieve from the camera and the laptop confirmed the blackmail we suspected. What I want to know is—did it name names? Did it say who Mountville is?"

"No." George sees my shoulders drop, and adds, "Sorry Catie. The blackmail letters were addressed to the same post office boxes you already know about."

"You next," says Bruce.

"Okay. Phyllis, the Gellermans' realtor, tracked down the realtor of the original Mountville sale. Although the other realtor is retired and a little senile, she says that she never met anyone from Mountville, just their lawyer. It turns out that the lawyer was the same one who represented the landowner of the Ashton superfund site in their dealings with the EPA. He later died in a car accident."

Both Bruce and George are very still for a while, staring at me. Then they turn and stare at each other. Finally, I say, "You want to tell me why that's so important? Or is this one of those police procedure, keep-it-close-to-the-chest, things?"

"It is," says George.

"This seems to be a lopsided exchange of information. Fine. I'm still trying to get some clue of who we're dealing with here. The blackmail letters didn't give any clues. What about the visits to the Best Western? Did you track down the name of the person who was staying there for one night stands and renting the meeting room?"

"It looks like someone was renting the meeting room without spending the night. My guess is that he was trying to make the Gellermans think that he was from out of town."

"Then it's somebody local?"

Bruce breaks in. "Your turn."

I have been saving the best for last in case I needed it for leverage. I reach into my purse and gingerly take out the plastic bag containing the note and the hunting knife. "When I came back to my car, after walking back up Two Rod Road, I found this stuck into the driver's seat." Handing it to them, I say, "I wiggled it out with a paper towel touching only the base of the blade." I show them the picture on my cell phone.

Suddenly Bruce and George start talking about how this changes everything. Apparently, if my personal safety is involved, they are obligated to share any and all information that will help me stay safe. How nice. If my life is threatened, we can all be friends again.

The pizza comes, and we start eating and sharing information more freely. They tell me that the blackmail letters were written to two men, since they were addressed 'Dear Gentlemen', and because Donald used phrases like, 'I saw both of you in Pine Hollow', and 'I have pictures of both of you.'

"By the way, he seems to have been bluffing," says Bruce. "We found no pictures. But he may have heard some commotion and gone down to investigate."

"Maybe he heard them throwing those big rusty pieces of metal into a pile," I say, trying to wipe some grease off my chin.

"Could be," says Bruce. "You know, you shouldn't have gone down Two Rod Road by yourself."

I'm happy that Bruce has welcomed me back into the fold. "After seeing that knife, I'm not going to the bathroom by myself."

"We are assuming that your bathroom companion will be your husband. Is he home?"

"No, but he'll be home at nine or nine thirty. I'll stay with my grandmother until then, and then we'll drive to the Rensford Inn and stay there tonight."

"Good," says George.

We decide that the leftover pizza should go to my grandmother. As we're combining all the slices into one box, George reminds me that the whole purpose of dinner was for me to tell him about something that happened to Jack and me this weekend.

"So," says George, folding his hands on the table in front of him. "Give us the story."

I turn to Bruce. "Let me back up a little for Bruce's benefit. Do you know about the arson thing last Thursday?"

"Everyone in the department has heard every detail, including how you look when you're dragged out of bed."

"Thank you, George, for sharing that information. Anyway, I thought that the reason for framing me was revenge. I figured that Terry, my neighbor, and his friends in the police department tried to uphold his name by tearing down mine. Or maybe Maureen was just trying to get back at me for yelling at her."

George smiles. "You yelled at Maureen Helms? She must outweigh you by a factor of two."

"Well, I didn't actually yell at her. I just told her she had done some things that had hurt my feelings."

"Whoa, that was brutal," says Bruce.

I ignore him. "On Saturday night, at the 4-H fair, Jack and I ran into Ralph, one of the guys who verbally roughed me up that night. After a jab in the ribs from his wife, he apologized. Then Amanda, Terry's wife, came over this morning and apologized, so it looks like that whole incident blew over."

"But we never found out who the third man was," says George.

"That's true. But I think that Ralph's wife could get the information out of him in minutes."

"And Maureen? She still mad at you?"

"Yeah, but not to the point of hiring a thug to scare the hell out of us at the 4H fair."

"A *thug*? At a *4-H* fair? That's not something you see every day," says George. "How did he scare you?"

"We had the feeling this guy was following us in his pickup. But then he went by us as we pulled into the entrance, and I saw that he had his finger in his ear, so we decided not to worry about him."

George and Bruce look at each other but say nothing.

"Then, at the skillet toss, I was just about to fling my second try when I saw the same guy down at the end of the red line. He was sort of smiling at me in a leering sort of way."

Bruce holds up his hands. "Wait, wait, wait. My wife came home and told me about this girl who threw a good first toss, but then threw the skillet straight in the air and it almost came straight down on her head."

"It wasn't that bad."

George is beginning to show some concern. "You're sure it was the same guy?"

"Not a doubt."

"Is that it? Or did you see him again?"

I recount how the pickup pulled out in front of us from a side road and then, halfway down a steep hill, slammed on the brakes. I told them that we were in a low sports car and that we almost slid under the pickup. And, finally, how the same guy got out and claimed that a deer had run across the road.

Bruce looks at George, and they are thinking in tandem. Finally Bruce says to George, "Decapitation by pickup."

"What?"

"We had a case a few years ago," says George. "A little sports car ended up beneath the bed of a pickup. Very messy. We had our suspicions, but in the end we couldn't prove anything. Tire tracks did show that the sports car had been following too close, but the pickup might have slowed down just before slamming on the brakes. And, of course, we couldn't prove that a deer had not darted across the road."

"What did he look like?" asks George.

I give them a description, as much as I can. "Remember, I only saw him at night."

Bruce looks at George. "Maybe, maybe not."

"What did he say when he got out of the pickup?" George asks.

"That's the weird part. He said something like 'A deer ran across the road'. But a normal person would have said, 'Are you all right?' He had a very calm voice and stared at us in a scary, in-your-face way."

George tilts his head and looks at me with raised eyebrows. "Someone comes close to killing you and you fail to mention it until now?"

"Jack and I talked about whether we should tell you, but in the end, we only had the vague feeling that he was trying to scare us. I mean, deer run across the road and people slam on their brakes, right?"

Bruce sighs, "That's the beauty of it. Happens all the time."

"That time before – who got killed? Who was in the sports car?"

"He was a local lawyer, Eric Brellin. He worked with the family who owned the superfund site in Ashton."

"Oh, my God."

"And who was the guy in the pickup?"

"Eugene Rendel, who happens to be the brother of Maureen Helms."

Chapter Thirty-Nine

"Maureen's brother? Maureen's brother was the one who almost killed us?"

"Tomorrow we'll show you a picture of Eugene, and we'll see if it's your guy," says George.

"I didn't even know she had a brother."

"He's kind of the loser in the family. Doesn't like to be pushed around. Takes a lot of odd jobs, but no one really knows what he lives on. An inheritance, most likely."

"How come you know about him?"

"Something didn't smell right about this accident. I guess a normal person would have been pretty distraught about the whole thing. He was just really, really nervous."

"Did they know each other? Was this Brellin guy his lawyer?"

George shakes his head. "Don't know. Judge wouldn't let us get a list of Brellin's clients unless we had reason to believe it wasn't an accident. But all we had was a feeling. There was talk that his lawyer wouldn't lie for him when Eugene tried to declare bankruptcy."

"But you wouldn't *kill* somebody because they won't back you up in a bankruptcy court," I say.

"We never thought that Eugene was trying to kill Brellin. Stopping fast is not a reliable way to kill someone, even if it's a low sports car in back of a pickup. We think that Eugene was just trying to scare him, and things went wrong."

"So, is that murder?" I ask.

"Second degree, probably."

"But if he's afraid that someone might take another look at the Brellin accident, why on earth would he do it again?"

"For one thing, he's not a smart guy. For another thing, you must have been making him really nervous, getting close to something that would lead us back to Brellin."

I nod. "I was poking around with Mountville Trust, which Brellin represented when Mountville was buying that land."

Bruce snorts. "Mountville Trust, with all that Cook Islands stuff? Eugene ain't got the brains or the money."

"But you said he had an inheritance, right? And Brellin could have been the brains. The land might be the asset that Eugene was trying to hide from the bankruptcy court. After all, only Brellin and some guy in the Cook Islands could trace it back to Eugene."

George is nodding. "And then years go by, and Eugene gets cocky again. Tries to pull a fast one on the Gellermans."

"Right," I say. "And then Donald says he has pictures. Eugene thinks that those pictures connect him to Mountville, and lead right back to the bankruptcy and Brellin."

"You guys are running off into fantasy land," says Bruce. "You're just piecing together a bunch of guesses."

George says, "Tomorrow we'll know if Eugene is Catie's 4-H thug. And if he is, we'll know that Eugene likes to stop short in front of people who are involved in Mountville, one way or another. That calls for a visit to Eugene, don't you think?"

"Can't wait," says Bruce.

George looks at his watch. "It's almost eight. My wife is going to kill me. She's got book club at our house and I'm supposed to take care of the kids."

"Get going then," I say, shooing him off.

"Bruce, could you follow Catie for ten, fifteen minutes to make sure there's no one behind her? If it looks okay, then just turn south at the 201 intersection. Catie, you are to go back to your grandmother's and stay there until Jack comes. Under no circumstances are you to go home, got it?"

"Got it."

Bruce follows me for a while, and then with a quick flash of his lights, he turns left at an intersection. I am going to follow instructions and go to my grandmother's and not go home. I just want to make one quick stop to pick up my birth control pills.

Chapter Forty

There is only one car in the parking lot in front of Lupien's Drugstore. I drive by the store slowly, but there appears to be no one in it. I'm not taking any chances, so I pull up as close to the store as possible. I park across several parking spaces, so that my car is parallel to the store and under the fluorescent light of the store's overhanging fixtures.

The bright light makes it hard to see the rest of the parking lot, but I wait a minute or so to make sure that no one has followed me. Then I look out of the passenger's side to make sure there's no one on the sidewalk. It's hard to see inside of the store because of the huge signs advertising a variety of things on sale, but the store looks pretty quiet, too. That must be Mr. Lupien's car in the lot.

I unlock my door, get out and lock it again. When I walk into the store, Mr. Lupien is in the back on his raised platform, and a Paul Simon song is playing in the background. The store is an old-fashioned drugstore, with the aisles defined by shelves about head high, so that Mr. Lupien can quickly see who's stealing what.

There is a man in the store with his back to me, staring at the wall that displays the cosmetics. As I walk to the back of the store, I see Mr. Lupien glance up at the man. I walk up to Mr. Lupien, tell him my name, and he walks over a few steps to retrieve my prescription. He still has his eye on the man. I look over, and see that the man has not moved.

I turn back to Mr. Lupien, and then look again toward the cosmetics section. About six feet away from me, at the end of one of the aisles, there are a variety of items on sale, most of them seasonal close-outs. One of them is a pair of gardening gloves.

I can see from where I stand that these are the same kind of gloves we found at the sandpit. Light blue on the outside, dark blue on the inside, and stripes running around the wrist. I'm tempted to buy a pair to show George, but I just want to pay Mr. Lupien and get out of there. Somehow, buying the gloves would require more courage than I have right now.

I pay Mr. Lupien and walk back toward the front of the store. From the very edge of my peripheral vision, I can see the man also heading for the front door. What I should do is hang back and let him go out first, but I find myself running. I open the glass door and his hand appears near the right side of my face. He is holding the door open for me.

"Nice parking job."

I glance over, and what looked like a man from the back is actually a tall, pimply kid. I give him a huge smile and thank him for holding the door for me. It comes out a little too loud and he looks at me as if trying to guess what drug I'm on. Then he says, "You're welcome," and walks over to the car in the parking lot.

"Catie."

I'm walking around the back of my car when I hear the voice. It's female and it's nearby.

"Catie."

I lift up my hand to shield my eyes and see only a dark form against the last bit of twilight. It's tall and wide, and standing about twenty feet away.

"Maureen?"

"I need to talk to you."

I push the button on my key to unlock the door, and my lights flash twice. It's enough light to see Maureen standing there.

"Please." Maureen's voice is plaintive.

I open my car door and stand next to the seat. "Come over where I can see you."

"I'm so sorry."

"Maureen, I'm not going to talk to you unless I can see you."

Maureen walks over slowly and when she gradually comes into the light, I see her face. She looks grotesque. One side of her face is swollen from her brow to below her cheekbone. The other eye is surrounded by dark green and her chin is purple. Her bottom lip is red and distended.

"My God, what happened?" I can't imagine Maureen allowing someone to beat her up, but there is no denying that her face has been hit, and hit more than once.

She starts to sob, so quietly that I can barely hear the rapid intakes of breath. "It doesn't matter."

"Did your brother do this to you?"

She looks up, but doesn't stop crying. She shakes her head and continues. "I saw your car and I had to come over." The sobs are starting to get louder and deeper. "I'm just so sorry. I'm just so sorry."

In spite of myself, I want to go over and put my arms around her, but I resist the temptation. "Sorry about what?"

She looks around and there is a dull fear in her eyes, like an animal in a cage that knows it will be hurt and can do nothing but wait. She shakes her head. "I didn't know," she says.

"Didn't know about what, Maureen? Just tell me what's going on."

She stands there sobbing quietly. I give up trying to understand her. "It's okay, Maureen. Whatever it is, it's okay."

"I swear I didn't know."

I feel like I'm talking to a small child. "I believe you. You didn't know. Now just go…"

She is looking at me, and then suddenly there is real fear in her eyes, as if the door to her cage has just been opened.

I hear a male voice behind me. "Maureen. Maureen, Maureen." He sounds very calm, almost tired. I turn around and see her husband on the other side of my car. "Now what have you done here, my sweet?"

"Gordon, please. I didn't tell her anything."

"Now that's odd, because I thought I just heard her say that she believed you. That you didn't know anything about it."

"She doesn't know anything." There is real fear in Maureen's voice now and it takes me a second to realize that she fears for my safety as well as hers. I duck down into my seat, slam the door, and try to jam the key into the lock. At the same, Gordon has gotten in on the passenger side.

"Get out!" I open my window. "Call the police!" I say to Maureen.

"Now why would she need to do that? Just because I sat in your car? She must have said some pretty bad things."

The safest place to go would be back into the store and I start to get out of the car. Gordon grabs my hand and pulls me back in, and I hit my head on top of the door opening. He yanks me down into the seat. Still gripping my wrist with his left hand, he shows me the gun in his right hand.

Chapter Forty-One

"This is my Glock," Gordon says, showing me his gun. "Stolen, of course, but mine nonetheless. When I first got it, I thought it was fake because of the plastic on the outside. But it has a steel barrel. Here, let me show you."

He releases my wrist and uses his left hand to gently move my hair away from my face. He raises the gun and places it against my temple. "Feel that cold metal? That's the steel barrel."

Maureen is frozen next to the car and gives a little whimper. I pray that she doesn't move or say anything that will startle him. I am as still as I can be, but I can't stop shaking. Even my head is shaking, making the steel circle pulse against my temple.

"There's another way I can show you it's a real gun." Gordon pauses, and then flips the gun on its side and hits me hard in the face. "See, it's really heavy."

For an instant, all I feel is shock, and then pain and heat. Maureen steps back and her whimper turns into a moan.

"Shut up! Go back to the office and wait for me."

I glance at Maureen. Her fists are up in front of her mouth, like she's trying to stuff her moan back down her own throat. She spins around and walks into the darkness.

Gordon turns his attention back to the gun. "Now, I want to show you something else. When I hit you just now, I had the safety on. I didn't want the gun to go off and attract Mr.

Lupien's attention. Now, I'm taking the safety off, see?"

I'm still looking straight ahead, afraid to turn toward him. My face is starting to get very hot, and the pain is seeping into my neck and around my skull. Turning my head to look at the gun makes it hurt even more.

"And, one more thing. There are 19 rounds in this one magazine. I don't get much target practice, but with this thing, I don't need much. Am I making my point here? I'm trying to scare you. Am I succeeding?"

"Yes."

"Good. Start driving."

It feels dangerous to turn the key and press my foot down. I want to be very still, as if there was a bomb in the car and I might set it off by doing something wrong. I can't control my shaking. Even my legs are shaking.

I drive across the parking lot and stop at the road. "Where to?"

"I think we should go see my brother-in-law, Eugene."

"Right or left?"

Gordon smiles. "He's at your house."

"My house?"

"Yeah, he's been hanging around there for a few days now. Except when he went to the 4-H fair with you and your hubbie."

I turn right and head toward the house. It will take ten minutes to get there, and that gives me ten minutes to think. My mind is crowded with physical sensations, the swelling pain in my face, and my heart pummeling the top of my chest.

I try and make my voice sound normal. "Maureen didn't tell me anything. Really."

I flinch as the gun speeds toward my face. Gordon stops himself in time. "I don't like liars," he says.

"She was saying things, but I couldn't understand her."

"Listen!" His voice is louder. "I know exactly what she told you because she only knows one thing. The stupid cow was listening at the top of the stairs when I was yelling at Eugene after that encounter he had with your little sports car. He was at least supposed to send you to the hospital, for God's sake." His voice drops and he almost sighs. "She heard it. I saw her face."

He is telling me this because he doesn't care that I know. He doesn't care, because I won't be alive to tell anyone.

"You know, Catie. It didn't have to come down to this. I tried to distract you as soon as you got interested in Mountville. I launched a campaign against the nudist camp, thinking you would get so caught up in defending the camp that you wouldn't be able to think of anything else."

"And Maureen got it all published."

"She thought it was a good career move. When that didn't work, I tried to get you arrested. I figured that getting arrested would focus your mind and make you drop everything else."

"So you set fire to Maureen's office."

"It was such a great set up and execution. Went down like clockwork until your friend the state cop showed up." Gordon sighs. "So next I tried to scare you off."

"You sent Eugene and his pickup."

"Which reminds me. Enough of this scintillating conversation." He transfers the gun into his left hand and points it at me as he reaches into his pocket and takes out his cell phone.

"Genie, my boy. You'll never guess who I'm bringing to you. Catie herself. You near the house?" After a pause, he asks, "Anybody around?" Then after another pause, "We'll be there in a few minutes."

Now is the time to think. Gordon is listening to Eugene, and

I have to use the time to think. Do I play along and wait until I see an opportunity to escape? What if time runs out and no opportunity comes along?

Gordon's voice is angry. "Don't try and weasel out of this, Eugene. You were the one who got this stupid toxic waste idea, and I had to fix that mess."

Gordon is making gestures with his left hand and the gun is pointing in all different directions. In spite of the gun waving around, I have to concentrate. Do I wait for an opportunity to escape, or do I create one?

"For Chrisake, it was just a nudist camp."

The hand with the gun is now resting on his leg. I have decided to try and escape. I'm worried that my body will not be able to act quickly, but I'll just have to risk it.

Gordon is shaking his head. "No, no. This one's on you. I'm not going to do all the heavy lifting."

He is not wearing a seat belt. I am. I wish the gun was in his other hand.

"Remember what we said. If we're both up to our ears in this, then neither one is going to cut a deal to get out of it."

We are turning into my driveway. The corn on both sides is about nine feet tall. I rehearse the sequence of motions in my head.

"Quit your whining, Eugene. You're going to be the one to pull the trigger on this one, and that's all there is to it." He puts the phone down and transfers the gun back to his right hand.

I step hard on the gas pedal, forcing him back in his seat. In the next second, I slam on the brake, twist the wheel so that the car goes into the corn on his side, and pull up the emergency brake. I do all this while I'm opening my door. Then I fall out of the car and start rolling diagonally across the driveway.

The noise is deafening. The gun gives off four or five rapid rounds while Gordon's finger is on the trigger and the windshield shatters. Then Gordon starts shooting out of the driver's side with the door open and the driver's window explodes. Some bullets hit the driveway, and I can hear them kick up gravel as they land.

The shooting stops as I crawl into the corn. I hear him throw himself against his door as he tries to open it, but he is pinned in by the corn. Then I hear him swear as he tries to slide over to the driver's seat before finding out that the parking brake is up. After a minute, I hear his feet on the gravel.

I've used this time to move into the corn. I'm in the triangle in front of the house, which is much smaller than the other fields in back or on the side of the house, but it will have to do.

"Gordon! What the hell happened? Are you all right?" I hear running footsteps on the gravel.

"Stop, Eugene. Go back and get a couple of flashlights from your truck," yells Gordon. I hear Eugene run toward the house and then I see him come back to Gordon. One flashlight is turned on, and then another.

Gordon and Eugene talk but I can't hear what they say. Then I see one bobbing flashlight go up toward the house and down the other driveway. As he walks on the gravel, I hear Eugene yell back to Gordon. "Just make sure you don't miss her and hit me."

"Shut up!" Gordon yells back. He walks down to the road where the driveway starts. The rows of corn run parallel to the road, and Gordon begins to methodically shine his flashlight down each row. Eugene stands at the other end of the row and shines the flashlight toward the house, lighting up the driveway to make sure I don't run out the other side.

I'm in the middle of the triangle, and Gordon is moving up row by row. I can't hide between the rows because the stalks are too thin. Quietly, I bend the corn stalks and move toward the house, keeping away from Gordon as he moves closer. But I am moving into shorter and shorter rows.

I don't have a plan, and now I'm wondering whether I'm going to make it through this. I might die sometime within the next half hour, maybe in the next few minutes. Tears begin to sting my eyes.

Gordon has moved about halfway up, and I'm still moving ahead of him. Soon I will run out of rows. No one is going to come to my rescue. No one even knows I'm here. Why didn't I think to grab my purse as I was rolling out of the car, so I could have called 911?

I hear someone crashing through the corn on the other side of the house. "Catie? You all right?" Terry yells from the darkness. He must have come through that secret pathway that Amanda told me about. Both Eugene's and Gordon's flashlights go dark.

"Terry, they're trying to kill me! Watch out! He has a gun!"

"Who's trying to kill you? Who has a gun?"

I don't want to tell Terry who these men are because it will mean that they will have to kill him, too.

"Catie, if I'm going to shoot somebody, I like to know who they are first."

He's got his rifle! "Gordon Helms and Eugene Somebody."

"Okay. Don't know them."

A few rounds of gunfire come from Gordon's side of the corn.

"Hey!" Terry seems offended that someone would shoot at him. I am assuming he's found a protected spot. He seems very relaxed about the whole thing.

"You there! Standing about a hundred feet away from me. I'm going to land one at your feet."

Terry fires a single shot and Eugene cries out in surprise. "Love that night vision," says Terry.

I hear a flashlight drop on the gravel. I think Eugene has put his hands in the air. "I give up. I don't have a gun. I didn't want to kill her. Gordon was going to make me – "

A blast of bullets flies across the corn and I hear a dull sound as Eugene falls on the gravel. There is silence again. I hear nothing from Terry and I wonder whether the spray of bullets somehow got to him.

I hear a fast rustling of the corn in back of me, almost like the sound of surf. "Terry, he's in the corn."

"Shut up!" yells Terry, but it's too late. I hear the bullets and then I feel one rip across the edge of my thigh.

"Catie, lie down." Terry's voice is from a higher position now and nearer to Gordon's side of the corn. "Lie down, and show me you are okay by moving one of the stalks next to you. *Quietly*."

I bend the nearest stalk of corn back and forth slowly. I hear nothing from behind me.

"Okay, we've got him pinned. Now, slither down your row toward me, on your belly, without a sound."

I try and find the exact center of the row because the dried leaves at the bottom of the stalks make too much noise. I'm heaving my weight forward with my upper arms and one knee. When I'm near the end of the road, I hear sirens.

"Okay. I see you. Stay right there. Don't get up," says Terry. "Now, you with the gun. I can see Catie now, and that means that I don't have to worry that I'm shooting the wrong person if I see any movement in the corn. So if one stalk of corn moves the slightest bit, I'm going to unload right on that site."

The sirens are loud and I can see some reflections of the flashing lights on the leaves of trees along the road. In a few moments two police cars are turning up the driveway. Their wheels pass right in front of my face, only a few feet away, then pull up in front of the house.

At the same time, I hear Gordon crashing through the corn. Then I hear his feet on the gravel, running away from the house. Three shots are fired, and I hear a sound that is almost a scream coming from him.

"One knee replacement, comin' up," says Terry.

The police floodlights are turned on and we can see Gordon rocking back and forth in pain with his gun about ten feet away. When the police go over to cuff him, Terry comes over to me. "Sorry about last week. We even now?"

The swelling in my face is making it hard to speak, but I manage to form the words. "Hell, yes."

Chapter Forty-Two

Terry steps back from me. "You don't look so good. Hey, Jimmy. Over here when you get a chance."

Captain Larini steps back from Gordon and lets another officer wait with Gordon until the ambulance arrives. The captain comes over to Terry. "I just can't believe it, Terry. Night vision or no night vision, he was running and you got his frigging knee."

"Shouldn't have taken me three shots. Listen, Jimmy. This here's my friend. You got that? You're going to take good care of her. I got to get back to Amanda. She must be worried sick with all the shooting.'

"How come you're here, anyway?" asks Captain Larini.

"I heard the automatic pistol. The only people with automatic pistols around here are you guys, so I thought I was coming over to provide backup. Amanda must have called 911 to make sure you were here."

Captain Larini is in awe. "Some backup, man. You handled the whole thing."

Terry shrugs. "Better check on the guy on the other driveway over there. No gun. Maybe dead. Shot by this guy," motioning toward Gordon.

Terry strides off and Captain Larini is left with me. "I called George Myers. Not my favorite person, but I figured he'd know who to call. Like your grandmother."

"Got a phone?" My words are garbled by my swollen jaw.

"What?"

"Phone," I say, holding my hand up to my ear.

He takes his phone out and I dial the number but hand it back to him, because my grandmother will not be able to understand me and she'll worry even more. "My grandmother."

He nods. When my grandmother answers, he says, "This is Captain Larini of the Rensford Police. I'm here at your granddaughter's house and I just want to tell you that she's okay. She—"

After a pause, he continues, "I assure you, ma'am, I am a police officer." There is another pause, and he says, "I can't prove it over the phone."

I hold out my hand for the phone. Captain Larini hands it to me, saying, "Not the most trusting person in the world."

As clearly as I can, I say, "Hi, Gramma."

"What are you doing at your house? You were supposed to come here."

I try and grunt an explanation.

"There must be something wrong with the phone. I can hardly hear you. Why in God's name did you go home? Everyone told you, don't go home, don't go home. And what did you do?"

"Sorry." It's all I can manage. I wish I could smile. It's so good to hear her yelling at me.

I hear footsteps running up the driveway, and then Jack's arms are around me. I pull away long enough to hand him the phone and say, "Gramma."

"Hi, Eleanor. It's Jack. She's okay. I'll call you back as soon as I can." Then he goes back to hugging me.

Jack pulls away to get a better look at me, and it gives me a chance to give Captain Larini his phone back. Then I point to my leg because it hurts like hell and I think it's still bleeding.

"Oh, my God, what happened?"

"Got shot."

Jack runs to the ambulance and brings back a paramedic, who notes that the pants are not sticking to the wound. The best course of action, therefore, is to gently pull my pants down. I'm trying to remember what underwear I put on this morning.

George arrives and I give him a little wave as he comes over to make sure I'm all right. My pants are down around my ankles, and my face is twice its normal size. "Great look for you, Catie." He smiles and starts to go.

I hold up my hands to tell him to wait. "Eugene?"

Captain Larini answers. "Eugene got shot in the hip, and went right down. Had enough sense to keep quiet."

George starts to move off and again I hold up my hands. "Maureen."

"What about her?"

"In her office." I'm struggling with the words. "Beaten up."

Captain Larini nods to George. "I'll send someone over."

George smiles at me. "*Now* can I go do my job?"

I shoo him away. In the meantime, the paramedic has confirmed what everyone can already see. The bullet tore off a piece of skin on the outer part of my thigh. I'm going to have a nasty scar, but that will be the extent of the damage. The paramedic doesn't think that any bones in my face are broken.

When the second ambulance arrives, I lie down on the gurney and get lifted up into it. The light in the ambulance is so bright it hurts my eyes. Jack holds my hand while the paramedics wrap a bandage around my leg and start an IV drip. The painkillers start to take effect and I drift off. I can't tell if I'm saying something, or just thinking it. I think I'm telling Jack that I don't like corn, but I'm not sure.

Chapter Forty-Three

"Nudist camp to stay." Gramma is sitting on the sofa in her trailer, reading the September 8 edition of the *Ashton Bulletin*. Her head is tilted all the way back so she can read out of the bottoms of her bifocals. Flo is next to her, bent all the way forward, giving herself a pedicure.

"It won't last," says Gramma. "They only voted that way because they realized they were being jerked around by that smear campaign. Once they get over that, they'll be all up in arms against us again."

"Whatever happened to that awful girl Maureen," says Flo, not looking up from her toes.

"She's out of the hospital and has gone to stay with an aunt in Pennsylvania," I say. Maureen and I were in the same hospital for a while, but neither of us tried to contact the other. I don't think I could have seen her without breaking into a major post-traumatic stress meltdown.

Flo lifts her head and looks at me. "Are you sure you don't want me to touch up that face of yours, hon? I've got a great little concealer that works on both the purple here and that dark green there." She is pointing to her own face to show me where she wants to hide my remaining bruises.

"Leave her alone. She's not exactly a sight for sore eyes, but that's good." Gramma looks at me. "You're piling up a lot of sympathy points around here. Come in handy later."

"Later?"

"You planning on walking around here naked anytime soon?"

"No."

"Okay, then. All I'm saying is that when they get pissed at you again, they'll hold off for a while when they remember that face of yours."

"If I were you, Eleanor, I'd be careful about slinging insults at her, being as she's now part of the Manure Mafia."

The Manure Mafia turns out to be a really nice group of people who are both farmers and members of the local gun club. By some strange logic, getting shot makes you an honorary member of the Rensford Gun Club, and since I am part owner of a farm, that makes me the newest member of the Manure Mafia.

While I was in the hospital, the Manure Mafia descended on our land and cut down and removed the corn for silage. Jack said it looked like some sort of farm equipment convention. When I got home, all that was left was beautiful brown stubble.

George came to see me the morning after I entered the hospital to tell me that both Gordon and Eugene are in prison hospitals. Gordon is being held without bail, and Eugene couldn't come up with enough money for his. George, Bruce and Kevin came to take a statement from me. Why the three of them had to be there, I don't know. I think they just like goofing around together.

Phil Demers came to visit and then stayed to assist the camp in selling the land back to the Gellermans for the $72,000 they paid for it. The Gellermans will now be able to put the land back on the market and get a good price for it. Jack helped by arranging for a contractor to get rid of the rusted items in the dump, and clean up the oil and paint with absorbents.

Jack spent three days in the hospital by my side, and then

went back to Washington and impressed everyone with his testimony. Since then, we have been working on our new joint effort to combine his ground penetration techniques with my soil science. So far, we haven't been able to come up with a name for our new venture. Gramma wants us to call it Down Deep and Dirty. We're still working on it.

About the Author

Like the main character in this book, Joan Dash spent much of her childhood in a nudist camp. She went on to get a Masters and a Ph.D from Harvard University where she studied microbial engineering using soil pathogens. Today, she and her husband use the ground-penetration techniques described in this book, helping archaeologists in Egypt and other countries decide where to dig. She and her husband live in a small farm community in Connecticut.

7214837R00188

Printed in Great Britain
by Amazon.co.uk, Ltd.,
Marston Gate.